DAVID PALIN was born in West London and lives in Berkshire. He is the author of several published novels, dark psychological thrillers, the first of which came out in 2006. David is intrigued by the things that hide in the shadows beyond the light of our everyday lives. As a fluent German speaker and having studied English & German literature, he believes we are drawn to darker tales and imaginings.

David has collaborated as editor and co-writer for various authors, as well as producing screen treatments and screenplays (including one of his own) for writers whose novels have sparked potential interest from film producers.

Away from writing, David loves sport, music, the theatre and travelling, many of which have seemed like elements of a fantasy tale in our recent tough times!

*The Armistice Killer*
Published in 2021 by Nine Elms Books Ltd
Unit 6B
Clapham North Arts Centre
26–32 Voltaire Road
London SW4 6DH
Email: info@nineelmsbooks.co.uk

www.nineelmsbooks.co.uk

ISBN: 978-1-910533-54-3
e-book 978-1-910533-55-0 Epub

Cover design Tony Hannaford
Book design Dominic Horsfiall
Printed in the UK

# THE ARMISTICE KILLER

## DAVID PALIN

NINE
ELMS

*To my mum and sister - girl power before its time!*

# I

The image of disembowelment flashed before his eyes – a sensory explosion, leaving a searing afterimage – and shocked him with its ferocity. He could almost feel once more the wave from the blast. By instinct, he ducked, putting out his hand on the bed for support and squashing the regimental beret, the sight of which had triggered the reaction as surely as if he had stepped on the IED itself.

The soundless bang scrambled his thoughts. Too many years away from the front line. Back in the day, he'd reacted with precision; calmness. He'd absorbed the chaos, given orders, organised the men; pushed everything else to one side. To a place he didn't know. Into the shadows. Seemed the bastard memories had waited there for a signal to reappear; now here they were in full bloody technicolor. They didn't spare him. The young private just a few feet to his left, looking in disbelief at the bloodied tufts of his own guts waving through the gaping hole in his torso, which had held them moments before. The devil's own surgeon, Mr Shrapnel, had hurried by. The awful sight, a little further off, of Lance Corporal Dean. Didn't look in the worst shape from the waist up. Then you saw the space where his legs had been – they'd paid the price for having led him a fatal few paces astray.

He pressed the thumb and forefinger of one hand to his

eyes, waiting for the gruesome reminders to fade. The blast-waves seemed to continue though, finding a muted echo in the Cornish winds which beat against the rattling windows of the old cottage. The blood was never the worst though: that would drain away into the sands of Iraq, Afghanistan, or damp soil of The Falklands. It was the shrieking. Any soldier would tell you that. Young men crying for their mothers, calling for help that didn't exist. It never left you. Like tinnitus, it just waited for a quiet moment to remind you of its presence. Again the winds mocked history with their wailing through the ageing glass.

That fucked you up. No civilian could ever understand that. Nor the brutality you needed to instil to create people – correction, soldiers – capable of coming through it. Because Mummy wasn't there to help. When, towards the end of his time in the mob, he had looked into the eyes of some of the Standard Entry recruits he had put through their Phase 1 training he'd felt better when he saw hatred – of him, for what he was putting them through. Okay, some of it went beyond the covers of the manual, but they would thank him one day. Just for being alive to give those thanks.

Opening his eyes again, he found the bland, beige walls of his bedroom. Dull. Indifferent. Like civvies. He gave a wary look at his other hand, or rather at the beret still squashed beneath it. Lifting his weight from it, he half-expected it to detonate like a pressure mine, but it just unfolded with all the slight gentleness of a night flower.

He straightened up again, breathing erratic, but calming. He shook his head, while something akin to a grin twitched at the straight-set line of his mouth.

"Hiding from phantoms. Images of flowers," he whispered. "What happened to you, soldier? To the hard bastard?" It was as if he had, as he trundled up and down the motorways in security vehicles transporting valuable goods in the private sector for the last ten years, worn away the stone of which he had once been made.

He'd known the coming event would unearth buried memories; had been prepared for that – or so he'd thought. The one hundredth anniversary of the end of the war to end all wars;

thank Christ that hadn't been true – he would have been nothing if not a soldier.

On reflection, he didn't want to think what he might have become.

It would be a day for sharing with the other veterans. It might just be a look, a glance exchanged, that spoke of horrors survived and shared; of the agelessness of death and the devil. The cheering onlookers. The cameras and interviews – he'd had plenty of them in recent weeks as the press had cottoned onto him: the hometown lad who'd gone and carved his name in history. Their words, not his. Deep down, he was relieved it wasn't true: soldiers' names were carved in one place only and that was on memorials. But he had pride in his chest again, instead of anxiety and bitterness. The names of heroes, both alive and departed, and even photographs of them which he could show to the interviewers and journalists. So much better than nameless fears, their features always obscured by darkness, whether with good or bad intent.

Even as he let his mind stray in that direction, a familiar voice taunted him, reminding him that the wars in which he, personally, had served his country were not the main reason people were spilling onto the streets and waving. Not why they were travelling for miles to look at ceramic poppies at the Tower. He was growing old, unlike those whom age would not wither. The Gulf, Iraq, Afghanistan – they did not appeal to the romantics. When things had been near the end of the road with his wife, she hadn't held back from saying so. *'What about The Falklands War, eh?'* he'd spat at her. *'Personal vendetta,'* she'd replied. Bitch!.

What really pissed him off was that she was probably right.

But what drove him fucking mad was that it didn't make the memories of blood any less traumatic when they emerged.

God, he needed some air.

He crossed to the window, shoved the curtains aside and grasped the latch. The strong wind now boomed and whistled across the fields that his bedroom overlooked, so throwing open the room to the elements he was met by another blast, but this one he was prepared for. His senses were alive, all of a sudden, as the gusts tugged him back to San Carlos and the long march towards Port Stanley.

"What the hell...?!"

The figure was just standing there, motionless in the chaos of the strengthening winds – what other sort was there in the peninsula if not strengthening – and the bending, clacking November trees. At first, he thought it might be one of the emaciated ponies that wandered about trying to graze on the stubble during the day. Perhaps one of them had realised it was more dangerous to be in that tumbledown stable in these gusts – but no, he could just about see that the figure was too tall to be a pony.

He narrowed his eyes. A combination of the wind, darkness and worsening eyesight meant he couldn't quite make things out. Out there in the coming storm, a ghost-white shape floated.

One of the ponies had a white blaze running down its face.

Yet even at this distance, he knew with strange and unnerving certainty that this was no pony, and that he was being watched.

He stood transfixed, neither able to see nor look away. Still as death, he and the watcher contemplated each other while everything else in their immediate world shook and blew and cackled. Inside, some perverse fibre of his soldier's DNA was thrilled by this, so much so that he had a sudden brainwave. Ducking away from the window for a moment, he reached into the trunk from which he had been removing his uniform and decorations. Finding the night vision goggles, he switched off the light and put them on.

Back at the window, he scanned the fields. The figure had disappeared.

"Where are you?" he muttered, head turning to right and left in a slow arc. "Where the fuck are you?"


He watched for at least an hour, senses more alive and alert than they had been in all the days since his retirement from the battlefields, but in the end he had to settle for a frustrated thump of his fist on the window frame. He'd left plenty of people with reasons to settle scores, as any hard-nosed Regimental Sergeant

Major might – indeed should have. Perhaps the Armistice centenary had caused a few old scars to throb. But whoever this was, he would be waiting.

★★★★

For Marshy, when the curtain had been pulled back the play had begun for real. Until that point the whole thing had seemed surreal, make-believe. The sudden appearance of the actor from behind the curtains had been a shock. Staring at the lit, shrouded window, with vague movements throwing shadows on the curtains, there had still been room for imagination and, perhaps, retreat. Not now. The figure standing staring out carried all its old threat. He'd even managed to turn the tables on Marshy, leaving the watcher feeling watched. Staying motionless had been the only option; the equivalent of lying beneath your blanket as a child, hoping the monsters won't see you.

As soon as that very real incubus ducked out sight, Marshy bolted towards the stable and took cover, better able to watch the window. God only knew what had prompted the decision to stand in the field anyway. Perhaps just the sense of space; freedom. The knowledge that turning and running was still a possibility.

Not any more though. Not now the beast had shown itself, staring from and into darkness. All the anger, which had risen like bile in Marshy's throat at the sight of the local military so-called hero being feted in the run-up to the Armistice celebrations, came spewing forth again. As the threatening shape had returned to the window, Marshy had fought hard to suppress nausea at the grotesque sight; creepy beyond belief with those blank, all-seeing shark eyes scouring the night for…for what? Another victim? Yet the night goggles had helped in a way. Though they made the hairs go up on the back of the neck, they had taken away the last shreds of humanity. Dehumanised the dreadful being that was RSM Tom Wright.

Some would argue it wasn't his fault. That war had made him the man, or beast, he was. They were wrong, misguided. Tom Wright and war had been made for each other. Watching him now, scanning the night fields around him with robotic precision, seeing how his senses fed on this tension, Marshy knew what needed to happen…

…and was way too terrified to move.

# 2

The car had been bothering him. Sure, it was just standing there, in no way different from any other morning...

...except this wasn't just any other morning.

You could say this brushfire of emotion had been smouldering for a hundred years, but for many months now it had been warming up, till it was difficult to avoid the heat – and who in their right mind would want to?

Jaroslaw had no reason to love the politicians of his adopted homeland – that was how he saw England, despite it being the land of his birth; in his heart as well as in his blood, he would always be Polish. It was those pedlars of empty words and not the military, who had treated the Poles like a dirty family secret seventy odd years ago. They who had held ace pilots from the east back, his father amongst them, in the Battle of Britain until there was no choice but to unleash them, and even then they had tried to veil and muffle Polish presence at the postwar parades, seeking in desperation not to upset Uncle Joe Stalin. The British soldiers themselves, though, were salt of the earth and likewise victims of the politicians. The same could be said of Britannia's people. It was these latter groups' acknowledgement of the part the Polish pilots had played in that historic air battle which had prompted his father to stay, eventually taking British citizenship. That and an encounter with a Yorkshire lass who Jaroslaw was proud to call his mother.

He looked again at his neighbour's car. His tenant. A troubled man, thought Jaroslaw. What was that expression he had learnt during that part of his upbringing in the north – a rum'un?

Jaroslaw chastised himself. He'd only known Tom Wright a few years, and the fact that the latter had rented the flat in middle age was suggestive of the downsizing that comes with a failed marriage. And it had taken until recent weeks for Jaroslaw to discover, via the eulogies in the local press, that the man had fought for his country in such far-flung places as the Falklands, the Gulf and Iraq. Highly decorated…and yet here he was renting a flat from an immigrant. Not that he hadn't worked honestly and hard to acquire his small property portfolio, no matter what the far right denizens of Little Britain would have you believe.

The papers had been full of information about the participants in today's centenary commemorations. That had provided a useful segue into a conversation or two with his taciturn, tight-lipped tenant. Yet despite his due respect for the man's past heroism, there was something in his demeanour – in his eyes – which had unsettled Jaroslaw.

A rum'un.

Perhaps the man had just seen bad things.

*Well of course he has, you old fool!* Once again the elderly Pole berated himself. And yet…and yet. It went deeper than that.

He pushed the thoughts aside impatiently.

Except they wouldn't leave him alone. During a nation's – a civilisation's – two minute silence he stared at Tom Wright's car, which seemed in tune with the respectful ritual, the sunlight reflecting from its immaculate exterior on what had turned out to be a glorious morning after the high winds of the last few days. Gradually it dawned on Jaroslaw – Tom Wright was supposed to be carrying the regimental standard of the former Duke of Cornwall's Light Infantry at the service at Truro Cathedral, so why was his car still here? It was four miles to Truro and although the ex-soldier kept himself in obvious good shape, it was unlikely he would have chosen to walk into the town in his full-dress uniform. That image brought back into the Pole's mind the man who'd come knocking at the upstairs flat's door that morning; also, a man in uniform –

soldier past or present – who had, he presumed, been looking for Tom Wright, but left without him just a few moments later. A visitor of any sort was a rarity, and the sound of heavy footsteps on the iron stairs had caught Jaroslaw's ears.

The Last Post at the service in London sounded on the television. Jaroslaw reproached himself for having become sidetracked by the fate of just one man instead of the millions who had lost their lives in war. Yet, on the other hand, his melancholy Polish soul found it only fit and proper that his focus had been on one former soldier who apparently had no family or friends to support him on this day.

As the final, elegiac notes of the trumpet faded, he turned to Sylvia, his eyes brimming with tears. Her loyal hand on his arm provided its unfailing touch of comfort and brought into a sharper focus the plight of his neighbour.

"Moving, my dear Jarek, isn't it," she said. "We British do these things so well, don't we?"

Like father, like son – he too had picked an English rose, and his love for her was far stronger than the temptation to correct her mislabelling of his nationality. It was a great sadness to him that he had never been able to raise a child with her, but, with a rueful twist of his mouth, he reflected that it had at least prevented any disagreements about what that child's mother tongue should be!

She pointed to the tears in his eyes. "I see thoughts of your family – their bravery, their sacrifices – are spilling over." Her lips pressed to his cheek.

"No, my dear…well, yes, and no. I was wondering about our military friend." His gaze lifted towards the ceiling and the upstairs flat.

Sylvia nodded her agreement. "Yes, he has done his bit for Queen and country."

"That's not what I meant." Jaroslaw pointed towards the car. Aware he had sounded impatient, he moderated his tone. "I've seen no sign of him today; heard no sound."

"Well, he'll be in Truro, dear."

Jaroslaw puffed out his cheeks. "You're probably right, but…" He looked again at the car, unable to pinpoint why its splendid isolation was bothering him. There was something beyond the fact that it hadn't been used to drive to town.

"Anyway he must be fine because he had a visitor, not long after midnight," continued Sylvia, prompting Jaroslaw to frown. "I heard the front door close."

"And how do you know that was a visitor? Do we only open and close our front door when we have visitors? Maybe he went out."

It was Sylvia's turn to frown. "No, I don't think so, because then I heard voices."

"Perhaps that was the TV."

"Who puts on the television when they have visitors, especially at that time of night?"

Jarek shook his head. You couldn't argue with that, but some flaw in the logic escaped him.

Sylvia did what she always did – sought the least troublesome explanation. She wasn't one of life's more inquisitive women. At moments like this it was a trait that caused him mild irritation. "He must have left early with someone this morning; must have had lots to do," she reasoned.

"So who was the man in uniform who called this morning – the man who left alone?"

They stood in silence, not quite sure where the discussion was leading.

"Why are you so concerned, Jarek, my dear?" asked Sylvia at last.

"Not sure." He chewed his lip. "I am just bothered." He shook his head. "Perhaps the day has got to me…and I can see in your eyes that I've worried you now."

Sylvia looked back at the television, watching the proud, serried ranks of men, in whose lined faces it was now almost impossible to see that they were once young and terrified. "This must have been a difficult day for any old soldier. Who knows what might come from all those memories, especially for a man who spends each night alone?" Now her hand made an involuntary movement to her mouth. "Oh, you can't think he's committed sui…no, surely not. He is a soldier."

"An ex-soldier. A man with no visitors. Someone for whom a large part of life's purpose has gone: the rules, the camaraderie that pointed him in the same direction as everyone else."

Sylvia took her husband's hand. "You always said there was something about him that seemed troubled. And you do read about it much more these days. What is it called – PDS…PTDS… oh, I don't know."

Releasing his hand, she walked across to an ashtray, took from it a key, which she extended towards her husband. "Well, as landlord, you are within your rights."

"I will call the proper authorities." Jaroslaw straightened his shoulders.

"On a day like this, won't they be rather busy?"

"On a day like this they should care about the possibility of an ex-soldier in distress," he snapped, followed by immediate regret as he saw the familiar bow of the head from his good wife. He gave a curt nod. "Forgive me."

"It's alright, my dear, I know how much you believe in the privacy of home. But you would be doing this out of concern for him."

The key was extended again towards him. He took it, being sure to give the hand that offered it a little loving squeeze.


Jaroslaw was astounded by the intensity of his heartbeat, triggered by this unexpected turn of events, as he stood in front of that door. This was an unexpected turn of events. With a hesitant finger he pressed the doorbell. It clicked, but he heard no ring. He pressed it again – click; silence – waited a few seconds and when it seemed safe to assume it wasn't working, having made a mental note to have it repaired, he knocked on the door.

He knocked again. After that morning's third minute of silence, he hefted the key in his palm as if it weighed a pound. Pandora's Box lay in wait, its contents whispering their murky secrets.

Jaroslaw opened the front door and was met by the aroma of unfamiliarity.

"Hello? Forgive me – hello?"

Despite the compact dimensions of the flat, the sound seemed to echo.

He took his first tentative steps.

"Hello?"

The silence brought unexpected comfort – at least he knew he wasn't walking in on anybody. Nevertheless, he moved with caution down the hallway, glancing into each room as he went. He knew the last door on the left was a bedroom and, though he believed the flat to be empty, still felt awkward as he peeped in.

Jaroslaw had been wondering which might disturb him more – to find the flat empty and feel like an intruder defiling someone's privacy, or to find a dead body. Looking into that bedroom, he had his answer soon enough.

This was no way for a fighting man to die – for dead he surely was. It was also neither suicide, nor natural causes.

Once his legs had stopped trembling, one of those wonderful, succinct British expressions sprang to his mind, but he didn't voice it, being an old-fashioned, decent man.

But this wasn't decent. This was obscene.

# 3

*Some days later*

Ben Logan almost smiled - in his world, where his freakish medical condition meant facial recognition was a luxury not afforded him, the rattling of the old Nespresso machine would have been as reliable a source of identification as a fingerprint or DNA.

"You hear that sound," he said, "you know Freddy Dessler must be somewhere close by."

The familiarity brought a certain relief. Whether these unofficial meet-ups did the same – now, of that he couldn't be certain. That wasn't the fault of his host; Logan just wasn't sure that catharsis could ever equate to comfort.

Freddy laughed as he busied himself with the cups and the sound was like the sea washing the beach clean of detritus and footprints. "Still makes damn good coffee. If it ain't broke, don't fix it."

"But what if it was always broken?"

"Well it didn't make this racket back in the day when you first…" Freddy paused, doubtless with the sudden realisation of what his guest was really implying, "…came to help me with my thesis." He nodded. "But I take your point. Some more pedantic people might see that as an inappropriate aphorism from a psychologist. I, on the other hand, believe that my role is to find out whether indeed something is broken, or just in need of servicing." He paused. "But not this evening – that's for the day job and my remit doesn't expand to coffee machines!"

As Logan heard him changing the coffee capsules, recognising this whole process of performing little everyday tasks, creating a relaxed environment, as part of Freddy's modus operandi, he wished he could switch off his own observational techniques. But noting the body language and behavioural patterns of others was a huge part of Logan's own survival mechanism, both in his work as a detective and as a sufferer of prosopagnosia; facial blindness to the uninformed…which was most people.

*Didn't do you much good in recent times, did it, Ben?* The self-critical, mocking inner voice always liked to have its say, though Logan found it easier to postpone those conversations these days!

Right here, right now, there was no cynicism intended in his analysis of Freddy Dessler's methods. Logan welcomed these… exchanges, particularly as they were unofficial; off the record. He and Freddy had been through some shit, to use non-academic terminology, together. Logan didn't doubt that their discussions were almost as therapeutic for the psychologist as they were for him. Their shared secret was dark; boy, was it! They no longer spoke about it, but it was a glue that would forever bind them. Each of them knew things which could finish the other person professionally. Not that they would ever have done that to each other, of course.

For all Logan knew, the woman – how Holmesian that sounded, but he couldn't bring himself to use her name – was also a not-quite-patient of Freddy's. Almost certainly he still had contact with her. Here, though, within these four walls, she was just a ghost and the tide of Freddy's laugh or humour would sweep away her footprints in the sand.

For a little while at least; she could never be washed from Logan's dreams and memories so easily.

Enough – for now. Where had he got to before the death rattle of the coffee machine had distracted him? Ah yes, the Armistice commemorations.

"So, as I was saying, despite my best intentions my focus had drifted a bit as the day wore on. Plus you get drawn into the emotions of an event like that. You can't help but be moved, end up with tears clouding your vision – as if facial blindness wasn't bad enough – even though technically you're supposed to be keeping the sharpest of watches for any remote suggestion of terrorist activity or anti-war protests. These days even environmental activists – in the current climate…"

"No pun intended." Freddy's intervention was accompanied by a little snort of laughter.

Logan raised his eyebrows in mock despair and continued: "I understood our heavier police presence, but you know it always seems that on Remembrance Day no one's looking for trouble. In fact, despite the general bonhomie, I reckon anyone disrupting that sacred event might well become the first casualty of an Armistice Day lynching."

Freddy returned with two cups of Lungo and placed one in front of his guest. "Yes, I watched a bit on the local news after the main event in London..."

Logan understood why the words ran out. On the day, Truro had, and rightly so, been awash with feelings of goodwill from young and old, official and civilian, tourist and resident towards the men and women in uniforms or blazers. Topped by a plethora of regimental berets, they had made their way towards the cathedral, some of them carrying so much medal -work on their ageing, frail chests, that their ability to stand tall and proud was worthy of applause in itself.

Freddy nodded as if reading Logan's thoughts. He sat down opposite again and fixed what Logan, on his mental crib sheet, had learnt to understand was a shrewd gaze on him. "But I know you – I don't mean this negatively, but emotion doesn't tend to distract you." Freddy paused, took a sip from his cup and seemed to be watching his guest. "I meant your own emotions of course. I'm aware you don't always pick them up in others without certain triggers." Logan did his best not to reach for his coffee: far too obvious a subconscious delaying tactic. Freddy's eyes narrowed very slightly. "But other things might have caused your mind to wander."

He recognised the tone in those last words and knew the question was coming. He gave a slight sigh that told his host the guard dog was off duty for the moment.

Freddy took the hint. "Did it not go well?" He paused. "The date? Was it an evening with none of the aforementioned triggers, just the bullets?"

Logan shook his head, but with a slight smile. He appreciated the humour. "Again."

"But it was a different woman?"

"And the same result."

"She must have made an impression on you if it was distracting you at a moment like that – on duty, I mean."

"I saw someone in the crowd who looked like her – as far as I could tell anyway; I mean the haircut, the distinctive red and green scarf thrown across her shoulders, the way she moved. Although unfortunately that involved her reaching the side of another guy against whom she then snuggled. Unlike the armistice, I'd clearly become forgotten history quite quickly!" He sipped his coffee again and grew thoughtful. "Wonder what he was doing right that I didn't? She was clearly on the market."

"Well," Freddy sounded reproachful, "phraseology like that won't have helped."

Though he hadn't meant it negatively, Logan was painfully aware that some of his slips might well be Freudian. Unable to offer a defence against the observation, he fell quiet.

Freddy did him the favour of moving on, though still along a muddy track. "So, do you think this string of failures is entirely your fault?"

"No, I mean…she was…" he paused, this time scrabbling in the vocabulary sack with care before settling on "…sanctimonious, shall we say? Spared me nothing, turning down a second date on the basis that I was – quote – weirdly needy. I could have dealt better with her accusing me of having halitosis."

"Needy." Freddy nodded. "An interesting apothegm. What do you think you did to provoke that?"

Now Logan did reach for his coffee. "Well excuse me, but isn't everyone venturing into the world of online dating in need of something?" He hated hearing the slight whine in his tone. "Don't we all have an albatross of some sort around our neck?"

*Except yours is more of a carrion crow, picking at roadkill; dead flesh.*

"So, tell me a bit about her. Presumably she has a name?"

He heard Freddy's analysis switch flick to the On position. "Felicity, and she was as hot as the profile picture. Of course, whether she was the actual person in that picture, my condition prevents me from truly knowing. But I'm still learning the dating game and I think the lesson from this latest experience is not to ask the hot ones out. Mostly they don't respond anyway, but it's becoming apparent that if they do it's to go on a date with themselves."

"Excuse me asking, Ben, but how do you define *hot*? It's to my shame, and that of much of my profession, that our understanding of prosopagnosia is still relatively limited."

"Facial blindness doesn't prevent me admiring a good figure, a nice haircut, cheekbones plus the other usual suspects. I stop short of marks out of ten!" They both laughed, but then he reconsidered. "If I'm honest, not that far short, but in my case it's not some arrogant macho process, or at least I hope not. It's more of a degree of difficulty score." There was further laughter, first from Freddy, which prompted an echo from Logan. His partner-in-crime had the ability to generate warmth, which was not necessarily a typical weapon in the armoury of a clinical psychologist. It gave Logan the strength to push on; open up. "Pretty eyes are in there, but mostly it's recognising something in those eyes – a look. The colour can sometimes pose a problem."

"Really?"

He nodded. Despite the awkwardness of focussing on his condition, his irritation was starting to subside and he felt a rueful grin spreading.

"What's amusing you?" asked Freddy.

"A couple of things I guess. I'm grateful I don't suffer the topographical agnosia that sometimes comes with the more extreme versions of what I suffer from. At least I was able to find my way home after being shown the door."

Though he smiled, Freddy now moved on with a swiftness that betrayed his professional curiosity. "What else?"

"Just wondering what conclusions she might be drawing about me, if she's got over herself."

"If I didn't know better," Freddy leaned forward, "I'd say you were a bit of a misogynist – except I do know better. You're wary, with good reason, and just not very good at expressing it." His eyes reflected their shared dark history.

"Better than needy."

It was a flippant response, but, in reality, Freddy's comment had given Logan pause for thought. It was all very well being judgemental, but he knew better than anyone that he wasn't an easy assignment. His prosopagnosia meant he was also very precise about meeting-places and times. Likewise, he fished for ideas about what the lady might wear, hiding behind the excuse that he wanted to come suitably attired, which probably came across as the *weird* part, but not as freaky as if he had turned up and stared past his date without a hint of recognition. Most of his compulsions were being brought under control. If any good had come out of that sorry, frightening business a couple of years before…

*He shuddered – surely nothing good could have come of it*

…it was that he knew his issues were harmless compared with some people. He still straightened coasters and cutlery; ensured his shirt was neatly tucked into his suit trousers; checked his tie length;

twirled his signet ring. They might be irritating manifestations of something deeper, though quite where *needy* reared its head amongst these tics was beyond him. At the commemoration service a few days before, he had looked around and wondered whether he should have joined the armed forces – nothing like hiding in plain sight amongst men for whom ritual and the minutest attention to detail were called discipline and a well-made bed. However, on reflection, he would have been mixing day in and day out with people in identical uniforms topped with regulation haircuts. Life would not have been easy! The early days in the police academy had been bad enough.

"What did she look like?" Freddy's question interrupted his thoughts. "I'm guessing not auburn-haired and green-eyed. None of your dates have been – hence my surprise about eye-colours confusing you sometimes."

There was a touch of teak in Freddy Dessler's tone. On reflection, perhaps ice might have been a better analogy as, despite the winter sun shining through the office window, Logan couldn't shake the chill his subconscious had just inflicted on him. Memories of Claire Treloggan – there, he'd said the name! - would doubtless tap him on the shoulder at unwelcome times for the rest of his life. Investigating that case had brought more demons cavorting into the daylight than even he could have imagined during his troubled upbringing – plus, there was nothing quite like having a gun pointed at your head by a woman you'd fallen for to destroy your search for equilibrium.

He returned Freddy's look with a steely one of his own. "You might be right, but can you blame me?"

"So it's a conscious choice?"

"Actually, truthfully, I don't know."

This dating game was one milder consequence of that catastrophic episode. He had been presented with proof undeniable that, despite his sixth sense for wrongness, which was perhaps the result of his brain compensating for the prosopagnosia, he seemed incapable of sound judgement where the heart was concerned.

He continued: "Look, I know I'm not the first man to find women an unsolvable mystery, but I'll take whatever help I can get and, while they might be economical with the truth, at least the profiles on online dating websites give you some sort of a handbook in advance."

"You're making them sound like cars now! In that case, maybe you should set your sights differently and go for the more comfortable ride."

"Now who's the misogynist?" Logan did grin as he said it.

"Didn't sound great, did it?" Freddy smiled and raised a hand in acknowledgement. "But I know what I meant – namely, given what I've seen, specifically in the woods not so many years ago, perhaps you might aim for someone with a thinner handbook. The less complex the machine, the fewer parts to go wrong. Perhaps settle for five on your scorecard instead of always seeking ten. What about someone more mature?"

"You never met my mother, did you?"

Freddy Dessler took another sip of coffee and leaned back again. It was a comment designed to leave him with nowhere to go. He seemed to pick up on it and know it was time to usher the ghost from the room, though doubtless it would return at some point. That in itself gave rise to another troubled thought for Logan – had Claire Treloggan sat in this very chair and, if so, when was the last time?

Truly, it was indeed time to move on.

"So," said Freddy, returning to safer ground, "just as Remembrance Day was drawing to a close, you got a call."

"Yes. Having just spotted someone in the crowd who I thought might be Mrs Needy…"

"There you go again," Freddy gestured with an upturned palm, "This almost bitter negativity towards women."

"I…" He didn't really know where to take things from there.

Freddy turned the outstretched palm downwards, more conciliatory. "Look, I get it. You used a label of expediency. All I'm saying is just be careful. This was one woman…"

As that sentence ground to a halt, it seemed to Logan that Freddy Dessler didn't know where to go either.

"Anyway, for a moment, I dared to believe in telepathy, wondering whether it was a text from her. but the phone kept buzzing and I recognised the station number. It was the news about RSM Wright."

### Some days earlier – 11th November

He stepped away from the noise of the crowd a little. "DCI Logan."

There were the usual contradictory emotions as he listened to the details, though today they were heightened; the sadness at the news of a life taken thrown deeper into shadow by it being an ex-serviceman, and one who had enjoyed a good degree of celebrity in recent weeks. Then the undeniable frisson of excitement at the thought of a murderer to catch, a riddle to solve. Something to silence his demons – the appearance of someone else's!

"I'm on my way."

Looking around for his recently-acquired sidekick, Detective Sergeant Andy Pascoe, all he saw at first was the usual sea of abstract faces. He was reminded, as so often, of the Edvard Munch painting, 'Anxiety'. Finally he spotted the tall figure, several rows distant, sporting the grey suit and distinctive lime-green tie Logan had clocked that morning. Pascoe was deep in conversation with an old veteran, judging by the row of medals; possibly someone who had known his much-decorated uncle.

He knew this day had particular meaning for the young DS, given that uncle's very recent death; so much harder-hitting against the backdrop of the daily countdown to the World War One commemorations.

This was not information that Logan had acquired from Pascoe himself, but rather from the Chief Superintendent, whom Logan had approached for a little background once he had been advised that the young Detective Sergeant would be joining his team. The request had been made on the basis of distrusting those above him less than those of lower rank, though it was marginal and hung purely on the premise that his rank superiors had nothing to gain from undermining him.

There was another reason for both Logan's curiosity and his wariness, though. Some weeks before, looking out from his office window, he had spotted Pascoe deep in conversation with Detective Inspector John Heath, whose slightly too skinny suits always clung to his gym-pumped physique. The latter was hardly Logan's biggest fan, having been overlooked for promotion to DCI himself and forced to play second fiddle to the young interloper from off-territory. If social media had applied in the police force, Heath would have been a troll. He had accepted his lot with ill grace for a while, but had then asked to be reassigned elsewhere in the county. It had taken a couple of years, but the opportunity had come up at last for him to move on. Still he was not going to do so, it seemed, without taking the chance to have a conversation with his replacement. Logan observed the glances Heath flashed towards his window during those few minutes.

All of which meant that, for a time, one of Pascoe's distinguishing features, for Logan at least, would be the 'Keep Your Distance' sticker.

It was a pity – he seemed personable enough and, from what the DCI understood, the deceased uncle had been almost a father-figure to Pascoe after the early death of his real father. Indeed Logan had considered granting the DS dispensatory time off for this day of commemoration and remembrance, but the word from above had been 'no leave.'

Seeing Pascoe engrossed now in convivial chatter with the ancient warrior, Logan wanted to believe that his young colleague's earlier edginess – he had seemed withdrawn and distracted – was simply the result of this whole event tapping into a deep-lying seam of distress at his recent loss. From time to time, Pascoe had appeared to look over the heads of the crowds in Logan's direction, and the latter hoped he was just apologising for his lack of focus, but having observed that conversation between him and Heath...it had stayed with Logan and he could never be one hundred percent sure what he was seeing.

It had been a relief, for more than one reason, when Heath had indeed been granted an opportunity to move on, as some comments about his interest in his commanding officer's history of cases had come to Logan's attention, including from Freddy Dessler, and that ran the risk of exhuming skeletons better left undisturbed.

Logan decided he would leave Pascoe to it for the moment and that, given the identity of the victim, the least he could do was start this one on his own right now. In many ways this was also how he preferred things.


Many crime scenes, in fact the crimes themselves, were like hard-boiled eggs – before you peeled them you knew exactly what you would find inside. You cracked them, rolled them. Some pieces of shell fell away with ease, others were more difficult to pick at; obstinate – but that was as surprising as it got.

As Logan pulled up in the car in Chadstow, a village on the outskirts of town, he found the usual - striped tape cordoning off the area; suburban reality masking something vague and sinister. A uniformed officer was talking with a smartly-dressed couple whom he assumed were the landlords - he had been advised en route of their Polish name and that they lived in the flat below. However, as Logan observed the woman, her looks, taken feature by feature and matched with those in his subconscious crib-sheet, appeared to be quintessentially English, as did the politeness in her interaction with the young policeman. The fact that she was not standing a deferential step behind the man in the smart blue suit and striking maroon tie', whom he assumed to be her husband, also seemed to support Logan's assumption. His few trips to the old Eastern Bloc countries had suggested feminism still had a wall, or Iron Curtain, to overcome.

Something about the husband's straight-backed stoicism spoke of his acceptance that life was, indeed, but a walking shadow – a wheel of misfortune which had come around again. Poland's recent history was nothing if not a catalogue of dark deeds on the doorstep by threatening neighbours. That knowledge may well have been passed in the genes from father to son.

Logan walked over. "Sir." The officer stood a little to attention.

Logan nodded to the couple. "Detective Chief Inspector Logan. Mr and Mrs Wolniek, I assume."

"Yes," replied the man with a slight stoop of acknowledgement.

Logan turned to the woman. "But you, Mrs Wolniek, look English, if I'm not mistaken."

"That's very astute of you, detective," she replied. "That renews one's confidence in the police force." She cast a surreptitious, almost conspiratorial look towards the uniformed officer, who seemed to be flipping the pages of his notebook backwards and forwards with a distracted air. Logan gave another polite nod, excused himself and took the officer to one side.

"Anything?"

"Not really, sir." The officer referenced his notebook. "The victim lives…lived alone. The landlady's wife, Mrs Wolniek – her husband is Polish, but was born in the UK and she's English, by the way…"

Logan gave an inner sigh. Mrs Wolniek's comments, or fears, seemed justified.

"…believes she heard the front door close sometime after midnight. It was very windy last night, as you know sir, so she can't be sure there was anything really. She did hear voices, though these may have come from the TV because actually he rarely had visitors. She said she assumed the victim had left early in preparation for the service at the cathedral today."

"Guess not." The heavy irony might have been inappropriate, but Logan couldn't help it sometimes. It was a shield for so many things and sometimes the humorous edge just helped him blend in.

A pause.

"He was due to carry a regimental standard there, sir. According to the husband, Mr Wolniek, a uniformed man came calling this morning around six a.m. and left alone." Logan gave a sharp glance at the officer. "He – Mr Wolniek - didn't think he went in, but if he did he wasn't here long enough to be our man, plus the team upstairs have said death probably occurred a few hours before that."

"So he probably didn't go in. But if he did, given he reported nothing, at the very least we have something extremely suspicious. And if he didn't go in, that makes it even more important to ascertain whether someone did call after midnight, as that's sounding like the time of death."

Despite the seriousness of the situation, it amused Logan to see the combination of enlightenment and embarrassment flash across the officer's features on hearing the DCI's words. Even reading aloud from his notes hadn't been enough for him to register the bleeding obvious. Some guys weren't made to be detectives. Perhaps it wasn't all his fault. Given the fact that neither his voice nor his mannerisms were familiar to Logan, he was probably some greenhorn, since most of the more experienced officers and detectives would have been on duty at the various commemorative events that day. Ideally, a more senior colleague would have been sent to the scene of a murder.

Nevertheless, with dogged determination, the young officer resumed his journey down the page.

"Um…the doorbell isn't working, so Mr Wolniek doesn't know whether the visitor knocked or rang, but he heard neither."

"So who did find the body, and when?"

"Mr Wolniek, late this morning."

Logan gave a short nod and turned, having decided he would speak with the landlord later after surveying the crime scene. He was about to put his foot on the first step of the iron staircase leading to the front door when he felt a hand on his arm.

"It's no way for a man to die. A soldier."

The suit and distinctive tie he'd clocked earlier told him this was Mr Wolniek.

"It must have been a horrible thing to come home to."

"Come home?" Mr Wolniek looked confused for a moment.

Logan gestured towards the suit. "I assumed you were at the service today."

Mr Wolniek stood up a little straighter. "This is showing respect for the day. No, I found him this morning, just after eleven o'clock, as we had observed the two minute silence. We live downstairs."

Logan found himself looking across with a hint of despair in the direction of the constable who had taken the initial details. Some of this information appeared not to have been noted down, or if it was, the young PC hadn't shared it. He'd be having a word with the sergeant about the training.

Logan had found himself wondering, given the old man's ethnicity, whether he would have made his original comment about a Nazi or Red Army trooper, but was now glad he had kept that thought to himself. From the cause of death outlined on the phone as he had been driving over, it must have been a tough thing to see. Discovering it, with the unpreparedness, the lack of warning that involved, added some notches of horror.

Wolniek's eyes were cracked mirrors, so many emotions did they reflect – and not just from this incident, he suspected. In the world the DCI inhabited, where blemishes and peculiarities fulfilled a role that faces could not, those flawed facets, those eyes, would, unusually, have been his markers for Wolniek.

"I'm sorry you had to be the one to find him. You knew him well?"

"A decent man."

Even at that moment, Logan had a gut feeling those words would return to haunt someone – he didn't know how that ghost might manifest itself, but had a peculiar conviction that it would.

Was this the first whiff of something rotten in the state of his boiled egg?

With a nod of acknowledgement, Logan headed for the door of the victim's flat It took only the clanging of his feet on the first few iron steps, as he made his way towards the front door, for Logan to know that the sound of that same door closing in the early hours was important; he didn't know exactly how right now, but he knew. It was a corner piece of the jigsaw, lying amongst hundreds.

Walking into the crime scene itself, he experienced a vicarious thrill, which had ceased a long time ago to be something of which he was ashamed. Oh, there was nothing Conan Doyle about that little chill along the spine; no anticipation at the thought of a worthy adversary; a Moriarty. Logan had no delusions about his abilities or motivations as a detective. This was not a vocation when you experienced the pulse of delight that came from confronting a challenge, as opposed to two-a-penny muggings, petty burglaries, bruising domestics and drunken gobshites, all of which had increased their profile in Truro in recent times. There was some dark poetry in this obscenity. He felt it; sensed it – as ritualised as an iambic pentameter. This was an execution and, as with any such act, it marked the beginning of the poem, not just someone's end.

Harj, the pathologist he'd been happy to hear was assigned to the case, stood up from the plastic-suited forensics team dusting for fingerprints and gave Logan a knowing look as he entered the bedroom.

"Anything?" He addressed the room, looking at the body, fascination overcoming revulsion. "I mean, apart from the obvious – the body tied to the bed with cable-ties, wearing night-vision goggles and choked … " he looked at Harj, " I assume" Harj nodded, "… by a swagger stick."

Logan walked over and tapped, with care – lots of care – the back of a fingernail on the brass end of the stick; the one jutting into the air from its base in the victim's mouth.

Harj took up the discussion. "Cause of death definitely seems to be the rather brutal pressure exerted on that swagger-stick, judging by the haemorrhaging and vomit, which would have assisted the choking. Some bruising around the neck suggests he was overpowered prior to the choking by expertly applied pressure, though I will need the autopsy to verify the stick as the sole cause of death, given the angle his head had to have been at to be able to force it in like that. I'll know more once we get him back to the morgue. The ligature marks on wrists and ankles suggest he struggled for longer than just the time it took to choke him."

"Fingerprints? Samples?"

"So far nothing," said one of the plastic-suited figures.

Another forensics officer waved an arm towards the carpet. "I've seen nothing that couldn't have been brought in on the shoes of the victim."

Logan looked around. "Unless the perp tidied up, there seem no obvious signs of a struggle. As he lived alone, we have no idea if anything has been taken, I guess, but my feeling is this has nothing to do with burglary."

All of them jerked their heads towards the door at the entry of the grey-suited, lime-green tied whirlwind that was Detective Sergeant Andy Pascoe.

"Sorry, sir – got here as quickly as I could once I noticed you'd gone!"

"That's okay, Pascoe. I saw you chatting to a veteran in Truro. On Armistice Day I thought I'd leave you in peace."

No sooner had he uttered the play-on-words – strange how so many officers resorted to black humour as a means of dealing with crime - than Logan regretted it, realising it might have been inappropriate. He was relieved when it appeared not to have registered with Pascoe, although that in itself was unusual – one of the young DS's more winning characteristics was being a sharp cookie where puns were concerned – and was perhaps further evidence for Logan of the day's impact on him. The only grimace from Pascoe this time was engendered by the sight of the horror he spotted now over DCI Logan's shoulder. "What the f...? What a terrible way to go! All the station told me was that something had happened to an ex-serviceman." He moved closer to the prone figure, shook his head. "Today of all days. I mean, dreadful on any day, but..."

Logan spun to look at the body again. "That's it though. I think today is the very point."

The DS frowned, but a sudden light shone in his eyes. "You mean because he's a veteran?"

"Well, yes and no. Not because of what he was, so much, as perhaps who he was."

"And who was he, sir?"

"I've been here about five minutes, Pascoe, though I am aware Tom Wright had become something of a minor celebrity in the local press. Now that you're here go and speak to the landlord and his wife again. One of the uniformed officers has already, but I'd like it done properly. Find out what you can, and then from the usual sources. By the way, when you are speaking with the Wolnieks emphasise to them that it would be best if they keep away from the press. Tell them the quickest way to justice is to keep those sniffing hounds off the trail of a story."

"Too late." It was Harj, who was pointing through the window at two cars of regrettable familiarity, which were pulling up further down the country road that ran between the flats and the fields.

"It was always going be tough, sir," Pascoe interjected, "I mean keeping the press at bay; once they found out you're on the case..."

Logan gave him a sharp look. "Meaning what?"

"You were a bit of a..." Pascoe hesitated, "...celebrity yourself after the whole Claire Treloggan thing – local lad returns and makes good..." now Pascoe looked somewhat embarrassed, as if he had overstepped the mark, "...sir. I mean the way you used those fibres to nail her attacker."

*'The whole Claire Treloggan thing' – how little Pascoe, or anyone, knew...with the exception of Freddy Dessler, and, of course, the woman*

*herself.*

Logan refocussed. "How do the press know about this so quickly?"

Pascoe shrugged, making a gesture towards the window. "Who knows, sir?"

"I realise Wright has been the local hero of late, but I took this call half an hour ago." He shook his head. "Our station should be rebuilt in the shape of a sieve."

Logan considered the untimely annoyance for a few moments. "We'll take the line with the Wolnieks, the press, or anyone else that the commemoration and all the other millions of veterans deserve better than to have this shadow cast over the Remembrance proceedings." He looked at the ghastly, prone figure of RSM Wright again. "Interesting. Today of all days, as you rightly said, no-one would dare lay a hand on a veteran. Whatever this is, it's premeditated and it's almost certainly personal."

★★★★

Pascoe stepped outside. He puffed out his cheeks and noticed his hands were shaking. That had been tough; the body.

That last couple of comments had borne out certain things he'd heard within the force – that Logan was a sharp cookie where second guessing motivations was concerned. That had been part of the appeal when the opportunity for this position had presented itself, though Pascoe hadn't expected to be at darkest depths the coalface quite so soon!

Logan had been succinct and focussed. He'd be worth observing. Heath had said something similar, but with a completely different nuance. Either way, Pascoe would be watching very carefully.

# 4

Pascoe thumped his palms on the steering wheel in apparent frustration at finding someone had already dived into the parking space he'd spotted becoming available on his third circuit of the one-way streets around that block.

"There's never anywhere to freaking park in Torquay, apart from on the waterfront itself. All bloody residents' permits."

"Better find one of those and pull rank then." Logan was getting fed-up of the endless circling too. Still, it hadn't really warranted the paroxysm of rage from the young DS, who to his mind had been in a peculiar mood from the moment Logan had told him they needed to head for Devon immediately. The Armistice commemoration had certainly awakened ghosts.

"I would if someone moved. Doesn't anyone here go out?"

"Perfect if she didn't want him to come calling," said Logan. He was aware of Pascoe's sidelong glance. "Well, they divorced relatively recently. She must have her reasons." He looked out of the side window at the uninspiring architecture. "Clearly moving in with a sugar-daddy wasn't one of them. But it's well-documented that some ex-servicemen have trouble readjusting to civilian life and are impossible to live with. That's hardly rocket-science or a revelation."

"Are you saying…?"

"I'm saying nothing; judging nothing." Logan's response was more impatient than he'd intended, so he sought to soften it with some humour as he pointed through the windscreen, "Except your inability to find a parking space."

Pascoe focussed again on the road, while Logan continued. "I've read recently that servicemen are coming forward more readily these days regarding PTSD, depression and so on. Perhaps it doesn't have the stigma it once did. But RSM Wright was old school."

"How do you come to that conclusion, sir?"

"Just a glance around his flat was enough. I'm surprised he didn't have a sign above his door, like the one at Anfield, but saying 'THIS IS SPARTA!' His study was like a shrine to all things military; regimental photos; sharp edges, ancient and modern; and an impressive collection of war movies. As for the bedroom – a more literal depiction I've yet to find; a bed in a room. Add to that the comments of his landlord, who never really managed to see inside his tenant's mind and found him remote and punctilious – my words, not his; my interpretation of them anyway. I think Mr Wolniek was allowing the sentiment of today to guide him. I don't think he wanted to speak with any negativity about a veteran.

"Anyway, for him – RSM Wright - to admit to any psychological issues – well, let's just say he'd have to have admitted them to himself first, and that might have been seen as weakness by him. I'm just asking you to bear that in mind." He pointed. "Look, there, on the right."

They dived into a space vacated by a transit van and then made their way on foot towards an unprepossessing terraced house; an address given to them by the local police responsible for Torquay. Though they were all members of the Devon and Cornwall Police Constabulary, Logan knew they would have to tread carefully, so as not to offend the hometown coppers.

Logan looked up and down the street. "Why here?"

"It's a nice enough street, sir."

"No, I meant why this town? She was born and brought up in Truro. There's no going west, south or north from there, so maybe it's as far east as she could get in the peninsula before getting her feet wet."

"So you're suggesting again that she's on the run from him and her past, sir? Not all ex-servicemen are monsters."

The DCI reminded himself once more that there might be the need for some care on this day. Pascoe's uncle had enjoyed a distinguished career in the Armed Forces, one which was beyond reproach, and it was the injuries he had sustained in rescuing a detachment of junior officers under fire in Afghanistan in 2009 that had eventually taken their toll and hastened his end. He had not been a man to whom Shakespeare's line applied, that nothing in his life became it like the leaving of it.

The wind bit as they got out of the car. It was small wonder the parking spaces had all been occupied – a combination of the Armistice commemorations on the TV and an east wind scouring the streets of Torquay would have convinced most residents to stay in once any local events had finished.

The front door was wholly unremarkable, and they fell silent as they waited for an answer to the doorbell.

If he had felt no shame when experiencing a thrill at the crime scene, Logan moved several paces outside his comfort zone now; enough that he struggled to hold her gaze as the door was opened by the athletic ex-Mrs Wright. Part of his embarrassment came from the hard-wired response to seeing her sweating, Lycra-clad figure, clearly used to the exercise they appeared to have interrupted; even at first glance she ticked enough boxes to place her way above the score of five for which Freddy Dessler had suggested he might settle. Then there was his presumption that she would look a certain way at fifty-one. As if he didn't have enough problems judging women and his response to them, there was now this inappropriate hormonal reaction; falling in immediate lust with a woman much older than him whose ex-husband had been murdered within the last twenty-four hours. It was neither professional, nor cool.

*There you go again*, mocked his bad angel. *Just your cup of tea…or poisoned chalice.*

He could understand the mockery. When he considered just how many opportunities for dates he had spurned in recent weeks, ignoring messages and winks, swiping left, what were the chances of this instant…*fatal?*…attraction? Was he cursed?

*Of course you are* – his bad angel wasn't finished yet – *you're carrying those twin millstones between your legs* – *the undoing of so many men throughout history.*

Still, he couldn't help himself. Even her former name was a taunt – Mrs Wright. He found himself wondering why no-one like her had appeared on those dating websites. Despite his recent rather dismissive comments in response to Freddy, he reckoned even in his priapic youth he would have found her maturity interesting and sexy. He couldn't help making a mental note to broaden the age range he had selected on said websites.

Logan was enough of a professional that only his conscience could have noticed the slight pause as he dwelt briefly on the inappropriate. He'd absorbed something else too, though; her eyes evinced no sadness. Rather there was a deep weariness, some of which was long-standing, etched into her features; ley-lines to a buried past. Intriguing - this woman would have received the details of her ex-husband's grotesque death within the last few hours; the father of her child had been executed, yet it seemed she was only fatigued, not traumatised.

More notable still was her relief – as insubstantial as smoke, but just as pungent. The fact that she had embarked on exercise, and with apparent gusto, also bore this out.

"Miss Scott?" Her slight smile of response betrayed a hint of discomfort. "Detective Chief Inspector Logan and Detective Sergeant Pascoe of the Devon and Cornwall Police. I assume you were told we were coming?"

She gave a little nod – "Yes" – and gestured them through.

The irony of it struck Logan between the eyes; this might have been his own flat, so devoid was it of ornamentation, family photographs and feminine touches. Had the RSM squeezed that out of her, or had they been peas in a pod? Perhaps monks in a monastic cell? Tom Wright's flat he could understand. Often it took men some time to bother rebuilding the den. Sometimes they didn't care, or didn't have a clue, and in the case of Tom Wright, he had lived huge chunks of his life in sterile regimentation. Yet he had observed that it was usually the woman's inclination to decorate that man right out of her life.

Looking through into another room, Logan saw a Concept II rowing machine, a treadmill and weights. The place was almost as Spartan and gladiatorial as Wright's; the one concession a little tray of scented candles.

It seemed Gill Scott had caught his questioning glances. "I've not been in here long." Now she saw Logan's frown. "Okay, I'm just not very girly. Bit of a show-home at the moment, isn't it?"

"Suits me," he responded. *You got your gym set up quickly enough.*

She waved them towards the sofa and offered them coffee, which both men were grateful to accept after the long drive.

As Logan heard the machine brewing in the kitchen and caught the aroma, he was reminded how smell, like music, had the ability to crystallize images from the vapour of memories. For just a moment, he was back at Exeter University, the voice of Freddy Dessler, although at that time still a postgraduate student and owner of a brand new Nespresso machine, barely able to disguise the intense excitement and curiosity engendered by his visitor's confessions. For Logan, taking up an offer of coffee was now part of the rules too, buying you time, putting people at ease, perhaps causing them to lower their defences if indeed they were up. He realised it was something he had learnt from Dessler, when the future Doctor of Psychology, a man who had proved himself more insightful than the police in at least one instance, had listened to a young student's cathartic unburdening of his troubled past.

He squeezed his eyes tight shut and tried to focus on the job at hand, but still his demons seemed determined to mislead him. An indoor gym and proper coffee – not only would she kick his butt in bed, she'd be up all night doing it!

And talking of kicking butts, when he re-opened his eyes he spotted a couple of pieces of memorabilia on an otherwise empty bookshelf; a photo and a certificate. The former appeared to have been taken at some martial arts event and showed three women clad in taekwondo suits. One of the women was several years older than the other two and sported a black belt, while the younger girls wore blue. Dishevelled, but beaming, they were giving a thumbs-up to the camera. The older woman was almost certainly Miss Scott, given the distinctive short, blonde hair with its severe cut. The certificate backed up why Miss Scott, or Mrs Wright as it stated, was wearing the black belt – she was at the very advanced sixth dan.

While she continued to prepare the coffee, Logan noticed that Pascoe, too, had clocked the photo and their hostess's ability to resist arrest. They exchanged a look – but where Logan expected to see a reflection of his own raised eyebrows, perhaps a nod acknowledging the hostess's impressive achievement, Pascoe just seemed troubled.

"So much for needing to put distance between her and her ex," whispered the DCI, his voice masked by the thrumming of the coffee machine. "She can take care of herself."


Logan replaced the cup carefully on the glass table. "Delicious." Gill Scott smiled; the only time so far that facial gesture had seemed to make it more than halfway to her eyes. Logan continued:

"So, Miss Scott, firstly may we express our sincere condolences for your loss. I know you were recently divorced, but…"

"Can I be brutally honest?"

Logan had half-expected something; it was just a mild surprise that it came so soon.

"Honesty's always welcome. It doesn't have to be brutal."

There was that half-smile again; some sort of ritual – to ward off intimacy maybe. Perhaps to encourage it. Who knew? Certainly not him. He'd seen the same facets of expression on the face of a couple of his dates. At best it was just wariness; at worst a curse above the door of a dusty, long-buried past. There was rueful recognition in the thought that a date with Gill Scott would have been another dismal failure. The damaged can survive without love – or at least that's what they tell themselves until it's too late.

*Where does that leave you?* His bad angel was at it again. *Except you've never known love, at least not at the receiving end.*

He was grateful her words interrupted that monologue.

"Tom and I had stopped loving each other a long time before we separated. It's probably been said thousands of times, but the army was his wife. Me? I wasn't even his mistress – that would have kept some passion alive. Oh, I'm sure he found some vent for his physical needs, but I wasn't prepared to be that." She rubbed her hands across her face and seemed troubled. "But I would not have wished that end on him. Whatever else, he did serve Queen and country with a true sense of duty. We were still in communication, and I'm even still looking after some of his stuff amongst my unpacked cases. Just things I guess we'd forgotten about that I found when I finally managed to sell the house this year and moved here. I was going to send them, but I doubt he's any space for them in that little flat he moved into."

She made a sudden movement, leaning forward in a rather masculine way with elbows on knees, coffee mug cradled in her hands, before continuing:

"But the army has mistresses too – whores that riddle it with diseases, which are brought home and infect family and friends; that drive people apart."

If Logan took anything positive from that intense confession, it was seeing the deadness - that fatigue - in Gill Scott's eyes being replaced by some of the passion she had been mourning the loss of just moments before. It was a peculiar revelation, the frightened anger transforming her for just a second or two into a thing of vulnerable beauty.

She leaned back in her chair again, her gaze transferring to the window; an opportunity taken by the two policemen to exchange the most subtle of glances, a subtlety singularly missing when Pascoe next spoke.

"When you mentioned diseases, were you only talking metaphorically, or had your husband…?" Logan saw Gill Scott's head turn towards Pascoe with a slowness born of disbelief and contempt - and in that, it mirrored his own. The DS was caught in a pincer. "Well, I'm just trying to…rule out reasons why you… might have…"

"Am I to understand I'm a suspect?"

"No, I meant why you had…separated…" Pascoe put down the shovel with a clang; went quiet. He didn't dare risk a look at Logan.

"Of course I was only speaking metaphorically." The delivery was a slow monotone, laced with disdain. "My husband…ex-husband…was a loyal man and I believe firmly that extended to his family. He…" she hesitated, "…loved us."

Logan didn't miss the contradiction – the man she had assumed, only moments before, had found an outlet elsewhere for his sexual needs, now described as true to his family. He made a mental note only, because he had spotted an opportunity to release Pascoe from his self-made shackles. "Talking of family…"

He broke off, observed how Gill Scott's features remained at the glacial end of the icy scale, no lines softening, her mouth remaining pinched, and then ploughed on. "How has your daughter taken the news?"

"I wouldn't know."

Well, that explained a lot. He just raised an eyebrow – an unspoken question.

"We haven't talked for some time."

"Some time being…?"

"Ten years." She appeared to pick up his unspoken response to this fact. "I believe that turns my use of *some time* into something of a euphemism."

Logan couldn't help but smile and wondered whether that reaction was *inappropriate* under the circumstances – and there was that word again. He had known Gill Scott just twenty minutes and already inappropriate had floated and spun through their interaction more than once. He allowed the feathery word to drift away along with his smile. For all Pascoe's rather gauche and clumsy behaviour moments before, it revealed a lack of awkwardness in the presence of a strong woman that Logan could only applaud; an absence of whispers, or echoes of screaming, that he envied.

Not for the first time in his career, nor for the last, he feared, Logan looked to regain his focus. "May I ask what caused the falling out – assuming there has been one?"

"Well, it started when she was a teenager. She fell out with the world. Don't they all? I should be ashamed to say this, but I'm not – we were never really close. She was the definitive daddy's girl. When he tired of me, so did she. Then, when army life did what it does, particularly in Afghanistan, and he came back not the quite same father, she took her leave of us both."

"Do you have a telephone number? Postal address? Email address?"

Gill Scott returned her eyes to the window, frustrating Logan, who had been trying to decipher the nature of the hurt lurking behind them; its peculiar tint. He fancied it might still have been iciness. Pain on the rocks; always a dangerous cocktail.

"Well, I hope you understand," he continued, "that it is our duty to inform her of recent events, even though she's probably seen it on the news, so if you do have the contact details..."

"I don't. You might have better luck if you try her cousin." The words were addressed towards the window.

Logan looked up. "Cousin?"

Gill Scott's gaze returned to her guests. "Yes, my sister's girl – Samantha. Samantha Ingle." She watched Pascoe note the name and gestured towards the pad. "Ironic."

"Ironic?"

"Yes, the way you've written her name – Miss S.Ingle."

"How so, ironic?" said Pascoe, speaking up again, perhaps wanting to move to safer ground. "Amusing, yes; probably a pain in the playground, but..."

"Ironic, because of the two girls, she was the prettier," interrupted Gill Scott. "Never any trouble attracting the boys – or the men – from a very young age."

Again, Logan felt that discomfort, this time in the delivery, rather than the words themselves. Once more, part of his unease lay in not being able to identify the exact cause of it.

*What's the other part, Ben*, his bad angel was on the ball today and in no mood for pleasantries, *memories of your sister?*

Not for the first time, he found himself grateful for an interjection from their hostess. "It wasn't a problem while they were best friends."

"I'm assuming the girls are of a similar age then," said Logan.

"Yes, just a year apart."

"You say they *were* best friends?"

"They fell out."

"Recently?"

"No, while they were still in their teens – at least it started then."

*Was there anyone in this family who saw eye to eye?* wondered Logan. "So actually you can't tell us where we can find Samantha

Ingle, and she probably can't tell us where your daughter is?"

Gill Scott gave a crooked smile and addressed her next comment to Pascoe. "Awesome. Watch and learn if you want to make DCI.

Pascoe tried to suppress a grin.

"Laugh it up, DS Pascoe," said Logan, not without humour. It was good to see the young officer loosen up a bit. He turned back to Gill Scott. "Call me Mystic Meg, but I assume you won't know where your sister lives, or am I allowed to believe in miracles… maybe…perhaps….?"

The heavy, exaggerated irony had been used in an attempt to further loosen the mood – and it seemed to work, because now Gill Scott threw her head back all of a sudden and burst out laughing; a sound that cascaded forth and then tinkled on for some time – tiny pebbles in a Chilean rain-stick. For her, it was perhaps simple comic relief. For DCI Ben Logan, there would never be simplicity in that sound – and what there was lay beyond the bounds of definition, out there in a dark, unmapped world.

Now he glanced at Pascoe and was thrown by how the young DS was staring at and through Gill Scott. He'd have expected Pascoe to be swept along by the moment; instead, his eyes had adopted the same enigmatic look evinced by the woman just moments before. Again, the DCI reminded himself not to underestimate the impact of this day and this murder on the young man.

He turned his attention back to Gill Scott; watched as she wiped beneath each eye with the back of a finger; a very delicate movement and a feminine reflex, unnecessary as she was wearing no mascara.

"I'm sorry," she said, still stifling giggles. "You probably think that's most inappropriate – a widow…" she made exaggerated air parenthesis of the commas, but Logan forgave her, given there was irony involved, "…of just a few hours laughing her head off."

That word again - *inappropriate*. Logan could have sworn he saw the feather spiralling once more in the breath of her laughter. He tried to banish the thoughts that circled with it. "Things are what they are. We do what we do to cope."

She levered herself out of her chair. "I'll just go and grab my phone – the address book of the twenty-first century. Hopefully I'll remember the name of my sibling." She paused, raised a finger as she remembered something. "Perhaps I should mention that my sister and her daughter don't get on all that well," she gave a rueful smile, "just to complete the set."

With an almost conspiratorial look that sent Logan's signet ring twirling, she headed for the bedroom.

# 5

There had been venues set aside for events that evening, but the three veterans, sated with too much noise and adulation, overwhelmed by the day's memories, had sought out somewhere quieter; a place where their need to be alone with each other and the ghosts of their fellow combatants would be understood. The Jolly Farmer, their local village pub, was that sanctuary. They'd not had to pay for a drink yet and had no problem with that manifestation of the British people's current love-affair with the armed forces. But their space was respected and now here they sat, late on a November evening, the vastness of their internal landscapes and of every battlefield they had trodden held at bay by the inconsequential chatter born of another drink and the light from the pub fire.

Around them, at the tables, at the bar, on the flat screen TV recommissioned for the day's events instead of the usual football, in the comforting hubbub of bar-side ramblings, there had only been one topic of conversation once the murder had appeared on the national news, just after the close of the live broadcasts. For the three of them, the subject was the same, but their slant on it was markedly different.

"'Ere's to whoever did it," said Lance Corporal 'Bovril' Bovis under his breath to the other two. All three raised their glasses and took a satisfying swig of Doom Bar ale. Bovis licked his lips with a relish that wasn't just the result of hops. "Couldn't 'ave 'appened to a nicer cunt."

The three of them laughed; a cruel sound, rather than hearty.

Sergeant Penney's smile didn't quite reach as far as it might. "What's the matter, Farthing," Bovis asked him. "You suffering an attack of conscience?" He paused. "'Ere, maybe this'll put paid to that."

Bovis leaned over and took an empty beer bottle from a nearby table. He placed it on its side in front of them and spun it. The three men watched the decelerating arcs of the bottle, thoughtful and mesmerised; lost, not for the first time that day, in memories of a distant conflict.

"Remind you of anything?"

"It's not conscience," said Penney. "Just thinking how it is really – life. You survive everything the Argies and the Taliban have got to throw at you, then die in agony on your own bed."

"How were you the first to find out, even before it hit the screens, Bovril?" asked the third member of the uniformed triumvirate, Corporal Bullard.

"The police contacted me as I was the one who should've picked him up this morning – which pissed me off, as you know. They couldn've chosen many people who liked him less, present company excluded. They just wanted to know whether I'd seen anything suspicious when I called at the flat."

A smirk pulled at the corners of Bullard's mouth. "What did you say? That you were too far back in the queue of possible suspects to see properly?"

They burst out laughing, drawing unknowing looks of good-will from some at the bar. Bullard continued, addressing Penney. "Anyway, you've hit the nail on the head. It's bad enough dealing with what those fuck-head fanatics are throwing at you, without another type of fanatic making your life a misery at the end of it all. I'll never forget what he made us do. All because we were terrified, when any man had a right to be. I'll shed no tears over him."

"So, who did it then?" Bovis' question was rhetorical. The bottle had come to a gentle stop, pointing to a space beyond the three comrades. "Well, there's three people we know didn't, God rest their souls."

They lifted their glasses again, saying, as one: "To Corporal Stead, Private Morgan and Private Best," before drinking their toast, followed by a moment of reflection.

"The thing is," said Bovis, "for all we know, the police might 'ave to cast a very large net. We might not be the only ones 'e did that to and, like us, the others were too scared to shop 'im. Somehow, 'is eyes 'ad that…brutality. Maybe war just brings it out in some men. I dunno."

Bullard took it up: "Yeah, he was a sneaky bastard. He'd have twisted it. Looks like he had support from above as well – all those commendations and decorations. He'd have said we made it up as some sort of cover for our actions. He was a survivor."

"Not today," said Bovis, his cruel grin finding a pale reflection in the features of the others.

Penney lifted his drink towards the others in turn. "No, the survivors – that'd be us then." His words prompted another swig of beer. He addressed Bovis: "So, back to your question – who…"

"…cares?" Bovis gave them all a look. Though there was the darkest of humour in the word, no-one smiled. "The RSM made us swear to silence – let's keep our word."

"Why were you asked to pick him up anyway?" Bullard addressed Bovis, sensing it was time to move on. "Hasn't he got a car?"

"Got bloody volunteered, didn't I. Bet the bastard did that 'imself, so I was forced to show respect to a former commanding officer, plus getting the hassle of finding somewhere to park, while 'e got dropped at the gathering point."

"Oh, I mean the guy had balls," admitted Bullard. "Some of his actions saved lives. It was just a heart he was lacking."

"Anyway, it's weird to think that I was calling on a dead man earlier today." Bovis looked around at the others, then reached down, spun the bottle again. "A stick rammed down 'is throat – sounds like the end was poetic justice."

"Meted out by someone who knew the poem," added Penney. He gave a knowing look around the table.

"Guess we'll let it all be buried with him. It can be everyone's little secret," said Bullard. "An oath of silence is an oath of silence, whatever the circumstances."

The three ex-soldiers sat in that silence once more, hypnotised by the spinning finger of fate on the table before them.

# 6

Instead of gazing, mesmerised, into a pair of gorgeous eyes, Logan found himself studying his cappuccino froth, confused. Forty-five minutes – that was the shortest date yet. What had seemed off-beat and quirky on the website had turned out to be just nutty face-to-face.

But even nutty he could have dealt with; likewise the fact that there was no spark. He'd have given it a go, at least for another hour, but her reason for having to leave so soon - she'd spilt tea on her duvet and needed to go to buy some stain-remover - was probably a new low; one that rendered *needy* a sublime compliment. Right now, he was of less interest to a woman than a tea-stain.

What was he doing wrong? Okay, he didn't think this particular instance was his fault, but clearly she had seen something that drove her away. He didn't suspect his looks – an ironic observation from someone with prosopagnosia perhaps, but he was basing it on comments from colleagues with whom he had a half-decent relationship, male and female. He guessed there must be some truth in their flattery because the dates kept coming, but it was the 'kept going' bit that he needed to solve. To use Freddy's scorecard, this time he had tried to settle for five, but he had still got no further.

Thinking again about those colleagues, while it was true that part of his motivation for playing the dating-websites game was the rock it provided in a sea of nothingness, the other reason was that using them was more the norm than the exception at the station and it offered him a way through the door to the in-crowd; the chance to seem normal and have common ground with them. Indeed, he had even tried to make it work for him. He made a note, wherever possible, of the women his cabal of fellow website users dated; kept up to speed on who had moved on, meaning those potential dates were now available. In one or two instances, his colleagues had even flagged an opportunity when they had been drawn by other temptations. A WPC, far too young to turn up in his pool, had helped him to pick his profile picture. He would look to link up. More often than not his request was accepted – he assumed the WPC had chosen well! Plus, he knew those dates had no issues at all with dating a policeman.

A wink emoji – a mobile phone number – a date.

A walk-away.

What were they avoiding?

If coming to terms with that weren't challenging enough, he was now trying to acquire a new skill – namely, looking like it was the most natural thing in the world that the woman with whom you had walked into the café had now walked out. What were the rules? He prayed for guidance.

Someone answered his prayers – the phone rang. A face appeared on the screen – a feature of the police phonebook which he'd kept so that he never had to answer the question of why he hadn't. As usual, he read and recognised the number.

"Pascoe…yeah, sure." He had told the DS it would be okay to call – had that been precognition, knowing there was every chance the date would go pear-shaped? Less explicable was the fact that he had confided at all in the young officer about his dating. He wasn't part of the cabal yet. Was it because he sensed something of the fellow outsider in Pascoe? The latter never mentioned a girlfriend, or seemed to hang out for a beer with anyone at the station. There was risk involved in this sharing of personal information, especially given his initial misgivings about the nature of the DS's interactions with Heath. Yet that awkwardness in Torquay, the question about the disease, had made Logan warm to him a little. On reflection, perhaps he had simply decided the surreal and mostly superficial world of dating would be a suitable No-Man's Land on which to try to build some common ground; a world in which reality was suspended so often that Logan would reveal nothing salient.

He heard Pascoe's voice and tuned in again, continuing: "Where?...okay, are you there at the moment? Right, I'll pick you up. Be there in ten minutes...no, no...I'm available. Yes, it went that well."

As he looked out at the grim surroundings of this particular part of Truro, far from the crashing waves, picturesque beaches and tourist tat, the questions were many. One of them found voice through Pascoe, who had been filling him in during the drive with the details of his enquiries: "I wonder what it is about the women in this unhappy family."

"Indeed," agreed Logan. "And you've already spoken to Samantha Ingle's mother, Bella...?"

"Yes. She lives in Denmark and has no contact with her daughter. Samantha was a driven, almost solitary individual, who went away to university and never came home again...and I must admit, given the slightly vacuous nature of the lady I spoke to on the phone, I have some sympathy. Sounds like Single is a high achiever, sir. Doctor of Laws, junior international in volleyball."

"Another sporty one! If the female of the species apparently conspiring to make me feel inadequate wasn't enough, I now get to feel embarrassed about my lack of exercise too," groaned Logan.

Pascoe frowned. "You look in good shape, sir – how do you manage that then?"

"I wish I could say good genes." Logan turned to stare through the passenger window, not wanting the momentary darkness in his eyes on show.

Pascoe laughed awkwardly. "Dare I ask, sir - what did happen on the date?"

Logan continued to stare out of the window, shaking his head in faux despair even as the real McCoy wandered its way through his thoughts. He puffed out his cheeks, deciding to keep the tone light. There were limits on how far in he would allow his junior. "What do you know about Vanish, Pascoe?"

"Is that what she did, sir?"

"Might have been better — and yes, in a way, she did." The DCI craned his neck to look at a sign. "Isn't this it?"

"Yes, Estuary Sports and Social Centre," read Pascoe.

They pulled into a car park alongside an unprepossessing brick building. Logan frowned. "I ask again, why here, in the middle of one of the uglier parts of the industrial estate?"

"Maybe it was cheap land at the time," ventured Pascoe, "relatively speaking. Certainly wouldn't be now."

At various points along their route through the estate they had been passing signs advertising how Cornerstone, the huge property investment company based in the south-west, were ploughing money into redevelopment of the tired businesses. New tinted glass and steel structures were springing up alongside the main thoroughfares; the bright young things on a vast, but ageing stage. Yet behind the scenes, at the back of the chorus line, still lurked old, tired sheds and huts; members of the original cast, careworn and grumpy, looking for a place in the sun, but lacking the solar panels to really make it count.

As they stepped out of the car, Logan took in the four artificial pitches; two of them occupied at that moment by hockey and touch-rugby training, while from the brick building came cries and groans that could only emanate from Hell, or a fitness club.

Logan saw another puzzle here, and mused out loud on it.

"There's money here – these four pitches wouldn't have come cheap," he gestured towards the car park, "but none of these cars smack of nouveau riche, or indeed old money. She must have been a highflier on the legal front but given it up completely for this."

Even as he spoke, another part of the DCI nodded to himself – he approved. This felt, sounded and looked like somewhere that did what it said on the tin. He was intrigued, because Pascoe's research had revealed this to be both the brain- and love-child of Samantha Ingle. She was a paradox; a highly qualified lawyer with a social conscience. He liked her already...and that spelt trouble!

They strolled over to the fence surrounding the pitches and observed as a group of as-yet-faceless figures moved against a surreal backdrop of giant cooling towers and grim factories. Art and life mingled, revealing a Lowry-esque world to Logan.

Both training sessions sounded and looked serious. There was something amongst the shouts of warning and encouragement in the rugby session that disconcerted Logan for a moment. He drew nearer, observing how one young, tall and powerful black lad, a teenager by the look of it, ran holding the ball almost with cockiness in one hand as he danced along the defensive line, feinting, inviting the opposition to get to him so he could release the ball and make them look stupid. One opposing player in a rather incongruous baseball cap seemed to take the bait, arriving too late, but appearing not to mind in the slightest as he crunched the muscular teenager with a fearsome tackle. The recipient lay motionless for a moment on his back.

"Uh oh!" Pascoe rocked on his toes, grinning. "That's what you call heavy touch rugby. Wonder if it will kick off now."

Only then did both men realise that the black lad was laughing, as were the rest of the players, who had given up any interest in the ball. Now the tackler got to his feet and removed the baseball cap to reveal that he was in fact a she, as an auburn ponytail swished out from beneath it.

Both policemen stood with their mouths open while the tackler offered a hand and hauled her victim to his feet. *Another candidate for Match.com*, thought Logan as it dawned on him what had been playing on his subconscious a moment before – the sound of a higher-pitched voice amongst the guys; more than one, in fact, as a careful look at the teams showed. There were a couple of other girls out there. Given the complexities of his love life, or rather the stark fact that he didn't have one, he wasn't sure which version of -pressed he should be, im- or de-.

Even if she hadn't looked across and then approached the fence with a certain confidence of stride and demeanour, the DCI would somehow have known this was Samantha Ingle. As she drew closer he noted, as far as his facial blindness would allow him, that, hair colour aside, she seemed to fit the Scott genetics – Ingle was her mother's married name. Her features were what he understood from his mental crib sheet to be alluring and attractive rather than pretty. Whether those features mirrored her mother or her aunt would have been a step too far for Logan to ascertain, but the lean, firm musculature, the apparent hardness of teak that marked the latter were manifest. As she neared them it occurred to Logan that two gawping men loitering near a playing field fence probably couldn't expect much of a welcome, and he steeled himself.

"Hello there. You must be the police." The greeting, if not warm, was polite. The women in this somewhat dysfunctional family not only seem determined to throw Logan off balance with their acumen, they seemed to enjoy it and were pretty good at it too.

"Don't worry," she continued, responding to their expressions, "I'm not much of a detective. It's just that you couldn't look more like *coppers* if you'd had your woo-woos on." She'd adopted a playful felon's accent when using the idiomatic term for policemen, quite out of keeping with her intense demeanour. "Given my uncle was murdered yesterday, that means you've had just enough time to discover that my aunt and her daughter have fallen out, and to do a bit of research into finding me."

Logan felt himself rocking on his heels, as if his body was determined to turn his police presence into a parody of one. The rocking was metaphorical as well as literal, exacerbated by the indifference of her language as she had referenced the horrific murder of a family member. He did his best to disguise his vertigo and take some control. Giving a polite smile, which mirrored Samantha's, he looked up at the top of the fence.

"Detective Chief Inspector Logan and Detective Sergeant Pascoe." He gestured towards his sidekick. "Any chance we could talk inside, Ms Ingle, rather than acting out some tragic wartime scene?"

"Sure. I imagine we've had all the wartime tragedies we can handle for a while." It was said without humour, and Logan immediately regretted his choice of image firstly given the crime and the particular time of year…

*What was it about November?*

…but also because it had handed further mastery of the moment to the obviously rather dominant Ms Ingle.

As if to emphasise the point, Samantha turned towards the pitches, gave a piercing whistle and yelled in the direction of the rugby players, who had not yet resumed play and seemed to be watching; waiting for her return. "Okay, I believe that was probably a penalty to the red shirts." There was much mocking laughter. "You've still got fifteen minutes to do – don't forget there's a game coming up."

Amid some general mickey-taking, play continued.

"Aren't your team a man…sorry, a player down?" Logan wanted to move on from his previous little faux pas.

Samantha was already striding towards the brick building and turned her head without breaking that stride. "No, I was just the ref."

Logan and Pascoe exchanged shrugs of shoulders while hurrying to try and catch up.

In the unpretentious but clean reception area, a large TV flicked from image to image. Samantha had stopped to chat with the receptionist about some issue with the showers. While he waited for her Logan took in the rolling credits; teams – hockey, rugby, football, volleyball, basketball, men's, women's, mixed – some players in action, some beaming at the camera, trophies in hand, medals around necks. Two young boxers sparred with each other. There were classes advertised – martial arts, boxing, yoga, the inevitable Zumba, which he couldn't help feeling was the wrong demographic, though what did he know.

Turning away from the screen, Logan saw Samantha was still deep in conversation at Reception, although now about bin collections. He was learning his place in the grand scheme of things today, for sure. It would be tea stains again next.

He spoke up. "We can come back later if you prefer – though we will definitely be back." He turned towards some photographs on the wall, effectively turning his back on her at the same time. "Things to do – murders to solve."

Despite his irritation, he found the pictures fascinating. They had clearly been taken during the renovation process and illustrated just what a difference refurbishment and enthusiasm could make to a tired building.

Now Pascoe pointed to a device in a glass case, standing proud in the middle of the reception area.

"What is that, sir? A telescope?"

Logan shook his head. "The youth of today." He adopted an old man's demeanour and voice. "That, young man, is a transit-level surveying tool, which is almost certainly what was manufactured here before Ms Ingle took over."

"Is that a pang of nostalgia I hear, sir?"

Logan raised an eyebrow. "For the beauty of the engineering, yes. But look at those pictures, Pascoe." He gestured towards the photographs. "This place was uncared for, falling apart. Going to the dogs. The death rattle could probably have been heard all over the Estate. Not all change is bad…"

He broke off, his attention drawn to another TV on which he saw something of a different ilk; the real reason behind the word 'Social' in the establishment's title. There were no pictures, just names and details; of charities, hospices, hostels, causes, some of them national, others local and less known, with no apparent differentiation between genders, colours, creeds, or indeed species.

A sudden rattling behind him surprised Logan. "You don't have to be a victim to join here, or pay a fee, but you do have to have a conscience and the only disability unwelcome here is short arms and deep pockets."

Logan turned and was surprised to see a warm smile, followed by the appearance of a collection tin, which Samantha held in front of his face. He turned back to the screen. "You support all of these?"

"Not all. We have links with some, particularly the hostels. This is a place where we nurture potential, predominantly through sport, and likewise harness and channel aggression, which is mostly a response to tyranny." She paused. "Which we shit on, by the way. If the latter manifests itself in any way here, we weed it out. Most of our members learn to do that themselves. The Centre is effectively self-policing, but not self-repairing. Nor do the bins empty themselves."

He ignored her slight dig. When no response came, she continued. "Of course, there are people that require something we can't provide…with demons we are in no position to fight."

"Such as?" He blurted it out with more abruptness than intended, but his fascination with Samantha Ingle's somewhat hazy history, combined with her use of the *demon* word, meant the question was out before he could stop it.

In response, her smile long gone, Samantha shook the tin again, on which the name 'Safebeds' was written, before saying: "Such as a bed. You'll note there's no address given. Take a moment to consider that there's a genuine need for an anonymous shelter for those who don't want to be, or shouldn't be, found by the curious…or vengeful. We give a phone number on request and ask nothing further."

He looked at the tin and then back at her. His arms remained by his sides. They exchanged a look. "Let me think about where I want to make my contribution."

With that, he received the look he expected before she turned and led them away from Reception, putting down the tin with rather a bang. Logan and Pascoe followed, reduced once more to exchanging silent glances which nevertheless spoke volumes. As they headed down the corridor, the groans and yells which they had heard outside were now indeed revealed as souls in torment, accompanied by the thumping of punch bags and trainers' pads, or the heaving of weights. Glances through the small windows in swing doors revealed fitness studios, peopled by the sweating hulks of tormentors and tormented of both sexes. The glass of those windows was reinforced, but Logan assumed that was just a health and safety directive – as Samantha Ingle had implied, this place could look after itself.

"You've done an amazing job, Miss Ingle," ventured Pascoe, "given everything…"

"Please, call me Sam." Logan had to admire her cleverness; that dimpled smile would have directed energy straight to Pascoe's loins – thereby lay distraction and weakness in all men, as he knew so well, but also it drove the slightest of wedges between senior and junior officer. Quite what Pascoe had been about to say was another matter. He had stopped mid-sentence, rather than Samantha interrupting him. Had he been planning something flirtatious himself, then thought better of it?

So Samantha liked her power games as well as ball games. Logan had encountered enough high-flying attorneys, or as he preferred to think of them, smart arse lawyers in his time, many of them obstructing the proper course of justice, to know that Miss Ingle, despite her protestations of conscience, had been trying to dictate the pace and direction of everything – the dialogue, the physical interaction, even down to the speed at which they had been walking – from the moment of his arrival. Once a devil, always an advocate, it seemed.

Well, he was up for the challenge. His presence here was, in theory, nothing more than an inquiry for information about RSM Wright's next of kin, but Logan's sixth sense always told him where there were buried secrets and this family had a graveyard full of them – he just knew. So, he was going to push a little harder than might seem merited. Okay, he couldn't deny there was a hint of irritation after several encounters with game-playing females in both his private- and now his work-life, but where Samantha Ingle was concerned, he knew already she was hiding in plain sight. As someone who had spent his life doing the same, concealing his prosopagnosia from the world, playing at normal, he recognised it in others. He would get behind the mask and find out what lurked there, even though it meant throwing the procedural book out of the window.

"Not quite the career path you seemed destined for," he said, almost mildly.

"No." Even though her back was now turned to them, the DCI knew her rather cocky smile had faded, which had been his intention. "I saw sense."

"Meaning?"

"Spot on, in one word. I wanted my life – my world – to have meaning for the first time."

"Yet you seemed so driven – in your law career, I mean."

"Driven away."

"How so?"

Their pace appeared to have quickened, as if a haunted past was in pursuit, and the conversation ground to a temporary halt as they reached the sanctuary of a break out area, devoid, at that moment, of anything breaking out. Samantha gestured to the coffee machine.

Only once three cups were filled and they had taken their seats did the dialogue continue.

She gestured around her. "My office. I don't believe in closing myself off."

Tempted though he was to respond to her with some quip, he knew it would have come across as unprofessional and decided that a momentary silence was the best way to restore some of the balance of power. As he watched her fold her arms, then unfold them again as the time-honoured defensiveness of the gesture dawned on her, reaching instead for her coffee, he took some obtuse pleasure now in the evident discomfort caused by that studied silence as well as noting with interest that it had happened at all. It was time to dispense with small talk.

"Your mother…"

"Ah yes. Mother." Rarely had Logan witnessed such contempt as oozed from those last two syllables. Clearly an emotive topic, given Samantha's preparedness to allow the mask to fall for a moment; stop playing the prosecution. She was studying her coffee in much the same way he had stared into his cappuccino froth only an hour before. Once more, he decided on silence and watchfulness. At last, there was a sigh. "Looking back, I think I was determined to break the mould. To be different." As she looked up again, her eyes were cold. "You see, Mummy-dear lost the fight for the brain cells to her sister, so she took what she thought was the only route open to women like her, the ladies-who-lunch brigade, and married my father, a very successful businessman, as doubtless you've checked."

Her cynicism regarding police procedures was sounding a bit jaded. Of course, they had fucking checked – that was their job! Logan let the jibe pass.

Samantha continued. "She lay back in kept splendour. I think I took the toughest university course there was, short of medicine, to prove I could be different. The trouble was I failed that part of the law syllabus which required you to discard your heart where ripping off poor or innocent people is concerned. Oh, I made a pile very quickly, but…" She stopped; took a thoughtful sip of her coffee. "At the risk of sounding a bit 'love-me love-me', I decided all that drive would be better directed towards helping those for whom the law is nothing but Chancery."

"Wasn't that a board game?" asked Pascoe, who for his trouble received one of Logan's despairing glances.

"That was from a novel, DS Pascoe." Logan turned to Samantha again and raised his eyebrows in mock despair. He might have been mistaken, but it seemed to draw an unwilling twitch at the corner of her mouth, that might have been a fledgling smile. "I can believe you did indeed make a pile. This land can't have come cheap."

"My father and mother divorced when I was ten, though she kept the name, of course, as it opened doors. Oh, he was far too intelligent to stay with a pair of tits for the rest of his life, but not completely devoid of a conscience. He was easy to tap up for a donation to my new project. Plus, he had plenty of connections with the big businesses around here. This piece of land was a piece of cake for him."

"As DS Pascoe alluded, you've certainly done his investment proud."

"A shame it's not him I'm making proud. His only active interest in this will be the one I pay him back – he loaned me the money. His conscience has its limits."

She broke off, leaning back in her chair and sipping her coffee, perhaps aware she had allowed an underbelly to show for a second or two. There followed a few moments of silence, filled with unspoken conjecture. At last, Logan said: "Still, a remarkable story…if a bit sad."

Samantha's eyes narrowed, a hint of steel and glass replacing their bricky brownness. Logan's eyes, on the other hand, widened in faux apology and he raised his hands. "Oh, I wasn't just referring to you." He watched how Samantha's head lowered, her gaze motionless; a lioness, but was she stalking, or defending? Seemed a different sort of pride was under threat here.

Logan continued: "I just meant that, well, quite frankly, the interaction between certain members of your family gives sub-zero a new meaning. My apologies if that sounds like I'm speaking out of turn." He looked at her in a way that challenged her to contradict him.

True to the Scott genes, she still had the power to unsettle him. Samantha threw back her head, but instead of a leonine roar, there was the most glorious laugh. It struck Logan that had he walked into the room at that moment, his prosopagnosia was such that only the colour and length of Samantha's hair would have differentiated her from her aunt in his eyes.

Logan glanced at Pascoe and was again surprised to catch him staring at Samantha in a repeat of the way he'd been staring at Gill Scott, lost in some moment that was causing his jaws to clench. Whatever his reasons, it suggested someone impervious to the distractions of a woman's charms, which as far as the DCI was concerned was something to be envied! Perhaps in both cases he had seen simply someone strong enough to knock a hard man to the floor? However, there was also an indefinable something, suggesting his eyes were focussed elsewhere. That the word *lost* had more than one nuance.

For once taking a lead from his younger colleague, Logan tried not to be distracted. He forged ahead:

"Anyway," he drew the word out, "your cousin." He realised the tone of that phrase was almost an echo of his earlier segue into the discussion about her mother, but it appeared to have escaped Samantha – already he knew she was someone who wouldn't have let the opportunity for a dig pass. Instead, her features settled. The smile was still there, but no longer convincing.

She puffed out her cheeks. "Right...my cousin. Well, what I meant to say to you outside earlier was, please come inside where I will tell you just how little I know about her life."

"I believe you were once the best of friends."

"Yes, then we managed to fall out, as girls do. I can give you her last known address – as in known by me – but I can pretty much guarantee she's no longer there."

"What caused you to fall out to that extent? I know teenagers have arguments, but they have been known to make up. Moving on without leaving a forwarding address to your family seems drastic, shall we say?"

"Oh, we just went in different directions. I love my sport, she doesn't. I liked the attention of the boys; she didn't get that, or at least not to the same extent. Used to accuse me of being 'the pretty one', as if I had some control over that."

"So did you fall out over a boy?"

"Over a man, yes."

Gill Scott's words had been one thing. To hear such a frank admission from Samantha Ingle was the latest in a line of surprises for Logan. As part of his attempt to get to the buried bones of this family's past, he had deliberately pushed the conversation more into the pattern of an interview at the station. Now he was grateful that he had adopted his usual pose under such circumstances, with his fingers interlaced to prevent the betrayal of hand gestures. As someone who was more reliant than many on body language, he did not want his own to give him away, though as a lawyer, Samantha was doubtless also a practised reader of these markers. Would she have noticed the slight whitening of his knuckles? DS Pascoe's pronounced discomfort on the other hand, required no specialist skills for interpretation. The way he shifted in his seat, spoke of an officer still learning his trade. His features were an open book, one he would need to close as his career progressed.

Words, on the other hand, were more easily controlled. "A man? I thought you said you were teenagers."

"But our friendship had started in another century; we had slipped across into the twenty-first by the time this happened. A lot can happen between millennia."

Despite his best efforts, Logan couldn't help but lean back in his chair. The sarcasm wasn't to his taste, but on this occasion his own naivety annoyed him.

It seemed he communicated this without words.

"I'm sorry," said Samantha, her ironic grin gone. "It was upsetting. I'm upset. Tom Wright's death…well, I didn't have any fondness for the man, but I wouldn't have wished that on Lara."

Logan felt a jolt as it occurred to him this was the first time anyone had mentioned RSM Wright's daughter by name.

Once the discussion had concluded and they had been led back to Reception, Logan popped a twenty pound note into a Macmillan Cancer Support tin that stood alongside the Safebeds one on the desk. He was making a point. Several in fact.

Having taken their leave, the two detectives settled in the car again and sat staring through the windscreen for a few seconds.

"Ever do Venn diagrams at school, Pascoe?"

"Yes, sir."

"Ah, so we still live in a time of miracles." He pushed on past Pascoe's openmouthed objection. "Well, a very interesting one has formed in this case already. Give me your notebook a second."

Once the DS had handed it over, accompanied by a puzzled frown, Logan turned to a blank page and drew three intersecting circles. Almost as an afterthought, he drew a fourth circle set apart from the others.

"Each woman is very much her own circle here," said the DCI. "That fourth one is Samantha's mother," he pointed to the last one he had drawn, "as I don't believe she has any significant part to play in anything, but right here…" he jabbed at the small area of intersection with his pen, "What sits in there?"

"Well," Pascoe paused, considering, "blood ties; the fact that they can't seem to get on with each other."

"Yes, but…for me, Tom Wright, or Tom Wright's death, lies in the middle there, and I cannot fathom out why."

"His death?" Pascoe seemed particularly thrown by the comment. "With respect, sir, that seems a stretch to me, especially as we've only met two of the four women."

"I'm not saying one of them is responsible. It's more what they're not saying, how they're not reacting to his death, that's registering with me. In particular the lack of response from his daughter, given Wright has been featured in the press quite a lot in recent weeks. It's almost a case of silence speaking volumes – but what is it saying?" He looked at the diagram and placed a fingertip thoughtfully on one of the circles. "We need to find Lara Wright."

# 7

Most nightmares didn't end Hollywood style, with the sufferer sitting bolt upright, crying out in anguish. Sergeant Penney could attest to that, nightmares being something he had to deal with on a regular basis. Mostly the screams were silent. That was one of the worst elements of the horror: the sense of smothering, the inability to vent the buildup of pressure and break free from the sticky, cloying webs of darkness.

Nor was there, in his case, the relative mercy of symbolism in his dreams – turning up at an interview wearing no trousers, or his teeth falling out would, in the comparative scheme of things, have been a blessing.

He would have been happy to become one of the new breed, those who didn't see it as shameful to approach the specialists – to face down post-traumatic stress disorder; to confront the bastard, hurling it from his bed like the infected whore it was.

Except…except the images were memories and he could think of no way of banishing them; well, no way that was acceptable to him. He wasn't prepared to allow the probing fingers of psychiatry to start fiddling in his brain; indiscriminate fruit picking that would take the good as well as the bruised.

Also, now more than ever, he feared the power of hypnosis. Who knew what brutal truths and deeds that might unearth?

That they had been sworn to silence was immaterial; the perverse demand of a brutal Regimental Sergeant Major would hold no sway with any Christian, yet the oath he had sworn tonight, over a pint, with the other remaining victims of that episode carried clout with him. Lying here in the lamplit semi-darkness – oh yes, the curtains were never drawn, post Iraq – having just dragged himself to the surface of another bad dream, he knew he would carry this one to the grave for the sake of his comrades. Revealing what they had been through and opening the door to unwelcome visitors…well, as his cricket coach had once said about wafting the bat outside the off stump, there was no profit in that shot.

RSM Wright had claimed he'd spared them an investigation into the events of that night and the potential accusation of cowardice from their fellow soldiers. Terrified, they had just done what he said. Only later did they really understand. He was a bully, pure and simple. And a bully is the biggest coward of all.

Cowardice had nothing to do with fear. God only knew what that bastard had put the recruits through during his later years of active service at the Army Training Regiment down near Winchester. No one joined the army expecting anything other than a tough time – everyone knew the almost caricature image of Regimental Sergeant Majors – but there was knocking off rough edges and then there was scarring for life.

Well, as they had said that night in the pub, it was all buried with him now. But that didn't stop the ghosts coming out to play, always in the strange hue that night vision goggles bring. He could still hear the spit of the sniper's fire; the screams from Corporal Stead, his bellowed commands punctuated by howls as another bullet sprayed his life away into the night sands. So far from home, yet not so far from help – except the sniper had them pinned down too. They'd had to turn in the end. Leave him.

Hadn't they?

Squeezing his eyes shut, Penney sat up, bathed in sweat despite the November chill from the open window. A lone passing car brought merciful distraction, dragging him back to the now – although what was *now* if you were standing in a fog, no idea whether you're facing backwards or ahead?

Despite the chidings of his own conscience, he could never forgive RSM Wright his brutality; his refusal to acknowledge that even trained soldiers could be subject to pure terror. So Penney would say nothing – hold his silence. As the three of them had said that evening in the pub, it was poetic justice.

He got out of bed, went to stand by the open window, reached for a packet of cigarettes. He lit up. Even the hollow click of the lighter that close to his face gave him a visceral jolt. He breathed shaky smoke into the night air. As always, that first drag performed an exorcism of sorts, but it wouldn't last.

# 8

Back at the station, Logan sighed with satisfaction at the after-taste of the police coffee, which always needed at least two sugars to make it more palatable. That sweetness was a guilty pleasure. Once he'd hit his late thirties and his trouser waist size had started to increase in parallel with his age, he'd cut down on sugar. Hence his preference now for more sophisticated Italian coffee at home, but there was no denying the primitive delight of a couple of spoons of artery-clogger.

Over the top of the mug, he stared at the whiteboard relating to Tom Wright's murder – the one in his own office containing his scribblings, not the one in the main space referred to by other officers. As yet it made little sense. His point about the Venn diagram had been all very well, but on another level, wasn't the murder victim always the point where every thread should lead, all circles intersect? Something nagged at him, but whatever it was remained beyond his gaze.

Nevertheless, the lack of any concrete base to the investigation had not stopped the lads at the station finding a name for case and perpetrator: The Armistice Killer. Kind of had a nice ring to it, he had to admit, even though he wasn't convinced it was a true reflection of the killer's psyche or motivation. Still, it couldn't be denied that the murder of a war veteran on the eleventh of the eleventh had to be more than a coincidence.

Another sip of coffee; another thought process spiked by caffeine and sugar. Logan couldn't shake from his mind the dysfunctionality of the relationships in that family. Mothers and daughters couldn't get on; cousins fell out; husbands left wives; wives left husbands. Of course there was more than a suggestion that Tom Wright had become difficult to be with. The words *whores* and *diseases* had entered Gill Scott's mind and vocabulary during their recent discussion in reference to the army, and PTSD was another known destroyer of marriages. Though where the latter was concerned, Logan suspected Wright was not a victim. His flat was almost a temple to the joys of soldiery; it spoke more of someone for whom the simple brutality of it all was his perfect world. Under those circumstances, Logan would have expected the women to form more of a supportive bond for each other.

He looked again at the disorder of the whiteboard. All of life was there in microcosm; so compressed it bore more than a passing resemblance to a Rorschach test, and he wasn't seeing the pictures amongst the random ink stains.

Some patterns, however, did have a certain inevitability to them, which was why, as he saw Pascoe entering the office, he knew the DS was coming to inform him that Lara Wright's address had been an even bigger blank than the whiteboard.

"There was a forwarding address, sir. Another blank, I'm afraid. It's been some years now since she disappeared." The DCI suppressed a grim smile that at least he'd been right about this.

"Married perhaps?"

"We're checking, sir."

"Okay, let me know what comes of it. Most peculiar."

"Oh, we'll find her, sir."

"Really?" The sarcasm was unmistakable. "That's not what's peculiar. Something doesn't correlate here. She fell out with her cousin, but that can't be the reason for disappearing off the face of the earth – unless the falling-out was over something monumental. No, she's exorcised herself from the whole family; become such a ghost that it was more than twenty-four hours before someone mentioned her by name."

"Doesn't that smack of shame, sir – I mean on the part of the family?"

"While I get your point, it struck me how Samantha Ingle mentioned her with almost a hint of sadness, perhaps regret. I mean, you may be right. It may be as simple as her being a black sheep. Or maybe in her own mind, Lara is Branwell Bronte." The look on Pascoe's face was so inevitable the DCI couldn't even bring himself to smile. "You have heard of the Brontes?"

"Give me some credit, sir."

"Well, in relation to his siblings Branwell was not really a success. He painted a portrait of his three sisters and himself, but became dissatisfied with it and painted out his image. Some say the motivations for that act go deeper. Look it up if you're ever in Haworth in Yorkshire; his outline, the space where he should be, has his spectral presence still."

Pascoe's interest seemed genuine, but Logan wasn't going to push his luck and moved on. "Maybe she did see herself as a failure, looking at her life through the eyes of her confident, superfit black belt mother, her decorated war hero father, her international volleyball playing lawyer cousin, her successful entrepreneur busi-nessman uncle – I've checked him out and he's loaded."

"Her aunt doesn't sound like she was any great shakes," ventured Pascoe.

"Pretty – and rich by osmosis."

"I take your point, sir. That probably would be enough to make an insecure person want to forge a new path and start afresh somewhere. I guess marriage would be one escape route – a new name at least, even if it does belong to someone else."

Logan put down his coffee mug with a bang, tutted as liquid

spilt over his hand. Reaching into a drawer, he took a tissue and wiped it dry, but he was smiling as he moved round the desk.

"Pascoe," he clapped his DS on the arm, "now I know why I value your sounding board more than any whiteboard." Pascoe looked like he was anticipating a scything coup de grâce, but Logan just tapped his arm again. "A change of name – there's more than one way of skinning a cat. Check into deed poll registers. If they come up with nothing, then see me again. I'll have a really balls' aching task for you as reward for your moment of inspiration."

"Right, sir. I have a contact to speak to at Wright's old regiment first."

"Ah yes – who have you managed to get hold of?"

"I can't say, sir." Logan was taken aback and it must have shown because Pascoe raised an apologetic hand. "I meant he would prefer to remain anonymous. I contacted the regiment and got left in little doubt that my enquiries weren't welcome. They gave me some answers, but not ones that were of any use – it will all be in my report. Then I get this one call. He insists it's off the record or he won't talk."

"Strange – and who the hell do they think they are anyway? This is a murder investigation."

Pascoe just shrugged. However, it occurred to Logan, given Pascoe's own connection with the army through his late uncle, that perhaps this unofficial conversation might be more fruitful. For now, he would let it go. Besides which, for more than one reason, he wanted to follow another path for the moment, and on that trail he, too, would prefer to be alone.

He headed towards the office door: "Ok, report back to me afterwards."

"Yes, sir. Where are you off to?"

"To see Samantha Ingle again. There's also more than one way of disappearing."

He really liked coming here. Strange how sports fields full of yelling humanity of all ages could bring some peace of mind. The closer he looked, the more Logan was prepared to view sport as the agar on which grew so many good cultures. He found it an additional source of satisfaction that football did not seem to be on the agenda here – that breeding ground of aggression; a reflection of so much that was sick in society, with its get-rich-or-die-trying mentality. Many of the activities available at this place seemed to channel aggression and turn it into something positive. Pascoe had been right to congratulate Samantha Ingle on what she was looking to achieve here; indeed had achieved already.

All the pitches were occupied, but he scanned the rugby field and picked her out, both by the baseball cap and by her having adopted what seemed to be her default role of referee and player. He saw she had noticed him and he gave a little wave of the hand that he hoped conveyed the right level of detached familiarity. He'd assumed she would keep him waiting; he'd perceived a prominent vein of stubbornness in her that doubtless served her well as a lawyer, but seemed to verge on the obtuse. So he was surprised to observe her issue some instructions to the players, hand over the whistle to one of them, and jog across to the fence.

"Samantha?" For a moment he wasn't sure how to read her look of surprise. For him, saying the name was just belt and braces, ensuring he had indeed recognised her correctly. Perhaps the informality of his greeting had taken her aback compared with his first visit. "Shall we?" He took the bull by the horns and gestured towards the building, wanting to take any initiative from her and also remove the fence as a barrier to their discussion. She just nodded and followed. Now a perverse side of him would have preferred less compliance – it was as if she knew this discussion would be fruitless and couldn't be bothered to protest.

With that in mind, it gave Logan some pleasure, as they sat in the breakout area again, to note that his next question had thrown her – there was that obvious fold of the arms. She gathered herself together, though, and countered with a rhetorical one of her own:

"Why would she have approached me about Safebeds? Are you suggesting she was in any way abused?" He noted she stopped short of indignant. "We were close friends at one time – I think she might have confided in me. Sure, Tom Wright was a tough nut – anyone better suited to being a Regimental Sergeant Major I've yet to meet – but his own daughter…"

"If modern times have shown us anything," said Logan, though not without some shifting awkwardness, "it is that all bets are off. It's not only a wise man who knows his own father, but a wise niece who knows her own uncle."

Though Samantha's eyes glowed with something that might have been resentment, she just tilted her head and let it go. "Please tell me when it was that she disappeared, by which I mean from public records."

"Well, she left her last place of employment when she was twenty."

"I last saw her when I was twenty-one, which was that same year. Bearing in mind I didn't get this place up and running until four years ago, when I was twenty-seven, that should answer your question about Safebeds."

"Twenty-one? I thought you fell out as teenagers."

"We did, but for some reason, as families do, there was a point where we decided an attempt at reconciliation might be a grown-up idea."

"Interesting." Logan ventured nothing else. He sat with fingers interlaced, leaning back in his seat, but very still.

"That's one way to describe it – and let's face it, we're at our most childish when we no longer have the defence of being children. We agreed that she would come to visit me at university one weekend, the result of which was a flaming, embarrassing row and her spending the night in the room of one of my exes. That was the last time I saw her."

Samantha's eyes were unreadable, except it was clear that, for just a moment, she was looking deep into the darkness of the past.

"So you doubt strongly that she would consider approaching you later in life."

"I don't doubt it, DCI Logan, I know it." She wagged a questioning finger in his direction. "Why are you fixating on Lara? Surely she's not under investigation."

"I don't see trying to locate the daughter of a murder victim as a fixation."

Samantha looked chastened – a unique moment in their interactions so far. Her rather defensive response was intriguing and did nothing to lessen Logan's sense that there was something parlous about the relationship between the women in that family. Whether it was relevant to the investigation, that remained a moot point, but he wanted to know more.

He decided to avoid any brick walls by approaching from a slightly different angle. He took a sip of his coffee. "Interesting, your turn of phrase just now: one of your exes." He smiled. "You make yourself sound like Elizabeth Taylor. How old did you say you were then – twenty-one?"

"I told you before, DCI Logan, I was blessed, or cursed, with having no problems attracting the opposite sex. I'm sure you can relate to that." She gave him a look, both knowing and undecipherable.

Fortunately his demons were strangely relaxed today and let him off with nothing more than a single twirl of his signet ring. "Perhaps – the cursed part anyway."

"Very Kafkaesque." She chose to take the line of thought no further, for now at least, it seemed. "I guess that's why Lara thought a good way to get back at me would be to sleep with one of my crowd. If only she knew…" She trailed off.

Logan raised an eyebrow. "That's way too cryptic, even for me."

"Oh, I just meant that back then, it was easy come, easy go.

I studied Law, not Psychology, but even I can probably piece together the reasons for that…well, the one very big reason – the few years I spent observing Father's and Mummy-dear's relationship. To quote Oscar Wilde, they knew the cost of everything and the value of nothing. It helped me concentrate on my studies, not having the distraction of that imposter, love, but I was still a sucker for lust."

Her words were cold, but not as depressing as her sad smile.

Samantha continued: "Whenever I see a paper cup being hurled from slipstream to slipstream on a motorway, I think of my love life back then – the only problem being I'm never sure whether I was the cup or the car, hurling would-be and ex-lovers in my wake."

Logan, his own recent experiences springing uncomfortably to mind, was thrown for just a moment.

He had watched Samantha's fingers knitting round another of those paper cups; now they unlocked, and she leaned back in her chair. Retaining that ability of hers to throw a man off-balance, she puffed out her cheeks. "That was dangerous."

He didn't twitch a muscle. "How so?"

"I don't think I've opened up like that in some time."

"Maybe I missed my calling."

She gave a sardonic grin. "Don't get ahead of yourself. I simply meant it was like those times when you open up to a complete stranger – the person you share a carriage with on a train – and know you can tell them anything because your paths will never cross again."

*Or if they did and I saw your face in the crowd,* thought Logan, *I wouldn't recognise you.* That scenario remained unspoken. Logan was certainly not going to open up to Samantha Ingle about prosopagnosia. He settled on something more prosaic, but couldn't let her comment pass without a riposte. "Well, if they do, let's hope it's not because they have to, Miss Ingle."

She appeared to give that consideration and continued with a less sarcastic tone, perhaps taking on board the tacit reminder in that final address: "So, anyway, all of that was a rather long-winded way of telling you that no, Lara didn't approach me about Safebeds, but if she had, as I said before, we just give a telephone number and then butt out – leave everything to the organisation itself. Yes, we communicate with everyone who advertises at our centre; of course we exchange stories of exciting, or worrying developments, but on the whole, the number is just there for people to note and use."

Back in the car park, they exchanged a handshake.

"Good luck, genuinely, DCI Logan, in finding Lara; if only because, if she has already seen the news, she doesn't deserve to carry that burden alone. If you do find her, tell her I'm still prepared to listen. To keep with the war themes, call it a Christmas truce – I'll step into No-Man's-Land with her."

Logan smiled his understanding and acknowledgement, then sat in his car and watched her head back to the rugby. If anything, despite unburdening herself, she seemed heavier of heart and legs, but then her uncle's brutal murder had to be affecting her; never mind the bravado.

And she was affecting him. The old twitchings – she might have been moving wearily, but the lean muscularity of those legs meant they were heavy only in the metaphorical sense. Every which way he turned, he saw the futility of trying the Dessler Method, as he had come to think of Freddy's suggestion that perhaps he should settle for less in his approach to women. He imagined going up to Samantha Ingle in a bar on the basis of her lovely set of pins, and boy, would you be in for some surprises from the collar up! He wondered just how long one would need to recover from her cutting put-down in that scenario. At some point, if too much time were spent on this avenue of investigation, he would need to ask himself, before others did, why he was pushing so hard to piece together this family. After all, he knew at first hand that it spoke volumes when you had changed your own name in an attempt to escape the dysfunctionality of your past! Then again, perhaps it made you the best qualified. When Pascoe had spoken at the station that morning about someone starting afresh with a new identity, it had been more than that moment of insight which had caused Logan to spill his coffee. Sometimes you buried things so deep, it took a ghost to remind you they ever existed.

Ghost – the word might be more appropriate than they realised. Logan knew he could be getting ahead of himself here, but the non-appearance of Lara Wright niggled at him.

He gunned the engine; stared through the windscreen into a place that might have been the past, but could so easily be the future. What the hell was it that prevented him from engaging with women in the real world, but not in the shadowy alleyways of criminal investigation? Then again, if dating websites were anything to go by, so-called reality was a play and, to borrow from Shakespeare, all the men and women merely players. So that begged the question: was the dark world of crime and murder the true reality? If so, did that explain the fatal attraction women seemed to hold for him in that place? The profiles on those dating sites were a fallacy; a series of bullet points – a presentation of the positives for the opposite sex. Was the final truth, the true nature of humanity, only to be found in the Stygian gloom of a murder case?

As a detective, he could not let that be so. He needed control – and he could definitely not let sexuality mislead him. Not again. Never again

# 9

Given Logan's comments about the time-consuming paper-chase ahead, Pascoe was now more determined than ever to finish treading another path. Like his original enquiries at Wright's service regiment, The Rifles, those at the training barracks in Winchester where the RSM had finished his army career had led down the road that he'd assumed they would: a series of way markers pointing towards the silhouette of an obsessive former soldier; hard, brutal in training and at war; displaying unswerving loyalty to his regiment; uncompromising in that allegiance and in his expectation of it from others. And yet every facet was presented as either desirable within its context or, at worst, a harmless quirk.

For many reasons, Pascoe's heart hadn't been in this whole process; he had guessed in advance which way the wind would blow and how ranks would close. Those who had stayed in touch with Wright – and there weren't many – seemed to sing from the same hymn sheet, one loaded with bland platitudes about the difficulties all former soldiers face in post-service civvy street. No one gave specifics and, as if they had been coached in which line to spin, all expressed the view that training recruits in Winchester towards the end of your army days was no substitute for leading them into battle. It was likened by one officer to the ex-player struggling to cope with coaching after years of running out under the flood-lights. Whether that was any sort of guarded reference to fractures appearing in Wright's private life, Pascoe could only guess.

His further probing away from the barracks revealed that Wright had, perhaps unsurprisingly, followed the long line of so many ex-soldiers and joined a company providing private security. After that, he had moved on to another enterprise that specialised in transporting bullion and gems. A few former colleagues there, ex-army themselves, said he had probably, like the rest of them, grown tired of standing around like a goon and a couple even ventured that he would have wanted it to kick off! None of this, however, was leading down any worthwhile avenues, just along paths of clay and cliché.

Nevertheless, it became apparent Pascoe's enquiries within the fraternity must have kicked some sort of wasp's nest in the dark and dust of a particular loft when he received a call from one of the top brass at Wright's former training regiment, the ATR, asking to meet off-site, off-record, and insisting anything mentioned would be denied with vehemence. That was more than fine by Pascoe. He had wondered whether he would incur the wrath of Logan for following this up on his own, but for now he had the go-ahead. He also had other reasons for preferring to do this alone, not least of which was that it got him away from checking deed poll registers.

The Shepherd's Crook in Barton Stacey seemed a suitable venue, both in terms of its isolation and the word 'crook' featuring in the name. As he stepped inside and looked around, he found further reason to smile, this time at his own stupidity as it dawned on him he was hoping to find a man in uniform. He thought back to the time he had visited the Ministry of Defence in Hampshire for a meeting with a major, who had marched into the conference room wearing desert camouflage. Pascoe had struggled to contain his laughter; the major was office based – he should have looked like a desk!

Pascoe needed reasons to smile. As he felt the reluctant easing in the lines of tension binding his face he realised how much weight he felt he was carrying. Life hadn't been good to him of late.

Now, as he scanned the four faces in the main bar, the faintest of nods from one of them, a man at a table in the corner, confirmed with almost masonic furtiveness that they might be seeking each other. He made his way over. As the other man stood to shake hands, Pascoe leaned across and enquired: "Colonel…?"

The second half of the question evaporated as the military man cringed and withdrew the handshake while glancing over Pascoe's shoulder with a reflex which suggested he had just spotted evidence of a sniper. Pascoe grimaced a silent apology; mouthed *sorry*. "Can I get you a drink?"

The colonel gestured towards the tomato juice on the table, which appeared untouched, so Pascoe ordered just a mineral water for himself. He could have murdered a pint – an unfortunate choice of verb under the circumstances – but was grateful for the moment to regain his composure after his faux pas and the cold glare it had elicited. When he sat down again, he realised what he had mistaken for frost was ice. Was this a man who saw too many ghosts of conflicts past, present and future? Or maybe it was the default setting for the colonel when confronted by non-military personnel, away from barracks or field of battle, and out of uniform.

The irony wasn't lost on Pascoe – this man wished to remain incognito, but couldn't have looked more like a stiff-backed regimental stickler if he had tried. It might have been mistaken for an air of privilege, not wishing to engage in conversation, were it not for the fact that he had called to request this meeting. Something was bothering him.

Nevertheless, much to his own frustration, Pascoe found himself cowed by the colonel's aura of authority. That was the military for you. Even his much-loved uncle had always been able to bring the young Pascoe to heel with a wordless stare, though almost always accompanied by an avuncular hand on the shoulder.

The colonel looked around. "Is this your local? Hmm."

That last syllable spoke volumes.

"That would hardly be a wise move," said Pascoe, "arranging to meet you somewhere I'm likely to be recognised. Besides, I'm based in Cornwall."

It was a decent riposte. The colonel's subsequent *hmm* was more conciliatory.

Pascoe continued: "So why are we here? I mean apart from the obvious, which is that this whole RSM Wright thing has stirred up a hornets' nest." He sipped his water – felt pleased to have put his early mistake behind him and seized the initiative, something he had observed Logan doing at the Estuary Sports and Social centre.

"Not enough of a stir if you ask me."

The agitation in the other man's features surprised him. "I'm sorry?"

The colonel leaned forward. "Despite your preconceptions, perhaps misconceptions, about me, I'm not one for allowing stuffy tradition and other bunkum to stand in the way of the truth. I'm somebody who, to use business parlance, has fought his way to the top from the shop floor – literally fought, in my case. I've spent too long surrounded by Etonians, Harrovians, and their old boys' mentality, to want to see it prosper." He seemed to take in the look on Pascoe's face. "Oh don't get me wrong; I'm not some spineless loony lefty – I would hardly have joined the army if I were – but, believe me, although it's not always possible to follow one's conscience into battle, the military is, or should be, a force for good. Within its own ranks too. Those who are not heroes shouldn't be feted as such."

The colonel took a sip of his tomato juice now. He studied the red contents of the glass. A peculiar, frigid smile twitched at the parade ground stiffness of his lips. "Blood – it's in the nature of combat that we have it on our hands. Some more than others." He broke away from the momentary meditation and turned his still cold eyes on Pascoe. "The top ranks, those at the rear, are naturally more vilified, of course; the blood that stains their fingers being that of their own men while they themselves often sit far removed from the immediacy of danger. But even for those at the front line, there are rules; bounds that shouldn't be crossed."

He leaned further forward; gave a suspicious look in all directions before continuing: "I know of a double injustice. Oh, I wasn't witness to the deed itself. I just saw the scab forming, concealing the open wound."

"So what are we talking about here?" asked Pascoe.

The colonel leaned back again, as if seeking to disentangle himself from the sticky threads of intrigue he had just spun.

"Oh, just rumours."

Pascoe tilted his head; said nothing.

"Ask the right people and answers may be forthcoming."

It seemed to Pascoe that the colonel was now backing away; having second thoughts about squealing in The Shepherd's Crook. He took a card from his jacket pocket, slid it across the table. "Well, unless your lines are tapped, you could probably have told me this over the phone. Here's my direct line in case you feel more talkative later."

The colonel's features hardened again. "I'm going out on a limb even letting you know that further enquiries at Wright's old regiment, The Rifles, may be fruitful, if frustrating."

"Well, they've certainly been the latter so far, and definitely not the former. I get the impression the expression *closed ranks* was never more appropriate." Pascoe allowed his impatience to surface.

The colonel looked at the card. "Detective Sergeant Andy Pascoe." Of a sudden, there was recognition. "Strange. This is either a coincidence, or…it just didn't occur to me before when I was put through to you at the station. I knew a Major Lawrence Pascoe. We were only nodding acquaintances, but we got on very well nonetheless. He was in the Royal Berkshires. He used to speak with great affection of his nephew Andy."

Pascoe couldn't help but smile. He leaned back in his chair, body language opening. "The very same."

There might almost have been the sound of a snap in the air as the colonel gave an unexpected smile. "Well – imagine that. He was a fine soldier." The smile faded, but an unexpected softening of the features followed. "Such a tragedy in Helmand."

Pascoe felt his own smile melt into the cracks and fault lines that appear when nostalgia is shaken by reality. "He passed away a month ago; never really recovered from his wounds." Seeing the colonel's shocked expression, he clarified: "I don't think he ever truly got over the ending of his career either. The army was his life. Just seemed to give up the ghost. The hospice staff simply found him dead one morning." He paused. "I miss him."

They sat in respectful silence; a moment of fragile empathy, each lost in different memories of a fine human being.

With a sudden movement the colonel slapped his palm on the table – it wasn't loud, but emphatic enough; a rare display of emotion. "You see, that's the thing; the sort of genuine loss that makes me want to speak out."

Pascoe tilted his head again. Once more, he said nothing. Despite his relative youth he'd already learned much from Logan's ability to use silence.

"All that bullshit in the press," continued the colonel.

"Bullshit?"

"About RSM Wright. Okay, it was a courageous act, no denying, rescuing those men against the odds under machine gun fire in the Falklands – a Distinguished Conduct Medal well earned. The wounds picked up in Iraq – oh, you might say he was a brave man…except, can someone who neither knows, feels nor understands fear really be considered brave. Not as much as the man who overcomes terror, in my opinion. He was made for the army – its unquestioning discipline, the – let's face it – brutality of its regimes, the camaraderie with your fellow man, but also the chance to bully the weaker ones. Yes, it made me sick to hear about him down in his hometown of Truro, riding the tsunami of public affection towards our armed forces in this year of commemoration. Luckily, he'd rubbed up a few glory boys the wrong way in his time and someone made sure there was no place for him in the big parade in London, but of course the Duke of Cornwall's Light Infantry had a strong tradition before the various mergers that made up The Rifles, so as a hometown boy he made a logical choice to carry the old standard into Truro Cathedral and light a flame of remembrance there. The military authorities couldn't afford to snub him entirely, given the circumstances.

"That last bit is rather cryptic."

The colonel hesitated, but then reached into the breast pocket of his shirt and removed a pen. Reaching for one of the beer mats on the table, he started to write.

"This is something I couldn't have given you over the phone, or, rather, I would not have risked it."

He slid the small square of cardboard across the table. Pascoe took it; scrutinised it. His pulse quickened.

"Who are these men, in the context of what you're saying? I recognise one – it's not a common name. Members of Wright's regiment in the Gulf, if I'm not mistaken?"

There was a further silence. The colonel gave him an old-fashioned look. At last he spoke, having taken some time to choose his words with care.

"None of these three may be approached as if this square of card is proof definitive of anything. There were just rumours and those only amongst the top ranks…but strong rumours."

"You've implied this before. Rumours of what?" Again, Pascoe found it hard to hide his impatience with the colonel's prevarication.

"Rumours of men unable to help a wounded comrade – their commanding officer, who had to leave him to die in the night while they retreated from sniper fire. Men who trained under a particularly brutal RSM. An RSM who had, as a young man, rescued comrades under fire and could not bear the thought of what he perceived as an act of cowardice. An RSM who would not allow the honour of the regiment to be besmirched by enquiries into that cowardice and so, in return for the silent consent of his superiors devised his own punishments."

Pascoe said nothing.

Now the colonel pointed to a particular name on the piece of paper. "You won't believe it at first, but I think he would be your best bet for further questioning." He raised a hand. "I don't imply any guilt – any involvement in Wright's murder – just that, despite his persona and attitude, I believe he is the closest to being a future candidate for the trauma of PTSD. Those who deny their weakness usually are. So, if there is anything useful to be uncovered regarding the skeletons in the RSM's wardrobe, he's probably your man."

The part about the denial of weakness bounced around in Pascoe's mind; words spoken already by one man, and now repeated in the voice of another. He puffed out his cheeks and stuffed the beer mat in his pocket. "I'll let you know how it goes."

"Please don't. If it goes well, I'm sure I'll find out everything I need to know in the press. You won't be able to phone me and…" the colonel looked around, "…I don't imagine myself coming back here for another drink."

He pushed back his chair.

"Before you go," said Pascoe, "you spoke of a double injustice. After all you've said, I can't think you count…" he paused, "…the murder of Tom Wright as one of them."

"Absolutely correct. No, I alluded to it earlier," the colonel counted on his fingers, "A, his bullying viciousness, and B, the cover-up by the top brass…in which I include myself, to my shame. I just hope that speaking with you serves as some sort of atonement."

Round and round spun the beer mat between the tips of Pascoe's fingers. He had long since stopped reading the names written by the colonel; they were already ingrained in his memory. His gaze was fixed on the flames of the pub fire, a backdrop against which his memories had danced like dervishes. Beyond the windows darkness had now fallen. He contemplated the paradox of the sunset, which drew in the horizons of one's world, yet opened it to limitless possibilities of the night; a repository for unspeakable, perhaps unimaginable acts.

Pascoe had arranged to meet the nameless colonel at The Shepherd's Crook not because it was supremely convenient, but because the last thing he wanted was to gain a reputation for assignations with different men in a quiet, out-of-the-way pub and all the ignorant, knowing looks from the publican that would go with that. In truth there wasn't much to choose between the two watering holes, and this could almost have been the same place. Now his thoughts drifted back.

### Three weeks before

The Jolly Farmer had been the *agreed* meeting place with Bovis. *Agreed* might have been putting it strongly; Bovis sounded as hard as nails, hadn't been at all pleased to be contacted, and had left Pascoe in no doubt that he wasn't up for this. It hadn't been an easy thing to do to someone who was a gnarled veteran of terrible theatres of war, but Pascoe had had to swing the lead a bit, reminding Bovis that the army's record of helping the police had taken a huge knock as a result of the Deepcut Barracks tragedy, when four privates had died from gunshots wounds in similar but suspicious circumstances and the enquiries seemed to open a can of worms regarding the barracks' procedures. He had stressed how he wanted to avoid having to make official enquiries via senior ranks in order to have a conversation which, he assured Bovis, was still possible to keep off the record.

As he sat in what he knew to be Bovis' local, Pascoe found himself hoping, in one way, that his deceased uncle's assessment had been correct; that Bovis' aggressive machismo, as displayed clearly over the phone, was a front. On the other hand, his uncle had also described Bovis as closer to the edge than the others. Edges were dangerous places.

There was no mistaking Pascoe's contact as he walked in. Still a serving soldier and proud of it, Lance Corporal Bovis arrived in uniform, sleeves neatly rolled up with the possible intention of appearing intimidating. Poking from them were forearms like Popeye and a swathe of fading tattoos that spoke of rites of passage in horrific places, not the pathetic faux-Maori efforts sported by indolent footballers and fashionistas whose only experience of the Middle East was a pad in Dubai. If this man was about to crumble, then Pascoe's next holiday would be to Egypt to watch the pyramids collapse – there seemed about as much chance.

There were cheery greetings from behind the bar and from several others who appeared to be regulars. Having responded with a few curt nods, Bovis looked around with narrowed eyes, perhaps expecting a man in uniform. Spotting a face he didn't recognise, the Lance Corporal made his way straight over.

Pascoe half stood, considered shaking hands, but just knew the offer would be ignored, so settled for gesturing towards the bar. "Can I buy you a…"

"So, what's this all about?" Bovis thumped down in the seat.

Thrown a bit off balance, Pascoe needed to remind himself he had nothing to fear from the truth. Bovis might have appeared to be made of granite with eyes of inlaid cold steel, but then so had his uncle back in the day. He just needed to gain the upper hand fast – so decided to play his main card, though in this case made of paper, pulling it from his pocket and placing it on the table for Bovis to see. It was a letter, folded so that only a tiny part, a short list, remained visible.

He watched the soldier's eyes as he read the three names;

studied those windows to the darkness of the soul with great intensity and in doing so saw what he needed. Just as in the military, so sometimes in the police; it came down to fractions of a second – the time it took a muscle to twitch, or a pupil to dilate. Pascoe hadn't worked long with Logan, but already he had noted the DCI's ability to spot the fundamental truths about some people during questioning. Curious about his new boss, Pascoe had asked discreetly at the station about him. No one professed to know the DCI well – he was a man who kept himself pretty much to himself and was viewed as a bit of an eccentric by some. However, one surprising revelation was that he was 'The Dude' when it came to the weekly poker evening held by some of the officers, caseload permitting. To a man and woman, all said he was an expert at spotting tells, those giveaway changes in another player's behaviour or demeanour. Taking a chance during the recent drive down to Torquay, Pascoe had tried to quiz Logan about this. Though not prepared to give away his own trade secrets, the DCI had advised him that – what was that expression he had used? – *Poker is less likely to deal you a shit hand than life, and even if it did you could still make it work!* Then, more seriously, he had told him to take certain lessons from poker into life, always instilling in him: don't watch faces, study the pieces of which they're made and the way they respond to their unseen motor, the brain. What was that other saying of his – don't seek perfection, seek imperfections.

Right now, at that table in The Jolly Farmer, when Bovis looked up again he was calm and enigmatic to anything but the trained eye; except, of course, thanks to that fraction of a second as he had read the piece of paper, Pascoe knew he wasn't. "What's that?" The Lance Corporal's tone was dismissive as he pushed the piece of paper back across the table. "Three comrades; comrades in arms." The final phrase carried the slightest sneer of exclusion.

"Well actually, I was hoping you could tell me."

A shrug; a turning down of the mouth. "I'm not sure what you wanna know."

"Let me just show you something." Pascoe produced a pen from his pocket; smiled as, for a moment he felt the smugness of the magician. He rewrote the three names alongside where they appeared on the list; turned it back for Bovis to read. "You see, it's not my handwriting. Now I could walk away from here, leave you a few days to try to get sample of handwriting from the top brass, and you can compare. Then you'll know this is serious."

Taking a sip from his pint of bitter, Pascoe watched Bovis and was impressed by how the latter again showed no fear to the unknowing eye – but the signs were there and the man across the table had evinced humanity like any other. That slight clench at the back of the jaw was enough, but Logan's main advice – the human face is active, never trust it when it is dormant – had never seemed more appropriate. Bovis had fought too hard to remain expressionless.

Although silences could be effective, he didn't want to let this one continue and needed to prod the bear. Callow detective though he was in some ways, Pascoe knew well enough that men of anger gave away more when that emotion surfaced – and boy, was Bovis a man of anger. "I believe there's a fourth name I should write on this list," he ventured.

Bovis leaned forward, biceps straining at the rolled-up sleeves. "I've no fuckin' idea what you're talking about." They just looked at each other, and Bovis blinked first. "A fourth name – you mean RSM fuckin' Wright?"

"Actually no." Pascoe steeled himself. He was about to perform a dirty trick – not one of which any conjurer would be proud. "No, the name of the officer who'd been picked off over the course of long, slow minutes by snipers near Basra." Bovis' fingers were interlaced, but the little movements, which appeared to be ants running through the veins beneath the skin of his bulky forearms, suggested they weren't still. "One more pointless death in the night, in a shithole in the desert, miles from home, but only yards from help."

Like all explosions that follow the lighting of a fuse, even though it had been half-expected, the thump of Bovis' hands on the table as he sprang up and reached for Pascoe's throat took the latter by surprise, though not so much that he wasn't able to jerk backwards out of harm's way.

"You fuckin'...!!!"

"Shut it!" Pascoe guessed all eyes in the pub were on them, most of them trained in anger on him. "Sit down, unless you want assault or attempted assault of a police officer added to your record." He didn't feel as calm or tough as he sounded. Bovis was leaning all his weight on one balled fist on the table, the other fist partway towards its intended target, but static. "Sit down!" Pascoe kept his voice low, but his teeth were gritted. "Believe it or not, I'm here to help."

"Why the fuck should I?"

Pascoe just waited, and waited, till the big squaddie thudded back in his seat. Now the DS chanced leaning forward again.

"My contact also said that RSM Wright was a bully; a nasty piece of work, well suited to his particular role in army life." Pascoe was careful to personalise the RSM's role – a blank dismissal of army types would have been unwise. As far as he could see, Bovis might also have been perfectly suited...except he had a feeling history was going to prove otherwise.

He gestured to the table and continued: "Look, let me buy you a drink."

The word *fuck* started to form on Bovis' lips, but it seemed he thought better of it. "Just tell me what you want."

Pascoe leaned further forward. "I just want the truth."

"The truth – hah! Seriously?"

"Yes – from what I've been told by my contact, the press's current love affair with Tom Wright is all wrong. The person who gave me this list..." Pascoe looked for the piece of paper, had a moment's panic when he couldn't find it, but then saw that it had fallen to the floor during the minor whirlwind of violence. He picked it up; gestured with it. "…that person was pretty adamant about that. This is more than just a list of names and the reason I'm here on my own today is because I've shown this to no one – not yet. I want to – need to – understand why it's been given to me."

"It's a fuckin' travesty!" Bovis blurted, before shutting his mouth again just as quickly, looking over his shoulder and around to check he wasn't under observation. Turning back, he resumed in a hissing whisper: "That the bastard is being sucked up to in the papers and the local community – it's a fuckin' joke."

Pascoe raised his hands in a placatory gesture. "Look – there's no notebook." To Bovis' evident surprise he unfastened three of his shirt buttons and showed his bare chest. "I'm not wearing a wire and this…" again he waved the letter, "…is just a piece of paper. I'm hoping it can become a map leading the way to justice."

Pascoe popped the list back in his pocket for now, just in case it might constitute an insurmountable obstacle to the discussion, and repeated: "I just want to understand. Look, before we go any further, let me tell you one more thing." Bovis seemed to be listening. "My uncle was Major Lawrence…" Pascoe was surprised to find himself all of a sudden overcome by the memory, and needed to compose himself, "…Major Lawrence Pascoe. Also badly wounded in Iraq; not fatally, but it did end up being the death of him very recently. He was an honourable man. He said it was a travesty that a bully like Wright was being feted by the populace. I have no love of men like that, but I understand a certain amount of that nastiness comes with the territory of an RSM. From what I can tell, Wright overstepped the mark. It was different with him somehow. As I said, I need to understand how." Feeling stronger, he lowered his head a little and spoke in a conspiratorial whisper. "Sometimes, my fucking job sucks. Too often, I see the wrong guy get away with it…but I see guys get away with it for the right reasons too. Let me tell you something – if there's some bond, a bond of silence and blood, that holds men together and quiets their tongues…" he leaned back and smiled, spreading his hands, "…

well then they're safe, aren't they?"

"What if they were forced to take that oath of silence?"

Pascoe smiled. "What if the facts are already known, as implied by the words and scribblings of someone high up; someone who, by the way, is ashamed of the actions of the RSM? Surely then no one is breaking the oath, because the facts are already out there." He waited for his words to sink in. "What do you say?"

Bovis folded his arms and leaned back. There might have been the merest hint of a smile. "I say a pint of Doom Bar."

His tattooed hand might have been around the pint glass, but his eyes were in the desert. If ever there had been a time for silence and just listening, Pascoe knew this was it. He just waited.

"We didn't see it all, but enough; too much. The six of us never did find whether that machine-gun post was there, or whether it was bad reconnaissance, but the fuckin' sniper was. Ready – sorry, that's Corporal Stead – instructed us to stay back and crawled ahead of us, pretty sure the target was over the next ridge of sand. 'E was like that – led by example. Of course we were on radio silence, but through the night vision goggles we saw 'im get to the top of the ridge and then look back for us to advance.

"As soon as we stood up, I knew it was a mistake. I 'eard the bullet whistle past, rip into – explode into – someone's flesh." Bovis' throat clicked as he swallowed. "An' I 'eard the gurgling shriek, turned to see Besty go down. Then came the other screams and knew that Ready must have been 'it. It was so quiet out there, every sound seemed amplified. Another spit, and Morgan bought it. That left three of us – Penney, Bullard and me. We could still 'ear the Corporal groaning, then there was another shot – we all pressed our faces into the dirt instinctively – and now it was screaming up ahead. That's when we knew 'e was bait.

"We'd taken shelter behind whatever scrub we could find, but there was fuck all cover between us and the ridge. I chanced a look up – Ready was nowhere to be seen. They must've let him cross that sandy ridge then taken 'im out; shot 'im in the legs probably. All we could do was lie there cursing, crying, arguing amongst ourselves, with ourselves. We couldn't just leave 'im in the 'ands of those fuckers, but we couldn't 'elp 'im neither."

Still Pascoe held his silence. He had been drawn into the night southwest of Basra, so had long ago given up watching the edifice crumble. It would have been to his shame at that moment, as thoughts of his uncle also came to him, to have retained a completely professional detachment.

Bovis continued, his voice a paradox, growing softer yet angrier. "In the end we made a decision – we'd 'ave to break cover in three directions; 'ope that by moving we wouldn't get 'it and pray – for Christ's sake! – pray that one of the others bought it and not you. Still, we lay there forever, terrified – you know?"

Pascoe just nodded.

"Ah, there's nothing worse than an enemy you can't see. Give me the days of bloody sword fighting. If you're gonna die in battle then die facing your enemy, fifty-fifty chance. Anyway, as if to 'urry us up, there was another distant spit of silenced gunfire – another scream from… Corporal Stead." Bovis voice caught at the mention of the name – the man they'd failed, in his mind. "But 'e must've bit down on them screams because now we 'eard him talking to us; 'e wasn't calling for us to come to 'im – just the opposite."

Now Bovis looked Pascoe in the eye for the first time. Even if the DS had not been engrossed in listening to this tale, there would have been no need to observe or interpret pupil dilation as Logan had taught him. Bovis was staring into the night and he was terrified.

"You know, you can't leave a wounded comrade, but at the same time, you can't condemn a fellow soldier to death. I know we'd said we would split into three, but we knew that meant at least one of us would buy it. So then we talked about just going all for one and one for all. I'll be honest with you though – we were so scared. The sound of bullets ripping flesh 'as never left me.

"Then, loud and clear, we heard Corporal Stead shouting: *"Go back! You'll never get to me! They'll kill me as soon as you come!"* Well at that point, a part of all of us wanted them to kill 'im – put 'im out of 'is misery."

Bovis fell into the silence of a man for whom words were inconsequential to a moment which was defying the usual strictures of time. One that had stretched across the years; a piece of elastic thrumming with energy and tension, closer to snapping the further it reached.

It was perhaps appropriate that the silence seemed to splinter when Bovis spoke again, his mind dragging through the shards.

"We were just stuck there – mice in the dark, knowing there was a big fuckin' bird of prey watching us from somewhere. You've gotta understand, we didn't know what the fuck to do."

Pascoe nodded in wordless response to the note of suppressed pleading in that last statement.

"None of us wanted to leave a wounded comrade in the 'ands of the enemy and none of us wanted to lead a fellow soldier on a suicide mission. No fuckin' virgins and eternal paradise for us." His fists balled and then his eyes returned to Pascoe and the present for just a moment, having tried that very British thing of deadening grief with black humour. "We needed focus. We needed a leader. Then Ready – Corporal Stead – showed us why 'e was our commanding officer, defying those murdering bastards. I'll never forget 'is voice – I 'ear it every night, like it's outside my window: *"Get yourselves back to base! That's an order. Take…the others with you. Who are you?"'*

Pascoe watched Bovis' back straighten.

*"Bovis, sir!"*

*"Penney, sir!"*

*"Bullard, sir!"*

The man of stone was close to tears. "We'd never been so proud to say our names."

*"Well then take Morgan and Best – make sure you bury me with them in your memories! The next shot you hear will…"*

Bovis' throat clicked. "There was another spit; another scream from Corporal Stead – but 'e wasn't 'aving it."

*"Okay…go now! The next shot…"*

There was silence for a few seconds. Pascoe realised, much like Stead, it must have been taking everything Bovis had at that moment to continue.

*"…you hear will be from me! They're not taking me! There's no Geneva Convention with these bastards! Ignore anything you see on the TV – I'll be back home before then!"*

There were now two men in that pub who would have to drag themselves away from the dust and blood.

"We 'eard the shot." Bovis looked straight at Pascoe with an honesty that made a mockery of the DS's original opinion of him. He doubted he had seen such openness in his whole time with the police, whether in the interview rooms or the offices of fellow officers. It was unnerving. "The sound made me…still makes me sometimes…well, question war. 'Ave I driven anyone to that point where they take their own life? A soldier so badly wounded 'e can't face the thought of the world? A mother, or father, who's lost a child, whether a soldier or a civilian casualty." The sadness was replaced with sudden anger, the more impactful for being expressed now in a hard whisper. "It makes what I'm gonna tell you that much tougher to take."

Bovis took a sip of his beer, his mouth clearly dry, before his eyes peered out into the darkness around Basra again.

"It was like the sound of that bullet flicked a switch. We needed to get back, so Corporal Stead's death wasn't in vain. Penney and me 'oisted Morgan and Besty onto our backs and then, on a count of three, Bullard raked the black 'orizon with gunfire, spraying bullets and screaming like something out of a poor action movie. I've no idea whether 'e got 'em, or if they were on their way to claim their prize, but even though they fired a few shots, all three of us made it away from there." He shuddered. "I tell you, it was 'ard to feel the odd bullet hit the bodies we were carrying. Even though Morgan and Besty were past caring, you take it personally. Yes, we were using them as shields, as we'd been trained to do, but still…"

Perhaps it was the strangest thing that Bovis' hand seemed steady as a rock when he reached for his pint glass, but on reflection Pascoe recognised that this was not a man who, despite confessing to fear, would be flaky in action, and he had just been body, mind and soul in that very arena. Pascoe knew this because he, too, had the smell of night and death in his nostrils; a helpless, poppy-wearing bystander.

It took some willpower for Pascoe to continue with being a policeman, but he allowed the sand to settle and the desert wind to cease before moving ahead.

"Look  why are you and I here, and why am I supposed to ask you about RSM Wright, at the suggestion of a senior officer; my uncle, Major Lawrence Pascoe?"

Bovis looked up and there was a sudden unexpected touch of humility in his voice: "I was sorry to 'ear you mention 'is death. I knew of 'im. An honourable man." Bovis straightened his back, his eyes narrowing, but in curiosity. "So 'e asked you to contact me?"

"In a manner of speaking, yes." Pascoe removed the letter from his pocket again and gestured with it. "This remains for my eyes only, because he handed it to me just before he died. Not knowing him, you wouldn't have noticed how shaky his writing was, but he felt moved enough by the press coverage Wright was receiving – is receiving still – to hint at things. I repeat – why?"

Bovis appeared to consider holding his silence, but then his shoulders loosened.

"'Cos Wright is an evil fucking sadist." Bovis' jaw clenched. "When we returned to camp and were debriefed, we found out there'd been more than one bird of prey waiting for us. 'E let us know in no uncertain manner that 'e thought we were cowards for leaving Corporal Stead and wasn't going to let it rest.

"'E ordered us to come with 'im in the middle of the night. It was weird; there was a small tent set up, a bit removed from the rest of the camp. When we went in, there was a table and three chairs. On the table…" Bovis hesitated, cold eyes darkening, full of contempt, possibly for all mankind, but more likely just for Wright. "…there was a pistol – a weird sort of snub revolver – and a bottle.

"Once we sat, Wright moved closer, enough to intimidate us, and said: '*Right, you three little mice are about to find out how it feels to wait for a bullet to take you out instead of running away and leaving your honour behind like piss in the dirt. We're going to play a bit of Russian roulette.*' 'E picked up the revolver – hefted it, almost with pride. '*In keeping with the Russian theme, this is the OTs-38 Stechkin, which the Russkies have just started making. It's a silent weapon, chambered in an SP4 cartridge, so this little party won't disturb other ranks.*' 'E gave this malicious, shit-kicking grin. '*It's double-action, so I leave it to you whether you just pull the trigger or add to the suspense by cocking the hammer.*'"

"Bullard spoke up for all of us: '*But Sergeant Major, we were…*'"

"Wright wasn't 'avin' it. '*Shut your fucking mouth! This is the only way you mice will earn any sort of right to be called men again.*'"

"With that, the RSM spun the bottle. '*Who'll it be, lads?*' 'E taunted us while the finger of death decided. '*Who'll you bury tonight?*'"

There was no stopping Bovis' hand shaking this time; in his memory and the telling he was like a man blindfolded and one false step away from oblivion. He clenched his fist again to hide the tremor and ploughed on.

"The bottle pointed to Penney first. Worse than anything that ever 'appened to me, I'll never forget 'is face as 'e was forced to shove that weird broad barrel right into his mouth, tears streaming down his cheeks while Wright bent over him, abusing him, calling 'im a coward, all in this whispered snarl. Telling 'im there would be much worse to deal with, from the RSM 'imself and the other ranks, if 'e bottled it. I tell you, Sergeant Pascoe…" He cut short; that particular musing lost forever. "I was still thinking *no way, he won't make him do thi*s, but he wouldn't let it go. *'Come on now, Penney – pull the trigger. Imagine it's that sniper you're shooting, like you should've done instead of running away like a fucking little girl!'*

Now, when Bovis leaned forward, his stare was almost too much for Pascoe. "I still don't know which is greater – the agony of 'earing Corporal Stead's death, or the shame that I didn't feel relieved for Penney when the gun just clicked. No spinning the bottle this time – there was just two of us now so I grabbed the gun. I couldn't imagine waiting to be the last one if it went that way. I'll never forget the feeling of that barrel sliding into my mouth; the strange wish that I could die in battle instead. For a moment I wondered why I didn't just take the gun and fire it at Wright. Of course, part of me knew that if I succeeded then I was a done man – and if it didn't fire…the same. It's hard to describe – Wright was abusing 'is power over us, but still, you're sort of programmed to obey; it leaves you nowhere to go. It's what sent men over the top to certain death in the First World War."

Bovis had to pause for a moment. As he swallowed, the noise was so loud, it might have been the click of a trigger. He continued:

"There was this joyful 'orror as death passed me by, then the fuckin' awful sense of betrayal when Wright pointed in Bullard's direction; the ridiculous 'appiness I felt when the gun just clicked for 'im too and 'e let it fall to the table, followed by threads of spit.

"I can't describe the anger neither, of realising we'd been put through all that as some sort of insane, sadistic, bullying joke. After 'is initial screaming at Penney, the devil 'imself didn't say a fuckin' word while 'e watched us. But 'e did something as 'e ordered us out of the tent which still brings me out in a cold sweat when I think about it…" There had been a look in Bovis' eyes Pascoe couldn't even begin to describe, although it wasn't hard to interpret. "'E took the gun, pointed it towards the sand and fired. Despite the noiseless report, all three of us leapt as the bullet spat."

"How the hell was he planning to explain it away if one of you had taken the bullet?" There was so much that Pascoe understood now, most of it, nonetheless, beyond his comprehension.

"Who knows? Maybe 'e'd quickly loaded the gun as we were 'eading out of the tent, but 'e would 'ave needed to be bloody fast."

"Or maybe it would have been just the word of two junior soldiers against a senior one. One coward who couldn't take the shame and two more lying to cover up theirs."

Pascoe shook his head. The sound of that silent gun had seemed to echo through The Jolly Farmer too, along with the laugh of a madman.

Words were inadequate once again – except Bovis had them anyway. His demeanour had reverted to the angry squaddie who had marched into the pub an hour before. He shook his head and gave a dry, humourless laugh. "And as if I 'adn't tried 'ard enough to forget, some fuckin' joker in the upper ranks 'as fingered me to be 'is fuckin' chauffeur on the morning of the Armistice commemoration." While Pascoe's jaw fell open at that revelation, Bovis leaned back, eyes wide for a moment. "Unless someone 'opes I'll kill him. I'll tell you this; if someone did it, I'm sure they'd be toasted for it by any number of squaddies."

It was a revelation that brooked no further small talk. Bovis downed the last of his beer, got up and left. The two men afforded each other a slight nod; a farewell devoid of words, but brim full of unspoken understanding.


With so much on which to reflect, as he stared into The Shepherd's Crook's fire on a late autumn's afternoon, finding warmth he hadn't known he needed, Pascoe decided, as he had done three weeks before, that the only proper lubricant for his thoughts was whisky. The whole world had become a minefield. How did a man move forward? There had even been discomfort in thinking about his own dear uncle's military career; not a man capable of such brutality, but had those beneath him helped to forge the glories of the nation on those same weak foundations of bloodstained sand? Of course they had, for what was history if not a reminder of what mankind would do next?

If Pascoe was learning nothing else in his short time as a detective, he was discovering that one of the prerequisites needed by any cop was the ability to suspend prejudgement. Whatever his first impressions of the anonymous colonel, the officer had proved a good judge of men in his assessment of Bovis. Outward appearances had been misleading. For Bovis, the army was family, every loss a bereavement, but where time to grieve was denied, the only thing left was a code of honour – a determination to ensure no death was in vain. Yet that was the sad irony – the military histories of the twentieth century and the first part of the twenty-first were chalices overflowing with lies and wasted lives. Despite the camouflage of tattoos and machismo, Bovis was a man of glass; fragile, transparent, and one false move away from shattering.

Pascoe was forced to contemplate the disturbing fact that he, a policeman, felt in his soul that the brutal wiping out of Wright's life was both justice and justified.

In the end, he was glad a whisky is soon gone, leaving less time for contemplation than a pint. He stood, removed the photocopy of his uncle's letter and the scrawled-on beermat from his pocket before placing them in the fire. Once they had disappeared as smoke up the chimney, leaving just the ashes of their history, he followed them out into the November darkness.

# 10

Gill Scott thought she might be feeling a little high. It had been so long, she wasn't entirely sure she could remember the sensation. A bit drunk, for sure, and not just on alcohol; she was a new face in a new town and her determination to keep in shape for her taekwondo appeared to have added benefits, judging by the reactions of the local guys, including some of the younger ones, in the bar where she'd gone tonight with her new work colleagues.

She was no longer caught in that pincer of despair, one arm of which had been her husband's failure to appreciate her, the other his propensity to want to inflict physical violence on anyone who looked at her the wrong way.

He'd been a brute of a man, who had *taken care of* his family with all the negative connotations of those words; a restrictive, bullying presence, even in his absence. She had put a brave face on it for the girls; for Lara and her erstwhile best friend, her cousin Sam. But there had been more than one reason why Gill Scott had learnt a martial art and honed it to the point where any wrong move could at least be repelled.

None of which had meant that every night he was by her side she hadn't lain there in fear, hoping he would fall asleep. And she'd counted every moment he was away on active service or training as a blessing.

It hadn't taken her long to forgive herself for being glad he was dead. The thing she had failed to silence – hoping it would grow quiet of its own accord – was the voice that condemned her for having noticed when his eye was wandering, where it was wandering, and just being glad that it wasn't undressing her.

Now she stopped; took a deep breath, feeling the anxiety tightening around her chest even after all this time. Thank God the man who had paid her attention tonight had been decent, to the point of disappointment when he had passed her his card and left for home. She might even have not cared if he'd been married, just as long as he wasn't a bully. But it had been a relief to find her libido was alive and kicking, not replaced by bitterness or bile. There remained the chance that some of the latter might have been reserved for her bad self, though.

If she could have aimed one of her incapacitating taekwondo Yop Chagi at herself for being a fool, she would have done so many times, and for being a coward – a blind one. Blind in so many ways. Despite rediscovering her ability to laugh, she could tell the period of recovery and catharsis would last longer than she had hoped, and, even then, you could never tell. Perhaps the hand of a good man might touch her when she least expected it and the first he would know of his mistake would be when he recovered consciousness from the instinctive blow she would deal him. Perhaps Mr Decent tonight had somehow seen that in her eyes and had decided to leave the initiative with her. She'd known little about him, after all. She would have to dig out his card again and check it didn't say *Psychic*!

She laughed; fumbled for her keys and dropped them. The clumsiness was just alcohol, which had always raced through her system. She scooped them up, tottered a bit on rising again, unused to heels – and then staggered back against her front door as the figure emerged from the bushes.

"You!" she gasped.

★★★★

Logan looked up from his paperwork at the sound of the knuckle tapping on his door, to find Harj standing there.

Harj was that rarest of things – a human being trustworthy enough that he had felt able to confide in him regarding his facial blindness. The confession had almost been drawn from him one day when the forensics expert had commented, only half joking, that the DCI's observations about living people seemed to mirror or utilise his own terminology for describing the dead!

Given Harj was the only Sikh in the department, identifying him required no quantum leap of analysis. "God bless the turban," said Logan. It was their private joke, and it drew its usual response:

"And Waheguru bless your tie." His colleague gestured with the folder he was holding before placing it on the desk. "Your forensics report."

"Thanks Harj." Logan grinned. "Let me guess – death caused by choking through a combination of vomit and severe downward pressure from a swagger stick in the throat."

"You missed your vocation. You're really a lab geek, aren't you, spotting all those subtle nuances like that?" They laughed. Logan gave a humph of agreement and opened the folder.

"There is one thing, Ben." Logan glanced up again. "Sure, that is the cause of death, but there's some bruising, just below the sternum, around the solar plexus. It's very concentrated, so probably caused by a single blow."

"Presumably that's how he was disabled?"

"Probably. He was in good shape for fifty-five, despite his war wounds, but a proper blow to the solar plexus will stop the most muscular mutt. What we also didn't see at the crime scene..." Harj stepped round the desk and pointed to the relevant line in the report, which Logan was now studying with greater interest than he'd predicted. "Here. It was disguised somewhat by the haem-orrhaging and the vomit; bruising on and a hairline fracture to the jaw, not caused by the pressure from the swagger stick. I'm guessing this was from another blow that knocked him out. Solar plexus, jaw, bang bang!"

Logan frowned as he continued to flick through the report, though the latter was more an empty gesture while he gathered his thoughts. "Doesn't sound like you think there was more than one blow in each case."

"No."

"So these were blows dealt by someone very strong."

"Yes," said Harj, "or who knew what they were doing."

"You mean like a martial arts exponent?"

"Can't be ruled out."

Logan reached for his phone, but Harj hadn't quite finished. "This is not that important in the grand scheme of things, but we did also find a fracture in the hyoid bone in the neck. This wouldn't have come from the blow that rendered the victim unconscious, in my opinion, but was probably caused by a hold on the throat from someone facing him, therefore probably while he was lying on the bed and having the stick thrust down his throat. It would have guaranteed his death. The killer may simply have been trying to stop him struggling. It's not of huge importance in this instance – it certainly wasn't being administered by someone who wasn't trying to kill him."

"Thank you Harj." Hurrying to dial out, he gave Harj the thumbs-up, signalling that forensics' work was done for the moment.

"Pascoe, how's it going?"

"All right, sir."

"Your shy army contact come up with anything?"

"Just the usual, sir – you know, hard bastard, might have made enemies, nothing concrete, that sort of thing. I'm not sure why he needed to be so secretive about it, though he suggested army personnel talking to the police don't do their careers any favours."

There was something in Pascoe's voice that gave Logan pause for a moment's thought. Then again, he sounded like he was driving, so perhaps he was just avoiding idiots. Logan continued: "You remember Gill Scott's alibi for the night of the tenth?"

"Yes, sir, though I wasn't aware it was an alibi – she just mentioned it in passing. She was at her taekwondo club in Torquay that evening and then went for a couple of drinks afterwards."

"Sorry, Pascoe, yes, it's something I've just seen that made me choose that word. Do me a favour and double-check that for me will you?"

"Yes, sir. You got a lead?"

"No, Pascoe – a lot of dogs running in the night, but none on a lead. Not yet."


As Logan hung up, he couldn't have known that his disquiet was mirrored by Pascoe's expression as he watched the call end on his mobile and its screen go dark.

# I I

These days, any ring of the doorbell seemed to set her fucking heart pounding. The thought of who it might be brought either panic or hope, depending where her mind had crept away to in the previous minutes.

She didn't deserve to feel hope. She knew that now – she'd been brought up better than this and if she could've turned the clock back she would have.

She was only glad it wasn't the sound of the key in the door; that would mean her torturer was home. She glanced at her watch – still a couple of hours to go till he was back from the night shift. Of course, she'd not always seen it as torture; not in the early days, when she'd wanted it as much as him and had mistaken rampant lust as grounds for marriage. She'd put it all on the plate and eaten her fill too. There was no part of her that she hadn't surrendered, willingly and every which way. But it had had to happen – one day she'd nothing left on the menu and he'd started to eat out. She'd wanted to say something – stop him – but the bottom line was that she was too scared: how did you feed the man who'd turned out to be a brute, when punishments you'd once been willing to receive became torments; your groans now screams, muffled by the very gag you'd once been so eager to wear?

Only one thing was worse – when the screams were not your own and all you could do was sit and listen, hating yourself for being grateful he was leaving you alone for now and the fact that it meant your life was going nowhere if not with him; never knowing whether you had created the monster, or just been too blind and stupid to see it.

But this was a ring of the doorbell. How she hoped. How she hoped! She almost didn't want to go to the door, because it would open onto the same hopeless fucking world as always. In many ways she'd given up thinking it might be the police. If Angelina had any fucking sense she'd never come back; just let this grim estate and this flat fade from her memories. How she'd love to do the same – forget.

She made it to the door.

Any memories, whether good or bad, were driven from her by the first blow, along with all her breath

So much so, she couldn't even remember the second blow when she came round. There was a vague memory of a figure in black clothing, wearing some sort of mask. Something wasn't right here. She knew where she was as she stared at the cracked plaster of the bedroom ceiling, but why or how she was there remained a fog. The shortness of breath was somehow familiar, but it wasn't a familiarity that brought any comfort, because now she knew she was gagged – it felt like her mouth was taped. She tried to reach to remove the gag, only to find her hands were fastened to the head-board by two sets of manacles. Again that weird recognition – this had been one of his favourites – but now there was only panic; not the dismay she felt when he had turned nastier in recent years, but huge fucking terror. After several thrashes of her wrists, she had to stop, snorting like a horse through her nostrils. She knew the manacles could be opened by the wearer – she'd worn them often enough! – but you had to be able to reach one hand with the other. Whoever had done this to her had fastened her hands wide apart. For a horrible moment, she wondered if it was him: had he come back early from his shift to play some terrible game of domination? She wouldn't be surprised; some of his demands, when he did bother with her, had become too much even for her.

Now, as she lay still, the pain kicked in; her jaw; her chest. Somehow it all told her this wasn't his work. Sure, he slapped her around, but he enjoyed her struggles and had never yet knocked her out. So that left the terrible question…

It was as if her body was regaining sensation by means of pain journeying down it. On trying to move her legs, she discovered her feet were tied so that she lay spread-eagled, like every pervert's wet dream – the concept, not her; she could barely stand the sight of her scrawny self in the mirror these days. Looking down, she saw she was naked. She thrashed again, just enough to confirm she was helpless. There was nothing for it; this had been done for a reason and she would have to await her fate. She lay there, listening to the flat; silent except for the usual faint voices, shouting and scolding through the thin walls. Ironic – even if her muffled screams for help could be heard now, the neighbours would just raise their eyebrows and put it down to that fucking, in all senses of the word, couple next door. Anyway, as far as she could tell, her attacker had gone. Why? What was this all about?

Unbelievable – she must have dozed off, or maybe passed out again, because she came to at the sound of the key in the front door. Wincing at the pain caused by turning her head, she glanced towards the closed bedroom door, imagining his brutal shape. Her stomach gave an instinctive lurch. It said a lot when a woman in her position wasn't relieved by her husband's return. Hearing the footsteps coming down the corridor, she recognised his tread; wondered whether her attacker was lying in wait for him. All sorts of thoughts and scenes raced through her mind. Perhaps the intruder was after him and had just put her here, like this, to stop her warning him. How she'd have liked to put her captor right. For reasons beyond her, she lay quiet anyway; that age-old habit of the prey.

"Sheila?"

He was used to silence when he came home, so he must have noticed she wasn't in the kitchen or the living room.

"Sheila!?"

Never in the best of moods – ever – but particularly after a night shift at the plant, he sounded ready for a fight.

The footsteps stopped by the closed bedroom door. Why the hesitation?

Then it was pushed open and in he stepped, in all his stocky, tattooed, dreadful bulk.

"What the fuck?!"

She lay still. What else was there she could do? At the moment, she had nothing left. That included answers. In fact, she wasn't even sure what the questions might be.

An absurd, but worrying grin spread across his face. In its horrible light, she felt shame, but pretty soon that was replaced by dread. Forgetting the gag, she tried to say something – she wasn't sure what – but all that came out was a muffled whimper. His words, however, made her blood turn cold.

"Well, what've we got 'ere?" He stepped further into the room. "Beats breakfast, whatever it is."

He started to unbuckle his belt. It dawned on her what he was thinking and all she could do was try to scream. She saw the impact of the sounds of her stifled terror in the growing bulge in his pants.

"Gotta hand it to yer – you've always known what a man wants." He seemed to nod in appreciation. "Nice bit of self-bondage."

He brought the belt cracking down across her stomach. Her body tried to double over, but the manacles and ropes jerked it back flat. As always, the thrashing and locomotive breathing were arousing him, but for her the real horror was the way she was echoing cries of the past heard from down the corridor, reminding her of far worse crimes. She deserved this punishment.

She fell quiet; watched as he removed his clothes, almost drooling with lust, struggling to release his throbbing erection from his boxers. She might almost have laughed at the thought of a husband who comes home to find his wife tied to the bed and can only think of fucking her, if it hadn't been so very, very sad. Tears welled up and spilled down her temples.

"I'd almost forgotten what a great body you've got for your age." He stood at the end of the bed; pointed to his pointer. "'aven't felt this 'ard in a long time – not since the bitch left town." Now he dropped onto his knees on the floor.

He untied her ankles. Part of her wanted to take aim and kick him in that ugly head, but the reprisals when she failed, which she knew she would, didn't bear thinking about. He held those legs apart.

"Jus' to prove it's not all about me, I think I'll dine at the Y. Remember 'ow much you loved that?"

As he started, she wondered at how much life and time could change to the point where the pressure of his tongue failed to excite a single nerve ending.

She turned her head to one side, but the movement made her jaw sing with pain. Only when she twisted it back did she see, over his shoulder, the figure which appeared to have emerged from the wardrobe. As a reflex, she screamed, but the gag robbed her terror of all specifics.

The monster she had married, oblivious to the real reason for her reaction', looked across her stomach. "That's right, girl – but now get ready to really scream."

Behind him, the man advanced, the creepy Guy Fawkes mask beyond all horror. On seeing the figure was holding some sort of old, battered sword, she knew that, although this should have been a nightmare from which she would wake up if she could only stay sane, this was all too real. If this had always been the intruder's plan, then either he possessed the cunning of the devil, or the mind of the beast currently scoffing between her legs that easy to read.

She yanked at the manacles, eyes popping as she howled against the gaffer tape, thrashed her legs, though the only effect of the latter was to excite the brute between them even more, judging by the noise he was making as he held her in a vice-like grip which she knew had strengthened through years of working in the factory. For one absurd moment her dark soul seemed to step outside her, long enough to hear the echoes and remember how this had once been the stuff that fed her appetites. The belt lashing once more across her stomach brought to an end those few seconds of release, and again she would have doubled over if she could.

And none of it mattered, or would ever matter, because through all of this the figure with the sword had advanced in total silence to stand right behind Kevin Miller.

Now Kevin straightened up to look at her, forcing her knees apart as he took her thighs in his iron grip – how that strength had once turned her on – getting ready to climb onto the bed. His penis looked harder than she could remember, and she knew the penetration would be sudden, violent and as painful as he could make it.

But the thrust never came; at least not from Kevin Miller. Just for a split second, it seemed he spotted something about her face that he'd never seen before. It could even have been a weird calmness, or acceptance. Now, his twisted features might have been mistaken for orgasmic frenzy, but not the blood-chilling scream. That, too, was cut short as the killer drove him face down onto the bed, pressed down on the bullish, tattooed back with one foot and continued to drive the blade downwards through the squirming body, while Sheila found the strength to scramble as far up the bed as the manacles would allow her. The battered blade was not the longest, and the mystery swordsman stopped when the hilt rested on his victim's back.

The body stopped thrashing. Sheila had also fallen still and silent, watching with gruesome fascination as the blood soaked and spread through the bedding. It was heading her way and she contorted her body to keep clear of it.

Now the killer – it seemed a harsh description, given the nature of the victim – lifted his foot from Kevin Miller's back and withdrew the sword; Sheila knew the sound of its exit as it scraped past bone would never leave her. He stood for a moment as if admiring his handiwork, the smile on the mask appropriate in its awfulness. Then – a dreadful thing to behold – he placed the point between the buttocks of the corpse and shoved. God only knew what terrible moment from his past had driven him to that action, and from somewhere in the pit of horrors where she found herself at that moment, she was surprised to find a tiny rock of sympathy. Yet her grip on that slipped at the sight and sound of the sword being pulled out again. The sucking of flesh on blade made her skin crawl. Then she could only watch as he wiped it on the duvet, as casual as a plumber cleaning his tools.

She lay still; once again, not only did it seem the best thing to do, it was her only option.

And then – the same peculiar sensation as earlier – she enjoyed a few seconds of calm. She was someone at the edge of a cliff and, just for a wonderful moment, there was only the breeze, the sighing of the sea and, for perhaps the first time in her life, no fear of falling.

A slight movement and the peace evaporated as the killer tilted his head. Through the eyeholes in the mask, she saw him watching her.

Now he edged around the bed. She started to scramble again, but between the restraints and the blood there was nowhere else to go. He leaned in till the mask was almost touching her head and she could smell the spearmint gum he'd been chewing.

The voice – she would never forget it. From that moment, both it and the damning words would live in her head.

"I was going to kill you too, but I see now you suffer enough – suffer in silence. You know all about silence, don't you?" Nostrils snorting, she gave a frantic nod where no agreement had been needed. "Men's primal urges cannot be forgiven, but they can be understood, if not comprehended. A mother's silence, on the other hand, cannot, if it isn't to protect her child. Never forget that and make a fresh start without this piece of shit."

The manacle around Sheila Miller's right wrist was loosened and her rescuer left, sword in hand.

It wasn't until she heard the front door shut that she dared move. She released her other hand and inched off the bed, away from the disgusting heap of flesh, which was how she had seen him towards the end of his life anyway, but still retching at the sight of it. She saw her grotesque reflection in the bedside mirror, gag still in place. The irony – the shame of her silence through the years – wasn't lost on her. She peeled the tape from her mouth, gasping with all manner of hurt. She'd have loved nothing better than to keep silent again, but she'd have to call this in. Still, she thought she could probably wait a few minutes. Long enough for the person to get away; that mercy killer who had relieved her of this sick fuck and, incredibly, spared her life.

As she contemplated how to explain what had happened it struck her – if she acted quickly, she wouldn't have to see her shame splashed across the front pages. She didn't give a fuck if the story of the murder was reported, but there was no need for anyone, from the neighbours to the trolls, to know what she had just been through. The past could be well and truly buried with this beast. It was nothing that long sleeves and a bit of makeup hadn't covered up many times before.

And then she had to look away from the figure in the mirror and hang her head. There were things makeup wouldn't hide and ghosts that would rise from the grave, refusing to pass away. You could stop the world from knowing, but it would offer no sanctuary to which you could run. To make a fresh start, was there someone she needed to find, from whom to ask forgiveness? And if so, she would need to decide, was it her daughter, or was it herself?

★★★★

The pathology report was still playing on Logan's mind when a shout from across the outer office snapped his chain of thoughts.

"Sir, we have another murder!"

The DCI spun round, leapt to his feet. "Another veteran?"

"I don't think so," said the officer on the incident desk, "but it's sounding pretty weird in its own way."

★★★★

Assuming the woman wasn't lying, the facts were clear, unlike the motive. As Logan wasn't one for assumption, this meant her reliability was key. There was a peculiar twist in that she, perhaps more so than the dead man, was a victim. It was written all over the bruise she had tried to cover on her face; in the complete exhaustion that dragged at every syllable she uttered; in the tiredness of everything he saw as he looked around the flat. Already mired in that, she had come home to find this gruesome vignette added to her life and was now fighting so very hard to hide her relief. It was Gill Scott all over again. That alone was something that convinced him she wasn't the perpetrator, setting aside the difficulty she would have had in overpowering that hulk. Was this the work of the Armistice Killer once more? Logan had no proof definitive of that, just the feeling in his gut as he had stepped through the door.

She had told him how she liked to nip out for cigarettes, or on any pretext, when he was due home from his one-till-nine morning shift, as he wasn't often in a good mood. She had come back about half an hour later to find him like this. Someone must have been watching; someone who knew their habits and timings – that's what she assumed. Again, though the DCI didn't like assumptions, this one seemed fair enough.

There was no sign of forced entry – at least not at the front door. The same couldn't be said of Kevin Miller's back door! Must have been some sort of sword, the forensics team had said. Given that was a military weapon, albeit only ceremonial these days, it provided another potential connection with the murder of RSM Wright. They would have to check whether Miller was ex-military. Thinking about his Venn diagrams again, Logan could see two muscular men found lying on beds having had various long implements shoved forcibly into them. Was there some sexual motivation here?

He walked through to the rather moth-eaten living room – it occurred to him they must have been desperate moths – where Sheila Miller sat curled on the sofa, dabbing a tissue from time to time at her nose. Looking around, Logan noted the absence of family photos.

"Mrs Miller." As she looked up, her eyes told a thousand tales of mostly evil. "Was your husband in the army?"

The question seemed to surprise her, as if it was less than meaningless, so her given answer was rendered almost superfluous. "No – why?"

"Oh, just trying to cross-link this with other…crimes. Is there anyone else who needs to be informed about this? Family, or…"

He stopped short on seeing such raw pain. This was a woman holding back so many things, but she was unable to mask this deep sadness, tinged, he was sure, with shame.

"No."

Logan dropped to his haunches in front of her, trying and failing to look into Sheila Miller's eyes. "Really?"

As he had walked through from the murder scene, he had glanced into the other bedroom and spotted enough of the usual flotsam and jetsam to suggest a teenager has sailed through. He had not sensed a happy passage; it was not the sort of room a loving parent left as a shrine to false nostalgia; the strops forgotten, the surly moods, instead everything kept in eager readiness for the return of the prodigal. The room hadn't spoken of love. If it ever had that tenderness had frayed, like the Twilight duvet cover and the rather tattered bear, sitting with immeasurable sadness on the pillow. There were no posters. There was a neat pile of magazines – too neat. Shoes were lined against a wall, but neither scattered in hopscotch fashion across the grubby carpet to suggest active occupancy nor cleaned and arranged with care. Some items of makeup stood on another shelf. Even his quick look through the door had been enough to recognise that room was a conundrum; a worrying one. It belonged to everyone and no one; the makeup speaking of a teenager, the duvet likewise…and then there was the neglect of the old, faithful bear.

Someone had left in a hurry, or without a backward glance.

The scene had left Logan rueful and it had taken an effort of will to walk away from it. He'd felt drawn into the vacuum. Would he have been a good father? He'd have liked to find out – still would in many ways, though if anything should have acted as juju protecting him from that madness, it was the succession of loveless homes he had entered in recent years. He hoped he would at least have been a better father than to allow this to happen…but then again, to adapt the saying, it was a wise father who knew his own child. That might have had a literal connotation at school run time, given his prosopagnosia. He gave a thin smile. Now something else occurred to him – it was a wise parent who recognised him or herself.

All of which had rendered this mother's one word response annoying, puzzling and pertinent in equal measures. She had refused to answer his disbelief-laden single word question that followed, so, although it might have seemed harsh, the next comment needed to be made: "We can check. I know you're having a tough time right now, but please save us the bother of having to."

In an obtuse way it was good to watch her face fighting against both her emotions and habitual mistrust of the police, which was a given on this particular estate. There was a flicker of defiance. "I dunno where she is now."

Logan stood, his legs driven by exasperation. Another one!? Mothers seemed to be getting careless. He paced across the room and back, gathering his thoughts.

Sheila Miller seemed to sense his anger. "It's better for her that way. She's got any sense, she'll stay lost, especially if she's got another bed somewhere she can call her own."

"How can you say that about your own daughter?" The words were out, but then again, as he looked at her, hunched on that sofa, the relief tangible that her brute of a husband was lying recently skewered in the other room, he realised there were different definitions of lost, and being anywhere that was away from here was, in all probability, a better place; somewhere *lost*, as in *safe*.

A thought occurred – he pushed it aside for the moment.

He ensured that his next words came out with more calmness than he was feeling: "Could you tell me why?"

"Why what?"

He frowned, thrown for a moment by the disorder of his own thoughts. "Well, why you feel that way, I suppose. Why she left."

"I'd rather not."

This wasn't helping him, but he could understand. He realised she wasn't being obstructive, just looking to shake off the dogs of the past. He knew that feeling; looking into that empty bedroom had set his own particular pack barking in his mind and memories, remembering how long it had taken his parents to finally stop treating his dead sister's goods, chattels and bed as holy relics in a shrine.

"How old is she?"

"Old enough." Despite himself, Logan felt the impatience rising again, but saw that she had sensed it too. "I mean, she'd just turned seventeen when she left."

"So how long ago was this?"

"Mebbe five months ago."

"She's seventeen and a half." Got there in the end! "Don't you think she'd want to know her father's dead?"

Sheila Miller gave a snort of laughter, which had nothing to do with humour, except of the blackest kind. It might even have been a reflection of her relief at being free. "Oh, she'd love to know. If you find her, feel free to tell her. He…bullied her." She stood suddenly; seemed impatient. "Please, am I a suspect? Cos if I'm not, I'd like to get on with my f…with my life. I told you all I know. I dunno who killed him. My husband's dead and, heaven 'elp me, I'm fuckin' glad!"

Logan compressed his lips, contemplating what she'd said. "No, actually, I think I'm done for now. Oh, I almost forgot – what was…is your daughter's name?"

"Angelina." She gave another snort. "He had a thing about that Lara Croft film that came out the year she was born."

Everything peripheral was lost on Logan for a moment. He was deep in woods he could see despite the trees. The name Lara had caused a jolt to run through him. He resorted to finger arithmetic for a moment – but no, Tom Wright's daughter had been born long before Tomb Raider and its virtual bombshell had hit small screens and parents' pockets. Much as he didn't believe in coincidence, this was one!

But that, if anything, convinced him that his earlier connection of dots from a few moments before was unlikely to be a second one. There was someone he had to see right now. "Okay, the forensics guys will be a while longer."

"Why? Isn't it obvious what happened?"

"It's obvious to a point perhaps." Logan would have noticed himself cringe as he made this unintended pun, but fortunately Sheila Miller was less observant. "But knowing how it occurred and knowing why are two different things. Also, we'd like to ascertain by whom it was done…so, we need to look at the exact nature of the injuries, get a better picture of the weapon and exactly how it was used, and that might help us narrow down suspects."

"Of course – sorry." She paused, looking a touch guilty. "I shouldn't say it, I s'pose, but I hope he gets away."

The assumption that it was a man, this person Sheila Miller claimed not to have seen, grated a little, though Logan could see how eons of violence had been driven by male savagery. He knew better than most the brutal acts of which women were also capable. He let it go for now, though there was more than a hint of admonition in his next words.

"I have to remind you, Mrs Miller, that this is a murder investigation, and we'll expect your full cooperation, irrespective of your opinion."

She looked at him – such a frank gaze that it unsettled him – before asking: "And what's yours?"

He wondered whether release from years of being dominated was responsible for the brevity of her question. Whatever the cause, it left him nowhere to go, but a myriad of possible answers. He settled on the one that got him off the hook for now: "As they say, Mrs Miller, I couldn't possibly comment."

So here he was, back at the social centre again, except this time his energies and thoughts had full professional focus. Okay, it was a shot in the dark to an extent. Sheila Miller's expression of hope that her daughter had found a bed, combined with his own translation of her definition of *lost* as being *safe*, had brought him into the presence of Samantha Ingle once more.

It came to something when your own hope was that the girl was hiding because terrible things had been done to her; it was better than because she'd done a terrible thing herself. It was a question he had to ask her, though. He had never heard of the charity till Samantha had flagged it to him, had no solid foundation to his own hope that he might find some guidance as to the whereabouts of Angelina Miller, but you had to start somewhere. Even if not with Safebeds, perhaps there was some other escape route for the girl, and the locally connected lawyer with the social conscience might just know someone who knew someone.

He'd expected the impatience, so didn't allow it to bother him. Instead, he focussed his energies on trying to see any traces of insincerity in her eyes. Then again, she had been a lawyer, those practiced masters of being enigmatic, social conscience or not!

"I told you before, DCI Logan, Safebeds is anonymous. Even if I had any information to give you, which I don't, I wouldn't pass it on."

He opened his mouth to speak; got no further.

"Oh, you could go down the legal route," continued Sam, "but I'm here to tell you, you'll fail."

"Okay. Well, was she ever a member of your club here?"

She sighed with exasperation, then beckoned him to follow her across to the receptionist and gestured towards the computer.

"Janey, not content with failing to find Lara, the DCI would like you to check whether we ever had any members registered under a combo of any or all of the following: Angelina, Croft, Jolie."

The sarcasm was dripping, and the receptionist stifled a conspiratorial grin, before saying: "Oh, strangely enough, there is a Brad Pitt on our books. Would that be of interest detective?"

"If you could just run the search for Angelina Miller that will be fine, thanks."

They drew a blank.

There was nothing left for Logan to do for now except to offer his thanks and leave. He was just opening the entrance door when Sam called from behind him. "If you do happen to find her, you will draw her attention to Safebeds, won't you?"

It was a comment too far. He hadn't planned to reveal his other reason for being there, but they needed to taste the seriousness of this situation. He stopped, though he didn't turn. "And if you happen to see her, you won't let her know she's a potential suspect in a murder, will you? If I'm finding it hard to get help then at least a lack of hindrance would be appreciated."

He walked on, only slightly regretting the tit for tat nature of the comment. He didn't need to look round – he could read the silence that met his words

# 12

Another day – another pathologist's report.

"Like London buses, these bloody reports," said Harj, dropping it on Logan's desk.

"And just as red," said the DCI, opening the folder and looking at the first picture.

"Thought you never read them," quipped Harj.

"I do, of course! I just value your between the lines opinions too." Logan started to read. "Bloody is the operative word! Death caused by blah blah blah blah…probably a long bladed weapon." He looked up at the pathologist. "That's based on?"

"Well, to cut through the technical jargon, the narrowness of the entry wound and the shape of the cuts where the weapon hit bone. Plus that final coup de grâce, shall we say, went in some way, though I believe the initial stab, the one through the heart, was almost certainly fatal."

"Hmm. The order matters you see, and I've been mulling over the possibility of a connection between this and the other murder, on the basis of them both being violent, penetrative acts performed on muscular men on beds. In Wright's case that was the cause of death, but in Miller's it was…violation of a corpse I suppose."

Harj nodded. "Indeed! And, of course, this time the weapon was taken away, perhaps suggesting someone other than the victim owned it?"

Logan contemplated this. "Doubtful the victim had a sword lying around, whereas, of course, RSM Wright had that swagger stick. Makes me think the first weapon was opportunistic and the second was indeed brought. Even if the crimes feel similar, this is something of a wedge that drives them apart. Unless…" Logan slapped his hand on the table. "I wonder if Wright owned the sword? Clearly, judging by the contents of the flat he had a keen interest in old weaponry, so what if the killer took it from him with murder aforethought? I'll have to check into that." Now Logan noticed that Harj was smiling. It must have been infectious, because he, too, started to grin. "What?"

"Despite the inevitable morbidity of the circumstances, it's always good to see DCI Logan on the trail again, viewing life through those bifocal eyes, split between reality and alternative reality."

Logan allowed his smile to continue for a moment longer. It was a rare – and appreciated – moment of understanding from a fellow human being. Then he regained focus. "In the meantime, any thoughts on whether this big brute was overpowered before the murder? Similar to the first MO?"

Harj pursed his lips; shook his head. "Unfortunately no bruising around the solar plexus region. It's puzzling – there were no signs of a violent struggle, apart from some bruising along the lower spine and lumbar region, which might have been a knee or foot holding him in place."

"Any chance he was unconscious?"

"There are no obvious signs as to how he might have been rendered that way – no narcotics in the system…"

"Clean living thug."

"…no bruising to head or neck. Plus, the distortion of facial and neck muscles are all suggestive of him being aware of what was happening."

Logan continued to scan the report. Something caught his eye and he pictured the scene in the flat again. "I think I know the answer to this, but was there any sign that he was…aroused at the time of his death? I see this…"

Harj looked to where he was pointing. "No, that's more common than people know – the slight inflammation of the penis is often there when the body is face down and as it says further down, there was prostatic discharge, but nothing more than that."

Logan nodded. "Think I need to pay a return visit to the first murder scene – view it from the vantage point of this second murder, if you see what I mean."

"Fresh eyes."

"In a manner of speaking; or maybe watching a movie for the second time, already knowing the plot."

Logan called Pascoe to the station, having decided they should travel together rather than meet at Wright's flat. There was more than one reason for wanting Pascoe in the private confinement of the car.

"So come on – what's going on?" he asked as the younger officer drove.

Pascoe's frown looked genuine enough, if you possessed a novice's eye, but intuition was sitting in the back seat again, prodding Logan's shoulder. He continued:

"Ever since you started making your enquiries at the barracks you have seemed a little bit…" he hesitated, "…preoccupied? In fact, correction – since a few days prior to the commemoration you've not quite seemed yourself. I'm allowing for the unfortunate passing of your uncle, but there's something else."

"Really?"

"Uh-huh." The inflexion mocked what he perceived as Pascoe's disingenuous surprise. "Did your discussion with anonymous officer bear any further poisonous fruit?"

"Well – it just seems Wright was one hell of a sadistic bully."

"A bullying sergeant major? Whatever next? This secretive contact wanted to meet you off-the-record just to tell you that?"

He kept his face turned towards his DS, increasing the discomfort.

"It just…disappointed me, sir."

"How so?"

"Well, as you know, I kind of grew up worshipping my uncle – it was gutting when my various allergies meant I didn't pass the medical requirements so I wasn't able to join up and try to follow in his footsteps." Pascoe's lips tightened for a second. "But anyway, as I say, I thought he was the ultimate honourable soldier. That hasn't changed, but…well, I'm not sure enlightening is the right word to describe my discussions; does 'endarkening' exist?"

"Do you mean the realisation that Empire and other passages of glorious colonial history have been built on foundations of horror and violence enthusiastically laid and abetted by men such as Wright?" Logan paused. "What do you think the subplot of the last few days' so-called celebrations has been? You've seen the poppies at the Tower. They represent lives lost."

Pascoe glanced at him. "Take your point, sir."

"So nothing other than that, Pascoe?"

"It seemed Wright was particularly brutal about ridiculing other ranks for showing any fear – you know, belittling them in front of the men."

"Anyone in particular?"

"No, sir, but I guess it does increase the possibility that this was some sort of a revenge killing."

Logan noted that Pascoe was shifting the topic slightly, but decided not to comment. "If so, it also increases the list of suspects to roughly the size of a regiment; if the possible motive for killing an RSM is that he was tough on the men, where the hell do we start?"

They had arrived; tyres crunching on the stony, potholed lane that ran alongside the converted cottages. They saw Mr Wolniek peering from his window. Was that just general nosiness from hearing a car's arrival, or was the old man checking it wasn't the press? Judging by the lack of detail in what articles there had been in the papers, it seemed everyone had decided to keep their counsel and circle the wagons when it came to the journos. For that, Logan was grateful. Perhaps, in these days of commemoration and greater awareness of the sacrifice of the armed forces, an element of respect had, for once, held sway. Logan raised a hand of acknowledgement towards Mr Wolniek. Of that man's sense of honour, there would never be a doubt. The hacks could knock on his door all day long without success.

Just as it had been on their first visit, Logan found himself in his element again as they parked up outside the flat. It had always held a fascination for him, to walk where the essence of a person's life had been separated from his or her body by violence. Even as a youth, he had developed, through close experience, an acute awareness of the forces that lingered when one man reached in and ripped out the soul of another. As childhood had passed, he had found himself drawn to old battlefields, fortresses and torture chambers. Walking in the bloody footprints of history, he felt the energy of malevolence and fear lingering centuries later. The knowledge had been a source of perverse comfort – that the dead would always make themselves heard; felt even.

In addition, on a more practical level, he savoured it once the scientists had taken their ordered chaos with them and you stood alone in the same killing field. Then everything returned, in many ways, to how it had been at that moment of taken life; as far as he was concerned, the respective energies of killer and victim never left the place where they had found their ultimate expression.

As he got out of the car and made his way towards the iron steps, even there, in that leafy suburb of Truro, a little gust of Atlantic wind tugged on the collar of his jacket, drawing his mind back to one particular time and place; a reminder that, for him, there was an otherwise innocuous stretch of cliff that would be forever death. Cornish coastal winds bore the echo of every life that ever perished on those rocky shores, be it commercial sailing ships that misread the currents and geography, the myths and legends of supposed Cornish wreckers, or unhappy, desperate suicides unlucky in love or lucre. But Logan would always think of at least two other lives lost to more violent actions. He had to fight hard to keep moving forward towards the steps of Wright's flat over the rush of memories calling to him from the rocky escarpments of his youth.

He waited for Pascoe to unlock the door of the flat. Once inside, he made his way to the bedroom.

He looked at the bed.

"Another mattress – another murder."

Pascoe grunted some form of agreement and then asked: "So what are we looking for, sir?"

"I don't know. We'll recognise it when we find it. Just anything that suggests the two murders of Wright and Miller are linked – other than the obvious of violent penetrative acts on beds."

Having scrutinised the flat, Logan crossed to the window; stared out at the really rather stunning vista of fields and farmhouses, complete with a distant church tower, across which played a constant interchange of winter sunlight and shadow. Out of the wind, it was hard to imagine violence being acted out on the periphery of such pastoral delight. Logan knew better though; he was aware that the darkness of night as a black canvas on which evildoers liked to sketch the nightmares of others?

Something glinted in the grass of the first field opposite. Probably nothing, but he would check anyway, since they were done here – Pascoe had continued to scan the room and indeed the flat, but found nothing of obvious relevance; and certainly not the other sword, indicating a collection, or, better, empty scabbard Logan had been half hoping for.

It was easy enough to clamber over the low wooden fence and into the field, which looked like it belonged to an adjoining white farmhouse. Technically, they should have requested a warrant before entering the property, but it looked like no one was home – no car out front, no windows open or lights on, and Logan had decided he would plead ignorance if they were confronted – the field might as easily have been communal ground.

The source of the glinting turned out to be a bottle of sparkling water, still half full. Taking the utmost care not to disturb any potential prints, Logan turned the cap a little; the hiss and reaction of the water suggested it was pretty fresh.

He looked up, noting how that spot had direct line of sight to RSM Wright's bedroom and lounge windows, yet was rendered invisible to the downstairs flats by a thick hedge. He addressed the bottle:

"Why were you here?"

"Couldn't it have just blown there, sir? There were some strong winds that night."

"It's still half full, Pascoe; unlikely to have just got picked up in a gust. And look around – doesn't seem to be any other litter. This isn't here by accident." Logan looked around. "But why just leave it?"

"Perhaps they were disturbed."

"In the middle of this field, on a winter's night – assuming this belongs to the perp?"

"Wright had those night vision goggles, sir. He must have had them out for a reason. Doubt the perp just happened to find them. Maybe Wright suspected something about that evening we don't know yet and was looking out across the field – our perp saw that and hid in a panic. Left the bottle."

Logan considered. "Sounds like a long shot, though I take your point about the goggles being out. Get the bottle checked for prints and DNA. What we'll also do is come back with some more men;

there may be more to find here. Get a warrant organised as well – technically we're trespassing."

Logan looked at the ground; it was hard, with no trace of a footprint – the autumn had been unusually dry. But for the bottle, there was no sign that anyone had been here. So, was this some sort of…what, playful clue? He doubted it – there had been strong symbolism in the actions of the killer, or killers, so far, never mind the brutality of the acts themselves.

Already, Logan sensed science would not lift the curtain, or if it did, little light would fall. The DNA testing of the bottle was unlikely to provide any immediate solutions. He could pretty well guarantee the perpetrator would not be on any police records. Yet how did he know that, other than through good old instinct? If the bottle was to be of any help, then that help lay in its being there, not in any chemical analysis.

He needed a moment.

"Pascoe?" The DS was lumbering around, surveying the earth more, it seemed, in hope than expectation – a suitable analogy for life perhaps – and looked up with a touch of both those emotions in his expression. "That other farmhouse we saw from the window; get over to them and ask…"

"Our guys already did, sir, on the day of the murder," interrupted Pascoe. "A couple of elderly ladies who saw nothing."

Logan took a breath. "I'm pretty sure you didn't ask them about this place." He gestured to the field and the rundown farmhouse. "What do they know about the owner? Have they seen him recently? There's no one here or we would have been challenged for clambering in over the fence. It's just a long shot, but maybe our killer hid near or even in the house that night."

As he wandered off, Pascoe's phone rang. He turned and headed back towards Logan, his features reflecting something of interest coming down the airwaves. "Yes, thanks very much for getting back to me, Miss Scott. Bye bye."

Logan's ears pricked up. "The sword?"

"Spot on, sir – RSM Wright did have one. Not a regimental one apparently, but an antique – a nineteenth century one. Given it wasn't in the flat just now, there might be a good chance it played a part in someone else's sticky end. Gives us a possible link between the murders, assuming we can find the sword."

"And you know what – my betting is, we will." Logan couldn't suppress a grin – and not just because of Pascoe's irreverent word-play. "Now, if you could just go and check out that other farm-house, that'll be great."

And thus he had that moment again for himself. He turned and looked around; went through a full three hundred and sixty degrees, trying to shut out the pied beauty of the scene; swap it for a howling wind, darkness pierced by lonely, lit windows; your stomach churning in dreadful anticipation.

This was a variation on a theme for Logan – a man who relished the post-murder scene because he read it so well; truth always seeping through its fabric and leeching from its stones. Here, instead, was the scene of the pre-murder vigil. Just the buffeting of the wind in his eardrums reminded him that the elements offered no differentiation of motives or time. He knew it somehow, but had to admit others would question him building his case on a founda-tion comprising one abandoned bottle. How he hoped, when he came back with more officers, the sweep of the field would reveal no other debris, proving this was no local litter dump.

"So who are you?" Again, he looked around, "Why pick this spot with such care so you wouldn't be seen, yet panic enough to drop the bottle or leave it behind? How did you manage to conceal any trace of your potential brutal involvement at two murder scenes, yet become so scared that you left us this calling card?"

When he thought about the ability to disappear without a trace, Lara Wright's name emerged from the fog, but when he thought about the brutality of the crimes, some ex-squaddie seemed more likely to march forward with pride; yet neither made sense – at least not on its own.

His mind wandered. It seemed the wind was picking up and it was, but only in the place to which his thoughts had drifted yet again. He experienced another sudden jolt from a suppressed memory; one he had tried to banish as being too dark, even for his dismal mind palace. There was a peculiar timbre to the moaning in the air. It disturbed him as it ruffled the surface of the lake, where he tried to submerge the things over which he had no control. He remembered a gun barrel being levelled towards his head, squeezing his eyes shut in that primordial wasted attempt to fend off death.

And this time too, relief and rescue came with the sound of the voice of another human being.

"Sir?"

He had no idea how long Pascoe had been standing there – he guessed no more than a couple of seconds. "Anything?"

"Well, I double-checked about the night itself and there's nothing new. As for the owner of this place," he gestured towards the dilapidated farmhouse and stables, "they don't really have anything to do with the guy. They've glimpsed him occasionally. They don't even know whether he's married, but said," Pascoe glanced at his notebook, "'He didn't look like he was,' whatever that means."

Logan wasn't sure he liked the conspiratorial smile Pascoe gave him, but allowed it to pass. The DS continued:

"They did say he's refused to acknowledge them the couple of times they've seen him turning onto his drive."

"Okay, let's head back to the station. We'll phone ahead and get the wheels turning for the warrant. I think it's worth us giving the place the once-over, inside and out."

Logan turned to go, but Pascoe hadn't finished: "However, one thing they did mention that might be of interest, sir, was that an RSPCA van and a horse trailer turned into the drive here the day before the murder."

"RSPCA?"

"They said it wouldn't surprise them if it was to collect the ponies. Apparently, there were three ponies in this field. The ladies said the animals were in a lamentable condition; half-starved, out in all weathers with no coats. Actually, they were a bit shamefaced about not having reported it themselves, but they hadn't wanted to fall out with our mysterious, missing friend."

Logan mulled it over, but not for long. He'd given up believing in coincidences in this case. "Okay, I'm bending the rules here, so we'll have to be quick, but let's just have a recce at the stables while we're here. If we find anything that looks at all suspicious, remember, don't touch it. If we do, I'll leave you here to watch the place," Logan pointed to Wright's flat, "while I hurry the warrant through."

They made their way to the outbuilding. Shelter wasn't a word that sprang to mind; a timber frame with putrid straw, no obvious signs of fodder, missing several slats from the roof – and missing ponies. From there they moved to the farmhouse itself and peered through a couple of windows before Logan walked off.

Pascoe followed, frowning. "Just curious, sir – why didn't you knock just now, or ask me to check here earlier?"

"Because there was no one home on the day of the murder and there isn't now, given there's no vehicle on the drive – or if there is, they wouldn't answer the door. Anyone who might be skulking in there clearly doesn't want to be seen, or they would have approached us, if nothing else, to ask us whether we have a warrant, which would have been awkward. Besides, sometimes, just sometimes, it's good to hear the opinions of others before you talk to someone. It gives you the social context of local life."

"Right." Pascoe's extended monosyllable suggested at least some of it made sense.

"Talking of which..." Logan knew Pascoe was probably hoping

the matter was dead, but then the DS should have known better.

"If we could go back to your discussion with your anonymous military contact." Even as he spoke, Logan made a mental note that Pascoe had the makings of a good DCI – his stoicism under the renewed inquisition and the mask-like demeanour would have given away nothing to anyone lacking Logan's intuition – and coping mechanisms. The 'tell' for Logan was a vein in the DS's temple, that became more prominent in such moments. He had read about other prosopagnosia sufferers who visualised human faces as landscapes and named parts, likening them to mountain ranges or canyons. Well, that vein was Pascoe's River of Dissemblance!

"What do you mean *back,* sir? I've told you such things as I was able to glean, bearing in mind the paranoia of my contact. Wright was a bully who would terrorise other ranks for any perceived lack of bottle. In fact, maybe this belongs to them," he quipped, pointing to the item they had just lifted from the scene.

"Elaborate on your use of *terrorise.*" It wasn't that Logan didn't appreciate the joke, but he wanted to avoid the distraction, whether deliberate or innocent.

"Shame them in front of comrades. He'd been decorated for his bravery in the Falklands – storming a machine-gun post, I think it was, in order to save his men."

"Any particular victims given as examples?"

"He mentioned a couple of instances, sir, but I didn't note the names down because the…contact told me they had all since died in action."

Logan sat back and puffed out his cheeks. "That was pretty slack, Pascoe. What if they have family who might be looking for revenge?"

"I'm sorry, sir. I didn't think. I wasn't able to keep notes, at his insistence."

"Didn't think?"

"Some of the stuff being discussed put me in mind of my uncle. Maybe I lost a bit of focus, sir. I apologise."

Intuition, that silent passenger, was joined in the car by silence itself.

Pascoe blinked first. "There was one thing that he said which did stay with me. He said RSM Wright was a man who knew no fear and therefore could never be truly classed as brave, since bravery is…"

"…overcoming your fears," concluded Logan, before deciding to take this up again at some future point when Pascoe's defences were down. One thing he had tried to instil into the DS was when to stay silent, so Pascoe's discomfort this time had been a giveaway. He changed tack. "Any luck with finding Lara Wright yet?"

"Nothing, sir. Zip in registry offices, deed poll applications. You don't think there's a chance she used her cousin's services at – what was it called – Safebeds?"

"Well firstly, it's not her cousin's services – they only advertise it. Secondly, by that point they'd apparently been out of contact for a number of years. You can give it a go if you want. During my last visit to the social centre I seemed to have become a target for glibness from Miss Bleeding Heart."

"Better than Miss Lonely Heart, sir." Logan caught Pascoe's wry grin and fancied he saw in it a bridge, or perhaps a deliberate diversion, being built. "Anything else booked on Mismatch.com?"

"Yeah, very funny." Logan gave a sigh of resignation. "I think I've got more chance of finding Lara Wright than Miss Right – or Lara Croft for that matter. I'm coming to the conclusion, Pascoe, if there's one thing more difficult than being me it's being with me."

He wasn't quite sure why he shared something so profound or private. Was that what happened when you probed for weakness in others? Clearly, it knocked Pascoe out of his stride, because no response was forthcoming. Logan took the opportunity to regather himself.

"Talking of Miss Wright, or whatever name she's going by now – maybe she's a ghost."

"Sorry, sir?"

"I mean we need to look at ghosting."

Pascoe frowned.

"The youth of today! Then again, I suppose computers are to blame. Ghosting is identity theft, except the identity is of a dead person, but not someone well known. You would need to be roughly the same age as the ghost so you can effectively use documents citing birth details and the like. Basically, you're replacing someone who's already on record. Don't look at it as stealing someone's life – if you can find a way to remove the record of their death, their existence reappears and is free for the taking."

"You mean like in The Day of the Jackal, sir."

Logan smiled. "There's hope for you yet, Pascoe – a classic movie. Edward Fox's finest hour. Yes, exactly like that."

Pascoe whistled, but that was followed by another frown. "If I remember the film correctly, it involved a lot of balls-aching ploughing through files...and if I remember correctly again, you have already used the term *balls-aching* in reference to something you had lined up for me."

Logan gave a slanted grin. "Think of it as retro-policing, Pascoe. However, my complaint about computers and digital records should actually work in your favour. The modern would-be ghost has to exist in a dark room where the lights can get turned on at any moment. Ghosting depends on wrong information, namely the lack of deceased status, remaining in the systems of one or more separate government agencies – and that happens, sometimes by accident or occasionally by intent. But, even then you're never safe – you need to get a passport, you have to hope no one runs a new check for a death certificate as a matter of course. The increase in computerisation means agencies can crosslink much more easily, but it's also created too vast a data swamp, and we all know checking between those different agencies is a lot less robust than they would have the general public believe, plus there are still many years' worth of backlog that haven't been computerised. Successful ghosting means falling between the cracks which are questions, and actually a woman has some advantages there – if she can ghost a dead woman who was married the death certificate and the birth certificate typically show two different surnames. Plus, fewer people will question a gap in employment history if it's explained away as a period of homemaking."

"I feel better already."

Logan laughed, and found himself feeling better too – he didn't like it when an atmosphere pervaded his dealings with the DS.

"It's an avenue worth following, Pascoe. I see no other way she could disappear quite so effectively. Doubtless it will lead in a straight line that just disappears off into the distance, like all our other threads, rather than knitting together nicely, making something substantial we can hold onto."

"Maybe she's dead, sir?"

"No." Logan was a little taken aback. "That makes no sense. There are no records of a hospitalisation or registered death. If you mean she might have been murdered…well, murders and murderers leave traces. Plus, I still don't see the motive. My guess is she's alive. I can't shake that – or my conviction that finding Lara Wright is key to…something."

# 13

It was becoming a well-trodden, or rather well-driven road back to the vicinity of RSM Wright's murder. And each return trip held a new surprise, one of which was that their process for keeping the press at bay for a while continued to work, as evidenced by their lack of presence around the cottages. Another was the weather, which on this occasion had taken a turn for the summery, in the form of torrential rain and that lazy Cornish wind that went through rather than round you.

Logan was armed with a warrant and three extra constables, each of whom had failed miserably to display their delight as he had selected them to trawl through a large field in this November deluge.

As they pulled into the driveway of Copton Farm, its dilapidated stones and moss covered roof tiles dripping with the possibility of wrongdoing, Pascoe was preparing to scoot from the vehicle to the front door to present the warrant, even though they assumed no one was home. Logan stopped him with a hand on his arm and said:

"You might have just been spared a day up to your ankles in pony shit."

Pascoe looked, astounded, in the direction Logan was pointing.

In the field to the left, standing proud in the gathering storm was a sword, driven point first into the soil.

Having signalled to the officers in the other car, all of them hurried across, their way marked by plumes of water which had gathered on the baked earth. The five men surrounded the object; pilgrims before the ghastly relic of some dark saint.

"Doesn't look regimental to me," said Logan, "or at least not a twentieth century army." He stooped, peering through the rain gathering on his eyelashes at the battered, double-edged blade, probably a couple of feet in length, and the cruciform hilt. "I assume that's a trace of blood." He pointed to the battered leather on the hilt, then nodded to Pascoe, who in turn gestured to one of the other officers. Having pulled on latex gloves, that officer lifted the blade with care, hoping to avoid disturbing any traces of blood, or other less appetising matter. They had all noticed the red marks in the grooves around the hilt.

"All the obvious tests please," said Pascoe, "though this bloody rain won't have helped. You three can fight amongst yourselves as to who takes it back to the lab, as we're still going to check over the field."

Logan added weight. "Obviously this is not some forensic analysis of every square foot of ground. I just want to know if there's anything here that looks like it shouldn't be."

The three uniformed officers exchanged a look that said: *we can't argue with a senior officer, but isn't a bloodstained sword enough?* The PC holding the sword decided that his return to the station wasn't up for debate and headed off. Logan addressed the remaining two.

"Sounds a bit strange, I know, but we have two murders; I believe they're linked and that the murderer stood in this field, possibly on this spot, watching RSM Wright on the night of the crime. My belief is you'll find nothing else. I think a drinks bottle I found lying here the other day has been the only mistake." Logan looked around the perimeter of the field, but his eyes were focussed beyond it. "That sword is someone showing off now; leaving a message."

His gaze alighted once more on the ground at his feet. "It's hard to tell whether there's a footprint under here now, but I doubt it. The sword was placed here sometime between when Pascoe and I left yesterday and now. That can't be coincidence and so the assumption is we were being watched. C'mon – let's check the farmhouse first. Maybe the rain will have eased off by the time we've finished."

Two knocks at the door brought no response. "In the light of the gruesome little souvenir outside," ventured Logan, "I think we can say it's in the best interests of the owner if we force entry."

Despite the rather tumbledown appearance of parts of the property, it took several applications of the strongest officer's shoulder before the oak door gave. The four of them checked through the rambling, stale rooms and each of them had the same tale to tell the others – it looked like no one was home.

"No surprise I suppose, sir," said Pascoe, "given his vehicle's not outside. Judging by the stale smell and the state of the plates in the kitchen, Mr…" he referenced the warrant, "…Alastair Foster doesn't appear to have been home for some while; since before the murder maybe." Pascoe's eyes opened wide. "You don't think…"

"That he did it? No, I don't." Logan answered the abbreviated question. He looked around the frayed living room. "Both murders show, in my opinion, a capacity for planning and neatness which is lacking here. He just strikes me as a reclusive bachelor with personal hygiene issues. Still, I guess we have to check into it; we know stuff-all about him. It's strange in itself that he seems to be a home-body, albeit that home is a monument to the pursuit of untidiness, yet has disappeared now. Could be linked to the perp; could even be another victim." Logan pulled an expression of sudden irritation and gave a little exasperated nod of the head. "Yet another bloody lead which is a contradiction in terms."

"Sorry, sir?"

"In that it's leading nowhere. I can understand the field being a good viewpoint for stalking RSM Wright, but why was the sword left there now, unless, as I said, someone was observing us yesterday and is cocking a snook at us? If Mr Foster was the perpetrator, he could have watched the RSM's windows from the comfort of his farmhouse. But maybe there is a connection. Maybe someone knew the place was going to be unoccupied, so perhaps Foster knows them. We know his vehicle registration. Let's see if we can at least track that down."

Logan's eyes swept one last time around the room. There was even less excuse for the mournful seediness than there had been in Boscawen, where they'd met Sheila Miller; as the owner of a decent sized piece of land in this part of Cornwall, Foster couldn't be short of money. Yet he seemed happy, if that was the appropriate word, to live, or at least exist, in this stained, threadbare, unhoovered disorder.

How Logan envied him this sense of abandonment!

Then again, on the plus side, perhaps it was Logan's inability to embrace disorder that made the photograph above the fireplace stand out.

It seemed out of place; indeed, it was unique in looking fresh; recently taken. A quick look round revealed no other photographs. There was one oil painting, but so stained by nicotine that it gave Glencoe, the subject, a sepia air; Logan assumed it might even have been left by a previous owner and never touched: there were no signs, visual or olfactory, of Foster being a smoker.

Logan crossed to the mantelpiece, pulled on his latex gloves and carefully picked up the grubby frame, only to discover that the photograph was, in fact, a print on copier paper, cut to fit and rest inside the recess. As it fell to the floor, he saw writing on the back.

"Pennyweather Farm."

He examined the picture, which showed a derelict house skulking in some woods. Unless Copton Farm had once been in even worse repair, surrounded by trees and subject to a name change, Pennyweather Farm it was not.

He showed the picture to the others. "Any of you know this place?"

"Yes, sir," said PC Rankin – a difficult enough name if you are in the police, Logan had thought earlier, never mind if you have a slight problem pronouncing the letter R, like the officer in question. God knew what hell he had been through during his time in the force. "It's a disused property out in the direction of Bodrean – at least I assume it's still disused. When I was based at St Agnes, we ended up checking it out a couple of times – kids were smoking dope there…and worse."

"Maybe Foster has been thinking of buying it," quipped Pascoe. "Looks like his sort of place."

The DCI waved the piece of paper, deep in thought. "I sense not. Let's get back to the station. Then you and I, Officer Rankin, will take a little jaunt. I think this overrides our need to check the field for the moment."

The word *derelict* might have been coined specifically for Pennyweather Farm, unlike its name, which conjured up the quirkiness of Merry England. The building must have been well enough constructed, since it was still standing despite many years of apparent neglect. However, the stone walls told only half the tale. You wouldn't want to approach it at night, since a pall of gloom hung over it even in the daytime, despite the feeble sunlight which had now broken through that day's earlier downpours. It would have looked better if the windows were boarded up, because the remaining pieces of broken glass gave them the aspect of dead, unseeing eyes.

"You'd have to be stoned to want to sit in there – I remember thinking that," volunteered PC Rankin. "We used to…"

Logan raised a hand of interruption; pointed towards some stables partly visible at the back of the farmhouse, in particular to a visible sliver of Range Rover, its colour just about identifiable as maroon beneath the caking of mud.

For a moment, Logan had to question the observational powers of the police officers they had selected today, since he had also been the first to spot the sword in the field that morning.

"Rankin, do you have that registration number for Foster's vehicle?"

The officer fumbled for his notebook, but Logan had known he had struck gold even before hearing the details read out.

He signalled Rankin to pull in by the stables. Picking their way between puddles, Logan noticed the ground, though slightly tackier here than back at Copton Farm, where the field was more exposed to sun and wind, was firm. He held out little hope of spotting a footprint, given that morning's rain had been the first in many days. And despite the car, he did not expect to find Foster – at least not in the mood for talking. In a moment of distraction, he wondered whether those blessed with intuition were also robbed of hope.

They peered inside the vehicle but saw nothing untoward; tried the doors and found them locked.

Perhaps because the place lacked a lightness of soul, they found themselves creeping, rather than striding, towards the farmhouse. It certainly wasn't to mask their footsteps, which were swept away by the wind when they weren't absorbed by the damp earth. Better safe than sorry though; if Foster was hiding here, then it didn't speak well of him. They had to allow for the possibility that he was a killer, even if that didn't ring true with Logan. Why leave an obvious clue – the photograph – as to your whereabouts if you were on the run? Logan found it hard to shake the idea of wrongdoing, whether by or to Foster, but there was no hard evidence.

Once his eyes adjusted to the gloom as he peered inside through one of the splintered windows, Logan found the apparent emptiness of the farmhouse somehow heightened the sense of danger. He signalled to Rankin to have his nightstick at the ready, only to see the officer had preempted him. Moving round to the front of the farmhouse, they found the main door open and pushed it fully ajar. Pennyweather Farm appeared to be deserted.

"He's got to be here somewhere." Familiarity with disappointment had not yet rendered Logan immune to the frustration of all leads in this case seeming to end down cul-de-sacs.

"You mean because of the car, sir?"

"No, his aftershave." The sarcasm took a while to filter through Rankin's earnestness, but the little nod that followed won him back some brownie points for at least acknowledging he had been slow.

It didn't take a long search to reveal nothing.

"Let's break into the car and have a look." Logan said it more in hope than anticipation.

Just as they were stepping out, Rankin stopped. He appeared to be listening.

"What is it?" No sooner had Logan asked, than he heard it too. The faintest moaning. "I'd lost that in the wind."

They stepped back inside.

"What the fuck?" It was all Logan could think to say, but it seemed a suitable summary of the entire case.

Rankin's face was full of sudden enlightenment. "Sir, there's a cellar. I just remembered. That's where we found the stoners. They'd heard us coming and tried to hide from us. Unfortunately for them, the whiff of weed was too pungent."

Now that Rankin had mentioned it, it was as clear as day where the cellar was located, even before the PC indicated with his nightstick. There was a battered rug, which, threadbare and stained though it was, looked out of place by its very presence. Pulling it back revealed a trapdoor, held by heavy bolts, which they forced open with difficulty, though not before Logan noted fresh grooves in the mould and rust on the backplates of the bolts.

Rankin put his mouth close to a crack where door met floor.

"Mr Foster?" The groan of response said everything and nothing. "Well, he hasn't gone to Gloucester."

It was Logan's turn to grin – Rankin was growing on him. Then he pointed to the bolts. "But he didn't stay by choice."

They both stood off to one side of the trapdoor, trying to grasp the edges rather than the handle. It made lifting it awkward, but was a necessity in the event of any booby trap that might be triggered by the movement. Once they were sure there was no such danger, they threw back the door.

Logan looked at Rankin's crumpled features, which he assumed mirrored his own. "Weed played no real part in my youth, but I know enough to know that smell ain't drugs!"

There were no steps down into the cellar, but close by lay a woodworm-riddled ladder which they had to assume had once been in place and could still serve the purpose. Torch clenched in his teeth, Rankin positioned the ladder. Rusty fittings showed it had once been attached to the frame, and it only just reached the ground, leaving no margin for error. Then the PC dropped down the creaking steps into the gloom. In no time he shouted up: "Better call for an ambulance, sir."

Logan stopped one of the paramedics. "How long before I can question him?"

"Well, he's certainly not making much sense at the moment. Hard to say. He's severely dehydrated and malnourished."

"It's important. He might have seen the Armistice Killer."

The medic wouldn't have recognised the reference, but neither did he appear concerned by it, refusing to be intimidated and maintaining his professional composure. "He's barely alive."

"He's lucky to be alive." Logan wasn't proud of his tetchiness but couldn't rein it in "By which I mean, I need to understand why he wasn't murdered."

The paramedic wasn't having it. "I'd strongly suggest that's what someone has tried to do. All the signs are there that he hasn't eaten or drunk for several days. There's a half-litre water bottle down there, long empty."

There was no arguing with that. Logan turned away. There must have been something in his eyes, though, that elicited some sympathy from one professional trying to do his job for another, because the paramedic added: "I'll let you know as soon as he's stabilised. It would be counterproductive to stress him now. He's been through enough."

Logan nodded his appreciation.

Now he approached Rankin, whom he'd designated as uniformed officer in charge of the scene. "Borrow your Maglite?"

"Sir." Rankin handed it over.

Logan clapped him on the arm. "Well done today, Rankin." He meant it too. Thinking about the PC's name again, combined with his slightest of speech impediments, Logan guessed he might well have been a fellow outsider during his life. He gestured towards the cellar. "When they get here, don't tell Forensics about what I'm doing – I do follow their lead…" he gave Rankin a conspiratorial smile, "…normally, so know how to not contaminate a crime scene, but technically this goes against protocol, and they hate that."

The PC just grinned and nodded. Then Logan dropped into the stale hole that passed for a cellar.

Life was just full of new experiences. As he stood surveying the scene, yellow circle by yellow circle in the beam of the torch, he found himself completing a rare set; he'd had a murder scene, then the place where the murderer kept his vigil and now the dungeon where a victim had escaped death. These walls were surely drenched in Foster's agony, but would that help Logan get into the mind of a murderer? Surely their killer hadn't simply locked Foster away so that his farm could be used as a base. That seemed not only fraught with difficulties, but also far too broad an incision for this perpetrator.

He found the first object he was seeking. Looking at the water bottle mentioned by the paramedic, he saw that it was the same brand, size and also expiry date as the one they had found in the field. It was proof of nothing, but when a ship was sinking, you grasped whatever flotsam came your way.

As he continued to pan the walls with the torch, for a mad moment he hoped the bat symbol would appear in the beam and he could then call on a superhero to guide him.

Guidance did come, but not till he had extinguished the light and clambered back up the steps, wary of their damp creakiness. Halfway through the opening he stopped, while cold lips kissed the back of his neck.

They had missed it in their understandable hurry to see what was down in the darkness, but it was unmistakable now – four parallel lines scratched very deliberately and recently into the trapdoor. Logan shone the torch down into the cellar again, but saw nothing that might have made those marks. They were too deep and regular to have been made by Foster clawing at the door, which would have been out of his reach in any case. Clambering out again, he looked around the floor of the main room and saw the rug they had slid to one side when they were looking for the cellar. Now Logan found cause to curse his own lack of observational powers: there was a knife lying beneath it, which clearly he had missed when they'd first arrived.

They were being toyed with – he was sure of it now. First the sword, left for them to find; now the marks and what he suspected was the tool with which they were made, just lying there. This was audacity. Catch me if you can.

It left him unsure whether to laugh or cry at this latest addition to his basket of soiled clues, but it did prompt an idea, which he decided he would keep to himself for the moment.

He headed over to the PC. "Rankin."

"Sir?"

"There's a knife on the floor. Please make sure Forensics don't overlook it." He winked. "Because we did."

It was raining again. The team had arrived to tow away the Range Rover, a cursory search of which had revealed nothing, and despite his faith in the scientists, Logan assumed a more thorough examination would only bring the same result.

Logan called Pascoe for an update. The bloody sword had been given priority, but so far all further tests had revealed nothing beyond confirming the gruesome stains as Kevin Miller's blood and faeces. Ghost hunting was also under way, but that avenue would require time, if indeed it led anywhere at all. In response to a question from the DS, Logan said:

"Well, we found Foster. Mmm, let's just say he's in a worse state than his house."

# 14

Having made sure the other end of the line had gone dead, Logan slammed down the phone, causing a few heads in the outer office to turn. He stared right back and heads dropped. Who had opened their big mouth? The call had been from his superior, demanding a progress report. It was apparent the shit was about to hit the fan in the shape of the press. Did this mean details would be continually leaking out from now on – information that might jeopardise the integrity of the investigation?

For Logan, the universe seemed increasingly perverse and chaotic. He was used to the day-to-day challenges of life, his difficulties compounded by certain distinct, ordered patterns he imposed on himself; patterns which had no coherent value except the very compulsion of them. The warped logic of the criminal or disturbed mind was normally his salvation, providing both an escape in its need for deciphering and proof that he still hadn't strayed from the path to redemption. Yet it seemed absent from this case, which appeared determined to confound him. There was no obvious method in the madness. Sure, there were leitmotifs – blades, beds, penetration and a family of strong, damaged women – but despite the origins of the German word, it seemed the leading motif actually led nowhere. It all lacked direction.

Unless, of course, the opposite was true and he was being deliberately led astray. It was akin to looking at one of those signposts found in certain key cities or geographical locations, which point the way and give mileages to various global landmarks. He'd never really seen the point of them, unless you had a path in mind.

So, was that morning's lethargy what normal people called waiting for inspiration? Was it detective's block?

Things must have been bad, because he felt not a frisson of irritation when Pascoe's lime-green tie burst in to interrupt his thoughts without a 'by your leave.'

"Sir, we asked the guys in Torquay to show a photo of the sword we found in the field to Gill Scott and she said she's pretty certain it was Wright's. All the tests have been completed and there appear to be no traces of any blood on the sword other than Kevin Miller's, nor other DNA for that matter. The rain might have removed a little dirt, but not DNA. Those streaks the Forensics guys found on the bed must have been made by the perp in an attempt to clean it."

Logan looked up. "Wouldn't you?"

Pascoe paused and then grinned. "Take your point, sir." He thought for a moment. "I wonder if those were Kevin Miller's last words."

Despite everything, Logan couldn't help but laugh. It didn't last.

"Pascoe, come in and close the door."

"Sounds ominous."

"Not at all. I just want to…oh man, I hate the buzzword, but I want to brainstorm." He tapped a manila folder on his desk. "Foster's incident report – yet another square peg in a round hole. Foster – locked in a cellar for days and starved. What are we looking at here?"

Pascoe frowned. "Do you mean why wasn't he killed?"

Logan pursed his lips. "That's the thing. We know this killer isn't squeamish; was this an attempted murder or not? If a torturous death was intended, maybe that bears a similarity to the other two. But I don't think he was meant to die. It wasn't as clear as, say, phoning in to the station, but we were left the clue about where to find him, the picture of Pennyweather Farm. Unless the killer was showboating again, we were meant to find Foster. He was needed out of the way for a while, but never an intended victim. In that case, why put him through hell? Why not leave him enough water and food till we found him?"

They fell into silence, stared at the whiteboard, which was the very embodiment of their enigmatic, blank puzzle.

Everything – Pascoe and all the items on the desk – jumped as Logan slammed his fist down. Though he didn't bother to look this time, he knew heads had turned again. Good – if the closed door wasn't enough, two unusual displays of anger would certainly notify the team he was an unhappy man. He gestured at the board in frustration. "So many leads, so little headway – too much reliance on intuition. I take back what I said the other day – there are no straight threads and everything is in one big fucking knot; a Gordian knot; impossible to unravel."

He breathed out. "For instance, why do I think finding Lara Wright is so important? Do I think she's the murderer? If so, why? Is it even a lead?"

Logan could both see and sense Pascoe's discomfort. That key element – finding Lara Wright – was in his care and, so far, he had drawn a blank. The sudden rise in pulse rate and evident agitation as he fiddled with his tie – *how he recognised himself, or at least the Logan of old in that!* – showed the younger detective felt his lack of progress keenly too. As he should! Logan had contemplated releasing some of that pressure from the DS, but decided he would keep the toe of his boot poised behind Pascoe's backside as he had enough issues of his own, so pushed on: "I had a call from the Chief Constable today, just when I was giving silent thanks for the absence of the press. Apparently the papers contacted him and they are about to rerun the story about a local veteran murdered on Armistice Day, except this time in full gore and speculation mode. It seemed the editor believes they've allowed plenty of breathing space to not appear disrespectful to the occasion of the centenary, but also word has got out about another man murdered in his bed. Bad enough, given I don't need journos clodhopping about and waving cheques for scoops. But then the Chief Constable mentioned that the press has decided the crimes must be linked, and they have hit upon a name for the double-murderer – The Armistice Killer. You are well aware of my feelings regarding coincidences, and also that this is a moniker bestowed by certain people in this station for this case. I would welcome any thoughts you have about this new cause for joy."

Pascoe sat silent, probably a wise move.

Integrity – the key word. Logan couldn't carry the burden of another albatross around his neck. He had escaped from the fiasco of his last major case with his reputation intact, but in private his mistakes still weighed heavily on him. Justice had seemed to be done as far as the public was concerned, but his own failings and miscalculations along the way – well they rankled and tore at him.

There would be no more misjudgements like that – not on his watch. And watch he would. Hence, he needed Pascoe somewhere he could measure and observe him. The conversation he had witnessed between the DS and Heath had not been forgotten. Perhaps there had been nothing to it. However, when you added Pascoe's military connection into the overall mix, were you left with cake or combustibles? His enquiries with Wright's old regiment had not been particularly structured or fruitful, perhaps, even allowing for sensibilities related to his uncle, to the point of suspicion. It required further investigation.

Possibly it had been an error assigning that area of the investigation to Pascoe, and he should have handled those enquiries himself. Still, Logan wondered whether he had he once again allowed a sixth sense to dominate his thought processes – this whole instinctive, intuitive conviction; because he remained convinced that this sequence of deaths and misdemeanours was driven by matters far from the battlefield.

Seeking anchorage, he gestured again towards the whiteboard. "This whole thing is full of hints and part-connections. There's the possibility of sexual motivation in the death by brutal penetration of two men on beds. Both of them were, it seems, capable of more than a bit of brutality themselves, so that implies someone pretty hardened took them out. But then where does the third victim fit in?"

He puffed out his cheeks before continuing. "Then there's the sword, owned by victim number one, used to kill number two, and then left in number three's field to taunt us."

"Or lead us, as you suggested, sir." Pascoe rejoined the conversation nervously with a safe play.

"Perhaps mislead. Either way it suggests a purpose to these killings and a single perpetrator. But then again, the first victim may have been Foster. He's been locked away in that cellar for some while, possibly since before the first murder took place. Certainly I noticed there were no footprints around the house, nor soil carried in as far as we could tell, suggesting he was moved there before the recent dry spell ended. Anyway, where does Alastair Foster sit in the paradigm? As far as we know he's a bachelor and childless. There are the two missing girls, Lara and Angelina, both daughters of brutish men, both nowhere to be found and both potentially with more than enough reason to want revenge. Then you put Foster into the equation and all the connections fail to add up."

Logan rose at last from his seat and moved to stand by the whiteboard, looking at lines and pictures again. If nothing else, these few minutes were helping him to express the dyslexic chaos of his earlier thoughts. It might be leading nowhere, but it was better than feeling like you were sitting in a darkness filled by whispers.

He pointed to a picture. "We have Gill Scott."

Pascoe inclined his head. "Are you saying she's involved, sir?"

"Ex-husband dead, daughter missing – I can't help feeling she owns a piece of this, even if unwittingly. And her husband was a bully…," he paused, "…which brings us back to the military."

Pascoe appeared to have found the tip of his finger of sudden interest. "Ah, yes sir. There's something I've been…"

"I know." Logan watched the interplay of emotions across Pascoe's features. "Something you've been meaning to tell me? You're a good policeman and I've been waiting for that fact to over-power your conscience."

"Well sir, it was really just rumour – but you remember I told you Wright used to shame soldiers he felt had let him down? The word is, Wright used to make them pay for it. Do penance of some sort."

Logan's head jerked up. "Names?"

"None, sir. Honestly, it was just rumours."

"No smoke…" He looked at the photo of RSM Wright, swagger stick shoved into his mouth. "Who did you say was desig-nated to pick him up on the morning of the Armistice celebrations?"

Pascoe consulted his notebook. "A Lance Corporal called Bovis."

"It's a bit strange that he knocked on the morning of the commemoration service and then just left. I assume you checked into him?"

"Of course, sir – later that day after you asked me to speak with the neighbours. He's a hard nut, sir, I can tell you. He said he didn't have time to hang around that morning and admitted it was a bit of a relief that Wright seemed not to be in. There was clearly no love lost between them, but to me, sir, it didn't sound like anything that would provoke violence. No one has spoken warmly of Wright. It sounds a bit like the Drill Sergeant in *Full Metal Jacket!*"

"And look what happened to him – shot by one of the marines he'd pushed too far."

"Can't help feeling too much water has passed under the bridge, sir. It's been eleven years since Bovis and Wright last served together."

"Nothing like a commemoration service to bring back memories; make them vivid again. Pascoe, don't you find it strange that Bovis didn't wait longer; didn't try to find out from a neighbour whether the RSM was at home, especially as his car was there? Sounds to me like you're right – like this Bovis was quite happy to believe Wright wasn't there, which might mean he knew he wasn't."

Pascoe's head hung a little. "I'll have another look, sir."

"Indeed. Not quite sure where he would fit into the other crimes though." Logan tapped impatient fingertips on the desk again.

"Are we guessing a bit at Foster, sir – I mean, couldn't it just be a coincidence that he was attacked? I know that's stretching things, but perhaps, as you've said, the person in the field was simply disturbed by Foster and took him out of the equation… then thought better of it and left us the admittedly cryptic clue for where to find him."

"I take your point absolutely, Pascoe, and it's the best way to make the pieces fit. Except for one thing: whatever the motivations, we're not guessing at a connection between Foster and the other killings. I'll tell you why – scraped quite deliberately into the cellar trapdoor were…" Logan lifted four fingers. "Four parallel lines."

"You've lost me?"

"What was the date of Wright's murder?"

Pascoe's eyes widened. "You mean four ones – the eleventh of the eleventh?"

Logan nodded and shrugged at the same time. "That's my supposition. No one else spotted the marks on the trapdoor, so let's keep that to ourselves for the moment. Okay, as well as being tenuous it also only connects Wright's murder and Foster's abduction as far as I can see, but it just might be a weird calling card from our killer. Only he – or she – and we know about it. Maybe we can set a trap."

"Aren't we hindering the investigation by doing that, sir?"

"Yeah, I'm taking that chance. But if it is somehow the killer's calling card I don't want any copycats to have that information and go printing some of their own."

"You mean the press, sir?"

Once again, Logan's head jerked up, puppet-like. The call with the Chief Constable that morning came back to him. "The press?"

"You said printing."

Was Pascoe just withdrawing his head quickly from the parapet, realising he might have given something away? Logan sensed not. "It was an extended simile." The look in the DS's eyes told Logan he might have been crediting the junior office with a bit too much sharpness of wits.

Silence – and then Pascoe seemed to move to firmer ground. "You said *or she* earlier when you referenced the killer. By that, you mean Lara?"

"We must find her, Pascoe, if only to eliminate her from the investigation. If she's safe and sound, living in Greenland or a kibbutz, then good luck to her." Logan looked back at the board. "At least then we could get back to the breadcrumbs."

"Breadcrumbs?"

"We're definitely following a trail – the murder on the eleventh of the eleventh, that leads to a bottle, that leads us to a field, that leads us to the sword and Copton Farm," Logan was tapping his fingertip on the relevant parts of the whiteboard as he spoke, "that leads us to Pennyweather Farm, to the cellar, that leads us to Foster, which leads us to another four ones. Perhaps the killer is incredibly resourceful and daring or defying us to find him – or her…but I don't think so. I think the breadcrumbs have just been caught in the wind. Yet they do say it's an ill wind that blows no one any good. I think we do have a trail, whether by accident or design." He paused. "I suppose there's a third option – that it's an act of catharsis. But it's just all such a jumble." Logan turned back to Pascoe. "Look, in the light of what I may or may not have found on that cellar door, let's go and have a fresh look at the RSM's flat."

"Wright's flat?" Pascoe seemed surprised enough to interrupt his superior. "Don't you mean Miller's flat? You know, so we can look for four ones there and link all three crimes?"

"No. Or I would have said Miller's flat." Taking pity on Pascoe, whose frown was in danger of creating permanent ageing on his features, Logan sighed and continued. "While the eleventh of the eleventh might seem a likely connection, it's just too ethereal. Whoever rammed that swagger stick down Wright's throat with such force was giving vent to some genuine demons, the sort that would only be satisfied by a physical manifestation such as the violence with which those lines were scored into the trapdoor imprisoning Foster. So that's why it's Wright's flat: to see if we spot anything new, now that we know what we're looking for. Strangely, I think that if we do it makes it less likely that we'll find anything of the same sort in Miller's flat."

Pascoe's brow, which had been gradually unfurrowing, knitted itself tight again.

"Later," said Logan, waving away the unspoken question. "For now, let's be on our way to Wright's. After that, and after you've spoken to Bovis again, you get back to pursuing your ghost, and I'm going to continue pursuing mine. I'll have another word with Samantha Ingle. She knows some of the protagonists and at least we know where to find her. We didn't part on the best of terms. If anything, she was being a little obstructive with her sarcasm – but there may just be something. I'll get off my high horse and see whether she reciprocates. I just need a break, and maybe she can provide it. It's a shot in the dark." He snorted an ironic laugh. "Amongst all the killing, that's something we haven't had yet."

The approach to Tom Wright's flat was now becoming eerily familiar. Logan wondered if it was just his imagination or whether the same wind which had scattered the breadcrumbs was now carrying the smell of death, just as bleach seemed, by association, tainted with the odours it masked. The weather gods had decided to flex their muscles and were thrashing the windows of the former RSM's home with gusting rain as an Atlantic front swept across the Cornish peninsula; the type that made waterproofs mandatory even for the short trip from car to front door. Both men peeled away their hoods on entering.

"Do we know yet whether Wright might have given his sword to someone, or even sold it or had it stolen?" Logan's distracted tone reflected his state of mind; the lack of any structure to this case was jumbling his thoughts. The uncertainty niggled.

"I should have asked Gill Scott – obviously I'll try again. Sorry," said Pascoe. "So is there anything particular you're hoping to find here, sir? Or just another set of four ones?"

Pascoe's question burrowed its way into Logan's conscious brain. "Yes…no…maybe. I can't believe we'll get that lucky – and despite what the guys at the station call the killer, if indeed it is one person, I'm sceptical about there being a straightforward Armistice connection."

"Could Foster have made those scratches himself while trying to get out." Pascoe asked the question over his shoulder as he moved on into the living room while Logan headed, as always, for the sacrificial altar – the place where brutality had met its match.

Once again, he failed to respond at first to Pascoe's enquiry, distracted by the need to sense something in this place of death.

"Sir?"

"No, the marks are too deep and regular; given he couldn't reach that trapdoor, it would have been almost impossible for him. Plus I asked the team to check for wood or paint under his nails and there was none" His eyes scoured the walls. "Okay, I guess we'll only know what we're looking for if and when we see it."

"Sir!" After a brief flash of irritation at another interruption it registered with Logan that Pascoe hadn't been chasing an answer. He was calling him. "You mean like this, sir?"

Logan hurried through into the living room and looked where Pascoe was pointing. Under other circumstances Logan might have smiled in vindication, but for now he was simply filled with dismay. How had he failed to spot this on his previous visit?

On the ledge of a small window, admittedly high enough that the item was silhouetted to some extent, was a framed colour photograph of a group of squaddies. The muddy mound on which the men sat, some with rifles held aloft as they grinned at the camera, suggested it had been taken in the Falklands. The subject of the picture mattered little, given the circumstances, but Logan had to be sure one of the soldiers was Wright. The geographical location suggested as much, but still…

He chose his words carefully – there were fewer people who knew about his prosopagnosia than there were soldiers in the photo. "So many years ago – see if you can spot Wright."

Pascoe pointed to one of the men. "Think that's him there."

"Yup," he tried to sound matter of fact.

In the picture, camouflage hid any indications of rank, but clearly it had also served to conceal a much later addition, certainly from Logan's gaze on his previous visits – the vertical black line drawn on Wright's chest and the lines of similar length to be found on the chests of the three soldiers to his left. Four parallel lines.

Logan should have been delighted by this apparent connection between the killing of the RSM and the attempted murder of Foster. Instead, there was anger and frustration. He wracked his brains, trying to remember whether he had looked at this photo with enough care on the previous visit. For a man trapped in the cage of facial blindness and the compulsions that were his fellow prisoners, it was hard to know whether to laugh or cry at the possibility of this oversight.

"Well done, sir."

"What for – missing this the first-time round? Two times in fact." There hadn't been a hint of irony in Pascoe's comment, but the balance was more than redressed by Logan's response.

His DS looked at him, seemed to understand. "But we were looking specifically for something like this on this occasion. Seeking with different eyes." It was an insightful comment that took the DCI aback for the moment. He was still pondering it, or rather trying to as the young officer continued excitedly: "Eleven eleven. Exactly the link you predicted! That changes things."

"Yes – I'm just not sure how." Logan chided himself; gathered his wits together. His voice was a whisper as he craned his neck towards the picture. "But you're right – it changes something." He pointed to the three, score marked men to the left of the RSM. "Who are they? Take that and find out."

# 15

She switched on the TV; liked it in the background as she cleaned. One of the music channels, or a cookery programme. She'd never been allowed that at home.

She had discovered a love of cleaning and left every room looking a million dollars. It was like making your world again, over and over. Fresh sheets, fresh pillowcases, fresh chocolates in the five-star rooms. Sometimes people even left her a tip – lovely of them, but for her it was almost enough that the work didn't involve a punch to the head, or worse.

It was a good hotel. Even the nastiest things a guest might leave behind couldn't compare with the average of what she had been asked to do in her young life. Plus, she had grown strong through the physical work. She could turn a mattress on her own in record time now, even a super king. It felt good. She felt good. Her world felt right – a place worth living for; one she'd grown up believing didn't exist.

She flicked through the channels; stopped; dropped the remote. She stared, while an involuntary motion brought her hands to her mouth.

The face of the beast had appeared on the screen. She thanked

God the volume was on; that it was the calming tones of the female newsreader which accompanied the picture. Otherwise, she might well have feared that he had found her. But for her, as she listened to the news, the sombre tone of the newsreader was all wrong – she should have been laughing; rejoicing at the news that the monster was dead.

Another face appeared on the screen; a man in uniform. He was a monster too – she didn't know him but recognised the eyes of a beast when she saw them. Of course, the first man's death shouldn't have shocked her as it did. He'd had it coming. Life balanced things out. It was just the unexpected appearance, as if she'd been back in that shithole of a flat and he was watching her in that way he'd always watched her.

A voice from the door startled her. "Alison?"

At first she didn't respond. So many times she forgot her new identity – plus it hadn't been suffixed with *bitch*. Then she turned to find one of the other maids looking at her with concern.

"You shrieked."

Alison, nee Angelina, realised her hands were still covering her mouth. When she let them fall, she found a smile had formed and this was mirrored now by the other maid. "Oh, I'm fine, thank you. It was a big, fat spider."

Throughout the morning and the afternoon, she tuned the TV to the news in every room she cleaned, awaiting the appearance of the face, which still never failed to give her a jolt. But as she listened to what they knew and what they didn't, she rejoiced, relishing every moment of that blade skewering the beast like some rotten kebab; hearing his screams of pain and agony until it was an adopted memory.

A passing thought brought her up short again. For a moment – truly just a fleeting wisp of time – she wondered how her mother was dealing with events. It shocked her that there was a hint of concern in that consideration. Oh, she didn't doubt that Mrs Kevin Miller, as she liked to think of her to keep any familiarity at bay, had been bullied too and had lived in fear. But still…if she had – just once – suggested they should run away, or stood up to that beast, it might all have been so different. Now Angelina would let the ship of her life drift by those dangerous, hidden rocks of family and forgiveness.

She did wonder at what point the TV news would stop giving her pleasure and she would want to be free of it, but for now she would enjoy the show. Truly, as she cleaned, her world was set straight, time and again.

# 16

A quick drive by the Estuary Sports and Social Centre found Sam absent. A glance at the pitches provided reason enough – the surfaces were waterlogged – and only the gym was open. The receptionist, whose wry grin showed that she remembered Logan, told him Sam couldn't be bothered to drive in through the pouring rain just to catch up with a backlog of admin she could easily do from home.

Logan didn't buy the excuse for Sam's absence, but it imbued his visit with a touch more purpose, if he was honest with himself. His reason for seeking her out in the first place had an element of the Chinese water torture about it – if she was hiding anything about the whereabouts of her cousin, he would find it by sheer persistence. If there was something else, he would sniff it out. Despite all her overt confidence he knew she was troubled; knew because she wore some of the same armour as him. It took a hider in plain sight to recognise another. And thus, her non-appearance at the social centre that morning spoke to him. Already, he fancied he knew her well enough to know the club was her baby and her salvation from the heartlessness that had been her world as a lawyer, so he'd decided not to call ahead, but rather turn up at her home unannounced and surprise her. Not a pleasant surprise, he assumed, but he would be civil. He had to hope she might nudge open a door, even by just stumbling against it.

Standing on a landing by her actual, front door now, he had to acknowledge it was one of many he hoped she might open.

As he rang the bell he was thankful there was no spyhole, as he assumed she wouldn't answer if she knew the identity of her visitor. The usual nerves assailed him and he cursed that inexplicable frailty, which seemed to beset him, no matter the occasion, when he found himself one-on-one with self-assured women. Perhaps it was more accurate to say they grew more assertive because of him; lampreys feeding on his uncertainty.

The signet ring was spinning now; his fingers pausing just long enough to ensure the tip of his tie aligned with his belt. That was one pattern he'd broken – it used to have to reach to his belly button! Change one thing…that's what they said. He'd have discarded the ring, if he could be certain his energies wouldn't find some quirkier outlet.

Movements beyond the door were growing louder. He braced himself for something less than a welcome and was both taken aback and vindicated by the nervousness in her features – the lines of tension drawn by lips that were a touch dry, perhaps through anxiety in the breathing pattern; pupils slightly dilated; a touch of redness over the cheekbones and around the nose in an otherwise pale face, possibly caused by the dilation of facial capillaries. Of course, who these features added up to was anyone's guess, as always, during those opening seconds before logical analysis, combined with the guidance of vocal tones, filled the void and prompted recognition. How strange was this life, where certainty could be swept away by something as simple as a haircut or a ponytail?

"Good afternoon, Miss Ingle." Again, the use of the name was as much about confirmation as politeness.

His sense of expectation didn't lessen as she opened the door fully to admit him without further ado.

"Come in; I've been expecting you."

"You have?"

"Yes. Janey in Reception called to say you'd probably be on your way."

"Of course." He felt foolish, reading something way too cryptic into her greeting. This case was causing his imagination to ferment.

She offered him a seat, then coffee, which she nipped into the kitchen to switch on. There was also a conciliatory gesture in her insistence that he call her Sam. All peace offerings having been taken up, amidst small talk about the weather, they stepped from the calm into the storm; she by means of an anticipatory look and the ensuing silence. Logan held the coffee mug firm, keeping his fingers occupied; sentries on duty against the onset of any tics.

"Okay. If there had been any bakers on my way over, I'd have popped in and bought some humble pie." Sam tilted her head and Logan imagined he saw a slight twitching at the corner of her mouth. "The fact is, I'm desperate."

Now she did smile. "Sounds like my typical date!"

He paused. "Mine too."

They laughed. It seemed genuine and heartfelt but was short-lived; smothered by the nervousness again.

He continued: "I don't have something specific, anything which I can put my finger on to say what I'm looking for." He thought again. "Well, not strictly true. There's your cousin…" Sam looked about to say something, but he ploughed on, "…but I'll come back to that. I just have these three murders…"

"Three?!"

"Sorry, three bodies. One of them's still alive…just."

"I knew about two – well, I assume you're talking about the skewered body in Boscawen that was on the news?"

"Yes. The other is a guy left very deliberately to starve; a Mr Foster. Might you know him?"

"I know a Dr Foster who went to Glouces…"

"Yeah, that joke's been done – at the crime scene." He kept his face straight but was amazed to hear this kind of remark from someone who was both a trained lawyer and overtly big on victim support. He felt she was trying far too hard, but why? Was she mirroring his own awkwardness?

"What makes you think this third attack is connected?" She was also fast at regaining her balance.

"He lived opposite RSM Wright's flat and I believe the killer hid on his property prior to committing the murder."

"Wow!" She was interested, but not as much as her response suggested. He didn't believe Samantha Ingle was a 'wow' person.

"And you see, I have all sorts of leads, but they don't seem to be heading in one direction."

Sam sat back in her chair. Logan had already noticed her tendency towards that defensive gesture, as if retreating behind a fortress wall. "So why do you seem to be of the opinion my cousin has some part in all of this?"

"It's gut feeling. Not something you can learn…"

A combination of hissing and gurgling came through from an adjoining room. "Ah, talking of gut feelings, it sounds like that coffee is ready?"

She headed off to the kitchen. Here he was again, wanting to say so much more; to put some meat on the bones of those last words, which sounded so clichéd. Was there a chance she wanted that too? Despite her defensive body language and his cynicism about the legal profession, he knew at least a few lawyers were victims rather than products of it. Some wanted to open their heart, not have it turned to stone. Sam Ingle had fled that profession. Would she be someone who wanted to share? Could he confide in her? Confide – a word that for him had only a shallow meaning outside the walls of the practice of a certain Freddy Dessler. Even then, within that sanctuary, he was always the one confiding. Sure, they had their shared trauma, Freddy and he, but he was aware their needs were different – what was cathartic for him was catnip to the curious mind of the psychologist.

For Logan, there was no intuition, just the piecing together of shards of the cracked mirror that reflected his world. As someone who, thanks to his prosopagnosia, could never rely on recognising someone a second time by their face alone, he compensated by feeding on the minutiae overlooked by others. Again, might this not have been something he and Sam Ingle had in common? In preparing a case, her attention to detail would have been key, whether looking for cracks to break open as a prosecutor, or cement together as the defence. Over time, he had learned that his weakness was also his strength. People might disguise their faces, but if the ship of their life sailed onto the rocks, he was the one who could gather the flotsam and jetsam. He disguised this perceptiveness as 'gut feeling' in the prosaic world of the police, knowing others might not understand.

*Wasn't much of a strength when the focus of your attention was also damaged goods, was it Ben?*

He was taken aback by the reappearance of his bad angel, which had been silent of late, perhaps driven away for a time by the complexities of this case. He tried shoving it to one side again, returning to the idea of a shipwreck. Wasn't the Estuary Sports and Social Centre above all things a safe harbour in which people could dock and seek repair?

He so wanted to share this part of him; allow himself what W.B. Yeats had described as a lonely impulse of delight and tell someone. It seemed he was most drawn to such moments in the company of certain women. Perhaps it was their emotional intelligence that tempted him, though now he had grown wary of the short road that led onwards to cunning. But he had been this way – alone – for too long. As he sat with Samantha Ingle, he knew the ground was as familiar as it was ever going to be and the fortress wall behind which she had retreated moments before, when she sat back in her chair and addressed him was just too high. Besides, for Ben Logan *familiar* was another term that held a different meaning than for most other people. He found it ironic that the word's origin was related to family. When he looked back on his own upbringing, he saw only four strangers sharing a house, reduced too soon to three by the tragedy of his sister's death and lower still by the greater estrangement that followed it.

But damn it! – Yet looking at this disastrous series of relationships he was trying to untangle now, this whole internecine war that was Tom Wright and those related to him, Logan realised he wasn't alone in the world of the fucked-up.

Sam returned with the coffees, sat herself down and said: "So, you were telling me where your stomach was leading you." She appeared to have topped up on confidence while making the drinks, if not a little cockiness. Wasn't that why lawyers took a recess?

Now, as he spoke again, his words sounded forced to his own ears: "I'm just trying to cover all the angles, like a good copper should." He tried to give the response some edgy humour, emphasising *copper* in a conscious echo of Sam's words at their first meeting." He held her gaze and she his; was hard pushed to tell who found it tougher. "I'm not saying Lara committed the murders."

"That must have taken a leap of intuition, DCI Logan." The sarcasm had likewise returned from its holiday. "From what I know of one and have read of the other, the two murder victims were both big brutes of men."

"I've seen women sending muscle mutts flying; one very recently on a sports field in Boscawen." Again, it was said with humour and this time appeared to be taken that way. "Anyway, look, I just want to eliminate her from the investigation, or speak to her and find out if she has any ideas. The same applies to you really."

"I understand your quandary. And I would love to offer some flash of insight, but I've told you all I know. What about your other Tomb Raider...Angelina – any sign of her? I apologise if I seemed frivolous before; at the Club."

The slight softening of tone was reflected in her eyes.

*This is the other door you were hoping to open!*

He ignored the bad angel on his shoulder. "Not a sausage."

Sam raised her eyebrows. "The age of technology, eh? You'd think it would be tougher to disappear these days."

Logan gave a rueful smile. "It, or rather I.T., may still help us. We're looking into the possibility of ghosting."

"Ghosting? Is that detection by séance?"

The tone was still friendly enough and Logan continued without affront. "The easiest way I find of explaining this to people is asking if they've seen the old film *The Day of the Jackal.*"

*Nice segue into talking cinema,* continued the bad angel. Actually, it wasn't wrong.

A light went on in Sam's eyes. "Ah, you mean stealing an identity? Well, I'm not sure our Lara, bless her, would necessarily have the – how can I put this without it sounding condescending? – know-how. I was going to say intellectual capacity. Whichever way, I'm not sure she would be capable. I wouldn't know where to start, let alone make a good job of it; from what you said a few minutes ago, would it be easy to trace?"

"Easier than in the past. Different departments can cross-link databases much more quickly these days. But that doesn't mean it's impossible."

"You really must be desperate, given that I just can't imagine Lara sitting at the centre of this web of intrigue."

Logan stood. "Yes – as I said right at the beginning, I am desperate."

*She might be too,* continued his tormenting imp. *Ask her.*

"Are you okay, DCI Logan?" It seemed she had noticed something in his demeanour. Time to hit the road.

He pushed on: "Again, if you think of anything – not necessarily relating to Lara – just anything that might give us a clue, please call."

Logan saw himself out. He knew he had to get away because, despite harsh lessons that should have been salutary in his past, and the good angel screaming from his other shoulder, he had almost asked Sam if she would like to discuss it over a drink. There was just something about her that was primal and alluring.

But God, didn't he think that about every seemingly strong, possibly vulnerable woman he had ever met?

It was something about him, not them – and it wasn't their vulnerability, because when he thought about it, Gill Scott could probably kick the crap out of him. Sam Ingle too, and also intellectually. And as for Claire Treloggan…he shivered. Always it came back to her.

He took the stairs two at a time; couldn't get down to his car and away fast enough. A pity he couldn't escape from his own company with such speed.

★★★★

Sam didn't move for some time after Logan's departure. It had been a peculiar conversation; unstructured. He had brought unwelcome visitors with him and they had chosen to stay, abusing her hospitality; imps repeating the same question to which there was only one answer – yes , he wanted to sleep with her. A part of her could deal with that; a small part.

The ringing of the doorbell a few minutes later made her head jerk to the extent that she realised she had been sitting motionless. She wanted to ignore it, but who can leave the door shut in the face of the devil.

The ache in her limbs as she made her way across the room again was not the result of the previous day's training run. As she opened the door once more, she felt as if she was prising herself open to reveal a thumping black heart.

The sight of her visitor left her even drier-mouthed than before. "I guess I've been expecting you too."

# 17

Lara walked in.

How could that be possible after so long – after everything – without some acknowledgement from the universe of the passing of time; a fanfare, perhaps her skin bursting into flame, or her body materialising from the stage of a transporter à la Star Trek?

"Hello cousin," said the stranger.

She moved to embrace Sam who, despite herself, hesitated. It lasted the merest of moments, but enough to derail the hug and leave open the possibility that Lara was a mirage.

"And how should I address you today?" Sam's words emerged drenched in weariness and doubt.

Lara thought for a moment. "Anna will do."

So it was true and Logan was as good as she'd feared he might be.

"They're onto you, y'know."

"Onto me?"

"That you're over here, or rather that they think you might be. One of them was here just a few minutes ago."

"I know."

"You saw him? Did you recognise him?"

"No – well, kind of. I mean, luckily, he wouldn't recognise me from any old photos. I saw him ringing your doorbell so just hung back out of sight till you let him in. But from Mother's description of the two detectives who called to see her, he sounded like one of them. The older one, who she said was quite hot!"

"You've been to see your mother?" Sam realised the tone of the question might have sounded surreal to an onlooker.

"She mentioned you'd come by."

Sam waited, but nothing was forthcoming. "And…?"

"And nothing. She said you had just taken the opportunity of my Father's death to see how she was. That's it. Was there more?"

"No…no."

This exchange was more surreal than even Sam could have imagined, yet in so many ways typical of the way their relationship had foundered. On reflection, should it have been a surprise that long-lost relatives could talk in anything other than soundbites, when none of the intervening years contained any common ground and the reunion came about against the most violent of backdrops?

Lara continued: "I stayed there for one night. I know I should have left the country by now, but it's difficult after so many years away. We shared a couple of bottles of wine and drank a toast to the death of a bullying bastard. I had a feeling the police would be looking for me."

"Had a feeling? What else could you have expected?"

"It seemed easier to lay low at Mum's. No one down there knows me. But I knew there was something else I needed to do – see you."

Sam fought hard to remain inscrutable. "Well, that does surprise me, given the terms on which we parted."

Having received no invitation to sit, Lara sat anyway before continuing:

"I'm tired – tired of having run so often; tired in anticipation of running again." She gave Sam a piercing look, yet somehow devoid of anger. "Tired of our last memories of each other being dislike, bordering on hatred. We should be reserving that last emotion for my deceased Father." Lara shuddered. "You have no idea how dreadful it is to even acknowledge that genetic link."

"I think I might, though of course having that monster as a father must be so much worse than as an uncle. But still…"

Lara gave her a look worth a thousand words. "But listen, strange though it may sound, I want to be the old Lara again. The one you could count as a friend. Just for a while."

With that, she reached up and pulled away a blonde wig, allowing her cropped auburn hair to breathe and scratching at her scalp with relief. With minimal difficulty, she removed blue contact lenses and placed them in a small container from her shoulder bag. When her now hazel eyes looked back at Sam, they seemed tearful, though that might have been the effect of taking out the lenses.

"Had you forgotten I wasn't a blue-eyed blonde?"

"I still know you well enough that I don't look at peripherals like appearance. But I had forgotten you wore glasses," said Sam.

"Yes, part of dowdy old me."

"That's not what I meant."

"I know – and I used to scrub up nicely as well, but dowdy old me is how I always felt when I was with you."

"And I know that. You resented me."

"You seemed to have a power over men – of course I resented you. I know now, that was just young foolishness. You were more like a magnet that attracted iron, but that included rust and nails. I look at you and I see you're troubled and your power hasn't brought you any happiness."

"Are you surprised?" There was anger in Sam's voice now as her other uninvited visitors started to chatter again. She paced across to the window and stared out. "I didn't welcome his attentions, you know."

"Didn't you? I think at first you did – a hormonal girl seeing attraction in a man's eyes, no matter how wrong it was." Sam sensed the great effort of will it took for Lara to stop there; shoring up her calmness before she continued: "Sorry – and I do realise I was a daddy's girl." From the corner of her eye Sam could see Lara's gaze lose itself in the grey clouds that lay beyond the window. "I stress *was*. How foolish young girls are." Now came the peculiar tingle that told Sam Lara's focus had shifted onto the back of her head. "So yes, given how often he was away, doing his job – killing people or making their lives a misery, as I now understand it – when he was back I disliked the attention you got, that I thought should have been mine." Her throat clicked as she swallowed. "Back before I understood just what a euphemism *attention* was."

"You'd have been welcome to it, believe me." Sam turned and then saw the look in Lara's eyes; raised a hand. "Sorry, that's badly phrased. Even when I liked you the least, that's something I never wished on you." She shuddered.

"Can't you sit down?" Lara gestured. Sam was rather taken aback by the request and more so to find herself heading to the chair. "Because believe it or not, I didn't come here to fight. I know building a bridge might not be possible, but I don't want the shadow of that bully to dominate our relationship, such as it is. If you want to dislike me, let it be for other reasons. He's dead – it doesn't matter how; he's gone and shouldn't be allowed to infect our lives anymore."

Sam was stunned – it seemed the cousin for whom she had felt little but contempt for many years had grown up. Everything seemed to have changed – she was sounding and acting stronger. It was something new for Sam to feel like the weak link. Perhaps it was time for her to follow Lara's lead, and yes, to stop running.

Still, the years had made her wary. "Well, let's hope this attempt at rapprochement works better than the previous one."

"It must – it has to. He's dead. How can it not?" Lara shifted in her seat. "If you had told me when I was twelve, I would be sitting one day with my mother celebrating the fact that somebody…" there was a look in Lara's eyes, "…had murdered him, brutally…"

"I can't say it surprises me that Gill finds some gladness in that.

I've always assumed there were plenty of reasons why she became so devoted to a martial art."

"And you?" Lara gave her a discomfiting look. "After all, you were the recipient of his lecherous uncle wandering hands. Those lovely family Christmases."

Sam's temples started to ache from the gritting of her teeth and she realised she was folding herself smaller in her chair. "If only it had been just his hands. You have no idea how much guilt I've carried around with me, wondering whether I led him on in some way. I admit, you were right just now; my preening girl's mind was flattered to have the eyes of an older man crawling all over me. I won't deny my sexuality has always been…"

"Seismic?" ventured Lara. It was said with a smile, but that soon faltered when she saw the response it drew.

"I hate that it's so difficult to control. As perhaps it was for him. Aren't men programmed that way? Isn't that what we're always told?" Sam sprang up. "I need a vodka! I know it's mid-afternoon, but…"

"Well then make it a double – in each glass."

Sam had to acknowledge that Lara was trying hard, and the shaking of her hands as she poured the drinks was as much suppressed relief as nerves. It was easier to air the next topic by speaking over her shoulder. "So, what was all that about at the university back then?" There was no immediate reply.

She brought over the drinks. They raised their glasses ever so slightly in each other's direction. "*Cheers* seems inappropriate under the circumstances."

"Likewise *bottoms up*," responded Lara.

They managed to smile through the pain, and finally their eyes met.

Lara took a generous sip and gave an awkward shrug. "What you never knew, or bothered to ask, was what happened once you went away to university. I became the target of his bullying; his frustration, I suppose, that you had escaped. I hadn't wanted to believe that he was sexually attracted to you; nor that his attention scared you. As I said, I was a daddy's girl, but once I saw what a mean-spirited bully he was all I wanted was to apologise to you; make up with you. That's why I asked to visit the campus in Southampton. I didn't want him to also destroy what had been a close friendship."

She stopped for a moment, as if remembering. "But then, from almost the first minute I arrived," she went on, "I saw again that hold you exerted over men; the way most of the male students in your circle were putty in your hands. And how you thrived on it."

Despite everything, Sam was fighting the recidivist temptation to dismiss Lara's claims. She managed to overcome it, knowing this moment was remedial in more than one way; for both of them. It added irony to Lara's further reflections.

"I got angry again. Why do you think I flirted with that computing PhD friend of yours, Pat, who followed you around like a lost puppy? I pretty much put everything on a plate for him that weekend. Men are suckers for sexual flattery at that age."

"Not just at that age," added Sam.

"Anyway, I didn't just want to show you; to compete for and win someone who was hot for you. There was already a plan forming in my head. I'd done a bit of research. I didn't want to be at home anymore, so I'd moved in with a friend for a while, but it wasn't far enough away and I wanted to make a fresh start. I couldn't afford university, wasn't sure I was bright enough anyway. And you know what? Perhaps I was also running away from myself." She stopped and laughed, though with little humour. "Well literally, I was! You mentioned the whole identity thing earlier on; who better than an IT geek – a bit of a hacker in fact – to help me cut some corners on the road to a new name for a new life?"

"He did that for you on the basis of one night's sex? Boy, you must be good!"

"Who said it was just one night."

Sam looked up, puzzled, but Lara just pushed on. "We saw each other a few times. As you had discarded him, I doubt you noticed he wasn't around for several weekends. I told him a tale about a psychopathically jealous ex-boyfriend, asked him to keep it quiet." She stopped for a moment to cast a reflective glance through the window and into the past. "He was a nice guy; didn't deserve to be used in that way." She looked back at Sam. "The Scott genes, eh?

"With his help, I was gone."

They sat in a pregnant silence, shocked by the contents of their very own book of revelations, until Lara read on: "I'm amazed that I've been able to unburden myself so easily. I just hope that I haven't passed an unbearable load to you." In the absence of a response she continued. "Australia might seem like a cliché, but that's where I aimed for. Once there, I changed my name again by deed poll. And here's the new me. It's ironic really – the men over there can be way more sexist than here, but I'm just more comfortable down under."

"So why did you come back?" Sam knew the response sounded bitter, but it was beyond her powers to prevent.

"It's still part of the Commonwealth. With all the news about the Armistice celebrations, I was curious. Technology actually was a wonderful thing…until I read the headlines – sorry, the lies – in an online paper about a much respected local military hero in Truro. I had to come over. It couldn't be allowed simply to pass. I just didn't know, as it turned out, exactly what I would do." She stared into the distance. "And now it's taken care of and I feel almost cheated."

Even to a non-legal brain that was a statement that begged a question or two, but the rebuilt ground of their relationship wasn't firm enough for Sam to ask them. She had to be content with feeling sure that Tom Wright's life hadn't been terminated by his daughter's hand: the bitterness told her that.

Lara took a long sip of her vodka, watching Sam over the rim of the glass, before adding: "And now you cannot allow him to get away with being a victim, a martyr; a brave, wounded veteran wiped out by some villain on Armistice Day. People need to know the truth."

Sam looked out of the window again. "The truth? A career in law taught me what a diseased lover that can be."

"As for who killed him, or any other violent abuser…who cares?"

Now Sam just looked at her, allowing another demon-haunted silence to pass.

Lara reached into her bag. "I brought you something; a parting gift, hopefully more acceptable than my last one." She produced a rolled up piece of paper. Battered, but tied with a ribbon, it looked for all the world like a precious, ancient parchment. "I remembered that picture you loved on my bedroom wall; how even when you were older, you said it encapsulated innocence for you. I kept it all these years – obviously, since I have it here." She laughed at her truism. "Perhaps, subconsciously, it was a part of you I could still hold onto; call mine…without needing to invest in closeness. Despite the hatred…"

Lara stopped; looked down for a moment before continuing. "Never mind the faults of men – why do we women do that to each other?"

"You mean putting conditions on friendship?"

Lara rose from her chair, came and knelt in front of Sam. "Here." She held out the rolled picture. When Sam took it, Lara enveloped her hand in both of hers. "I hope it brings you some happiness."

Sam looked down at the parchment, clasped in three hands, and watched as two spatters of tears landed on it. "I don't think I can look at this now. I need to be ready."

"Of course." Lara released Sam's hand. "And now, as you intimated right at the beginning, I need to go. I have no desire to talk to the police and my plane leaves in twelve hours, at least four of which it will take me to get to Heathrow." Sam could see a deep sadness in her eyes. "I wish I could say don't be a stranger," she paused, "but truly, I think in distance there's less danger."

★★★★

For the second time that afternoon, the departure of an unexpected visitor left Sam sitting motionless, her insides churning with conflicting emotions. She looked at the rolled-up picture, which still sat in her clutching hand; Pandora's box tied with a ribbon. One visit to the past was enough, surely. But she'd meant what she said – she wasn't ready. She placed it to one side. There were far worse things to contemplate in the here and now.

"Oh Lara," she whispered. "What have you done?"

# 18

Pascoe found it hard to contain his excitement as he leaned in through Logan's door forty-eight hours later, consulting what appeared to be a shopping list.

"Loads of stuff, sir."

"Don't forget the washing-up liquid."

Pascoe ignored him. "First, yes, official confirmation – the blood on the sword belongs to Kevin Miller, blah blah, we knew that already. Second, there appears to be some bruising around the sternum on Mr Foster – suggests a similar MO, doesn't it, sir?"

"Indeed! Good to know, especially in light of the four ones link. And?"

"I took the photo from Wright's flat to the regimental barracks and managed to get IDs for the other three soldiers alongside Wright who had the lines drawn on them." Pascoe looked again at his list. "Think we can exclude them from our investigations on the grounds of one not having survived the first Gulf War, one happily ensconced on the Costa del Sol from where he hasn't moved in months, and one, um, now being a vicar in South Shields."

The two of them exchanged a look, as if that phrase was some sort of euphemism rather than an epiphany, before Pascoe moved on.

"I contacted Bovis about why he wasn't more curious when Wright didn't come to the door on that morning. He was refreshingly frank — said he hated the RSM, had been pissed off being asked to pick him up and was…" again Pascoe referred to the paperwork, "…'only too glad the bastard seemed to have overslept and missed his free ride.'"

"Do we know why he hated him? Seems a perfect motive."

"I did ask, sir, and he just said he was far from alone in feeling that way about Wright." Pascoe gave a rueful smile. "Whatever the reason, his account of his movements tallies perfectly with Mr. Wolniek's, which means he wasn't there long enough to have done the deed. Besides, I seem to remember Harj reckoned the crime was committed some hours before."

Logan considered, tapping his finger to his lips. "Could be a double bluff; returning to the scene a few hours later. What's his alibi for that night?"

"Doesn't seem the sort for that kind of complexity really, sir… anyway, he was with a couple of vets having a few beers until gone midnight — seems that with the Armistice and everything his local wasn't being too strict about closing time for ex-soldiers"

Again, Logan was silent for a few moments before continuing: "Okay, that makes it difficult but not impossible for him to have been the murderer…and in any case they might cover for each other if Wright was so unpopular. We may come back to this, but as I don't see Bovis as having any motive for the attacks on Miller and Foster, we'll move on. Anything else?"

"Thought I would save the best for last, sir — I think we've found our ghost." Now Pascoe had Logan's full attention. "Took a little longer than we hoped. Clearly, she had some help — someone with some expertise, because the cross-linking of databases brought nothing, and we only found it via a manual search. Anyway, we got her: looks like Mandy Woods combined a stint in St Mary's Church cemetery in Basingstoke with applying for a passport and buying a ticket to Australia in 2008. Again, there was a bit of a delay because of the time difference with Oz, and they had to do some further checking because she'd changed her name by deed poll once she was there."

"And is she still there?"

"Yes, sir..."

"Fuck!"

"…but…she was here."

Logan jumped up, cracking his knee on the drawer unit of the desk. Swearing, rubbing his leg, he moved around to the white-board. "What's the name?"

"Anna McGinty."

"And when did she return to Australia?"

"Three days ago."

"Damn these fucking delays!" Logan took in the look on Pascoe's face and clapped him on the shoulder. "Well done – I know it wasn't easy. Right – when did she arrive in the UK?"

"Ninth November."

Logan turned back to the board, wrote Anna McGinty next to Lara Wright and circled it several times in angry red. He tapped the pen against the swirl of colour. "Is this our Gordian Knot then? I knew it. I knew it!" Now he looked at Pascoe and frowned. "I just don't understand it."

A sense of vague resolution seemed to draw near and he continued. "Pascoe, if she was here for that length of time, I cannot believe she wouldn't have visited old acquaintances – consider that last word to be qualified appropriately, as I refuse to lower myself to making quote marks signs in the air." It was good to feel able to smile for a moment. "Old stomping grounds. Contact Gill Scott – I know it makes little sense given their estrangement but try to find out whether Lara was there at all. It's one of very few options we have as things stand. Go down to Torquay and do that. Speak to her face-to-face; I want to know whether she's lying." He saw the look on Pascoe's face. "I'm trusting you – remember some of the key facial and other responses we've discussed."

What Logan kept to himself was that Pascoe might have greater success, and for more than one reason. Gill Scott might have her defences down – see Pascoe as less of a threat. Above all, though, Gill Scott's face already showed so many signs of stress, misery and conflict that Logan's examination of parts might be swamped in false positives. Pascoe's less forensic approach would, he felt sure, be more likely to spot something awry compared with his previous visit. Some paintings didn't warrant being analysed; their impact was impressionistic.

He continued: "Meanwhile, I'm off to see Sam Ingle again. For all I know, her cousin was sitting in the other room while we spoke. That's not based on any logical premise either – I'm back with the intuitive thing; there was just something about Sam the last time we spoke. She seemed ill at ease; perhaps a little defensive again. Have you asked the authorities in Australia to watch Anna McGinty?"

"Yes, sir. I told them just to observe for the moment."

"Good man." He grabbed his coat and strode past Pascoe. "C'mon Watson, the game's afoot."

The club was thronging. A couple of days of unexpected sunshine had dried out the pitches and the entire lot appeared to be occupied that afternoon. Though he scanned them all, Logan looked in particular at the rugby pitch. There was no baseball cap, and the couple of female voices he heard turned out to belong to girls of different build, in one case, and different race, in the other, to Sam.

As the DCI made his way towards Reception a teenager in rugby kit came jogging towards him on the other side of the fence. "Excuse me; is Sam Ingle in today?" he asked the lad, who stopped and thought for a moment.

"You mean Marshy?"

"Um…maybe. The woman who runs this place."

"I think she's in." The lad jerked a thumb in the direction of the building. "She was in the boxing gym."

"Thanks." Logan smiled. "Why do you call her Marshy?"

"Short for martial."

"That's not her surname though."

"No, as in martial arts." The lad laughed and jogged on again, responding to the shouts from his teammates.

Logan, on the other hand, was rooted to the spot, cursing the condition that made it impossible for him to remember or recognise the faces of the two younger women in the photograph in Gill Scott's flat.

★★★★

Sam loved the banter of the boxing gym, where being treated as an equal was an honour bestowed by her on the lads, not vice versa, even for those who had graduated to national championship-winning level.

Today, however, she had asked for an hour alone. The journey she would take in that time – the rage that needed release and the channelling of anger – was not something for the eyes of others; they would have sensed – known – that something was going on.

Once, she had hoped that time would heal. Now it seemed the images were scars on her retina. Her only healing was to be found in this club and, today, in this room.

She swivelled; transferred her weight as the bag came back towards her.

*BOOFF!!*

*Her taekwondo side kick…*

*…lands square and precise in the solar plexus of RSM Wright. She had counted on having those few seconds as he opened the door; that he would stare in shock and allow her in – it's the only part of this night that you could call planned; that and the cable ties in her pocket. He doubles over, all*

*strength gone, struggling to breathe, his jaw in the perfect position for her to kick again, knocking him out.*

*Funny how you can take out someone strong with one well-aimed blow but then struggle to move their deadweight. She drags Wright through the hallway to his bedroom, panicking a little at the thought of him coming round before she can secure him. Getting him onto the bed is also not the easiest thing, but at last she hauls him into position and is able to step back, panting and sweating – the baggy training top and tracksuit pants she is wearing have made her hot, likewise the Thinsulate hiking hat, holding in her hair and the latex gloves. But they are serving the dual purpose, she hopes, of disguise in the event she is spotted, and of keeping DNA from the scene. All can be disposed of later with ease.*

*And this is as far as she has ever come in her wild imaginings; while she was standing in the field just before, and in the preceding days when she felt the bile rising at the thought of him being feted. Perhaps she will just say her piece to her captive audience; get it all out of her system. She knows some demons will just crawl right back in and take up residence again in dark recesses, though.*

*She has a sudden fear of seeing his eyes, looks around for the night vision goggles, spots them and tugs them over his forehead and into place. Already that makes things easier; he is dehumanised – the monster from the window is back.*

*It's now a question of waiting. Unable to stand in that room, the breathing of the beast a good deal more terrifying than the wind rampaging beyond the windows, she wanders through the flat. Small, sterile rooms that constitute a shrine to the regiment. There is a dagger, ivory handled; its fearsome blade concealed in a primitive wooden sheath. It was doubtless taken from some Middle Eastern tribesman. She remembers enough from having read Macbeth at school to wonder whether the weapon is tempting her to murder. Like all humans, she finds it impossible to resist lifting the blade and, as if there is innate power in that shaft of steel, she considers whether the threat of it might scare her prisoner – for that is what he is – as he once terrified her with it when she refused to play ball.*

*She hears a groan from the bedroom and decides that, if nothing else, the dagger might guarantee his silence, so takes it through with her.*

*As she waits for him to recover his senses, she hopes the shaking will stop and curses the universe for allowing him to have that power over her still.*

*At last, he raises his head to see her standing at the end of the bed.*

*"What the fuck? Sam!"*

*There is so much she wants to say, but it seems the unspeakable nature of his deeds has left her speechless.*

*"What are you doing? Why?"*

*That last word is a blessing as it gives her anger at least. "How can you ask why?" How she wishes her voice wasn't quivering.*

*He pauses as if thinking. "Okay – why now?"*

*She brandishes the dagger, pointing; accusatory. "When I think of you being lauded at the commemoration like some sort of hero, it makes me sick to the pit of my stomach. If it weren't for my own name being dragged through the muck, I'd tell them the truth about Regimental Sergeant Major Wright."*

*"Look, Sammy…"*

*"Regimental Child Abuser Wright!"*

*Wind rages into the void that follows, accusing with more eloquence than her words could ever muster. From another flat downstairs the sound of a television filters through and serves as a grim reminder to her, not just of the need to keep her voice down if she wants her presence here to remain undetected, but of other desperate times – the commanding whisper from behind her, telling her to be sure she stayed quiet, so they could hear if her cousin – his daughter – returned; her head being forced into the pillow when he sensed she might be about to scream.*

*He breaks what passes for silence in the storm of the elements and her mind. "What do you want?" He tugs at the cable ties, though he desists soon enough as she brings the point of the blade to his throat.*

*"Pathetic!" she spits. "That might have been an acceptable question if you'd been wounded badly enough to have clinically proven amnesia – but you seem to have recalled your heroism in fine enough detail for the press in recent weeks."*

*She shakes her head. "At first, in my naivety, I did see you as some sort of hero. Maybe my pubescent mind was even flattered by your eyes wandering over my body – proof I was becoming a woman. How right you put me on that one." She lifts the dagger point so it plays across his lips. "There's nothing like a gnarled old cock being shoved into your mouth to destroy innocence and hero-worship."*

*His response is sibilant, as if he dare not move his lips near that fearsome, sharp blade. "I have no idea what you're talking about."*

*She steps away, fearing she might just plunge the dagger into his face. "Perhaps you don't. Perhaps you see innocence and youth as something to be purged; beaten out of recruits; fucked out of girls."*

*She walks across the room; wants to open the curtains, throw wide the windows and allow the night and the wind to cleanse that space of its stale air and fetid imaginings – but she remains paranoid, fearing being seen or heard. Then turning again, she sees a picture above the bed. The content of the picture is immaterial, but its position serves as a reminder of the one sweet thing to which she had clung during all those foul acts. Of course, it was another room, another house, another life – another picture. Strange how, no matter where you chose to live, from time to time four walls could revert to being a prison.*

*She heads for the door.*

*"Where are you going?" he demands. "You can't just leave me here."*

*She turns in the doorway. "Oh, don't worry – I'll be back, as they say; just like you used to be – and maybe you'll wish that I wasn't. But if you don't want me to come back and cut off your dick, you'll just lie quiet."*

*The memory of that picture, reappearing after all these years, has taken her aback, as if she had forgotten to blink for all that time. She needs to breathe for a moment and cannot let Wright see just how he, or the idea of him, still terrifies her.*

*From the bedroom come the suppressed sounds of exertion. They leave her feeling exposed, so she dashes back through. She can tell by the veins on his neck and the ligature marks on his wrists that he has been struggling to break free of the cable ties. Thank goodness they seem strong enough. It isn't that she doubts her ability to defend herself, but it's one thing to incapacitate a brute with an unexpected blow, another to confront him if he's on the attack and angry.*

*Just in case he has managed to work himself loose and is waiting to strike, she runs a little test, bringing her fist down onto that tender spot on the solar plexus once again. He convulses, all air driven from his lungs so that it sounds like nothing more than a wheezing cough, but his body is unable to double up as the cable ties hold firm.*

*"Just checking," she says, relishing the lightheartedness of her words. "But I enjoyed it anyway."*

*He gasps: "I don't know what you think you're doing, Sam…"*

*"Don't you use my name again! Don't you dare!"*

*"Alright — I don't know what you think you're doing…bitch."*

*"That's better," she cajoles.*

*"…but I have no idea why you're here and why you're doing this to me."*

*And now she feels brave enough, if only for a few moments, to reach down, lift the night vision goggles from his face. For this next bit, she needs to look into his eyes.*

*"What's the matter, Tommy-baby?" There were some reflexes the human body couldn't avoid. The eyes have it. "Ah, I see you remember that — how you used to make me whisper it before…" her courage falters for a moment, "…before the vile things you made me do."*

*She replaces the night vision goggles.*

*"You're fucking mad! I don't know what you're talking about."*

*She feels the tears coming. No! She's not going to let that happen, though she can't keep their echo from her voice. "You know, what is mad is that, for a time, I even questioned myself; wondered whether somehow I led you on. Not at the beginning, but as the years went on and I awoke to my own sexuality. How did I let it happen? Who was I protecting by not telling the police?" Despite herself, she has to wipe her eyes. "But if you would just stop denying that it happened, then maybe, just maybe, I could walk away — because believe me, I've tried. But I've been treading in quicksand…even at those times when I have managed not to think about it for a whole day."*

*He raises his head to look at her. She is grateful the goggles are in place once more. "What — you want me to confess to something that didn't happen; to something I didn't do? You looking to cash in somehow? Are you wired for sound? Oh, I wonder what they'd pay, the tabloids, for a story about a war hero who's accused of being a paedophile – and it being sex with his own niece."*

*Sam steps back, almost stumbles, weakened by what she has heard and the poison in this beast's veins. She looks around in a literal and metaphorical attempt to find something to grasp; realises she has taken the dagger back to its resting place and knows somehow that isn't the solution – or rather, it isn't the tool to finish the job.*

*Because there is no doubt this unrepentant monster deserves to die.*

*And then she spots what she needs, puts it out of sight but within reach. This crime requires poetic justice, and with something akin to a click of the fingers she has everything she needs – motivation, cause and, above all, anger.*

*She climbs onto the bed and, though it repulses her, straddles him, sensing his immediate unease. "What's the matter? Scared to try something different – well, in the sense that I'm on top. You liked to dominate, didn't you? To terrify. Oh, you're silent now. You asked if I'm wearing a wire. I noticed you moderated your language just in case "*

*She unzips her tracksuit top; gives him a knowing look. "See, no wire." She drops the top around her waist. She looks at her breasts and back at him; provocative." You remember these puppies, don't you?" She gives a pointed stare in the direction of his groin. "What's the matter – cat got your cock?"*

*She thanks the fates for the shield of her angry purpose, because the thought of him pulsing beneath her is almost enough to make her projectile vomit across him. DNA can be a bummer sometimes.*

*She is not sure how much longer she can stay there, but the thought of what is to come gives her strength. Time to up the ante. "Tell you what; if you can get hard, I'll let you go."*

*Despite every instinct of revulsion in her, she starts to rock gently on him. After a few seconds she stops and gives a mocking pout with her bottom lip. "Hector doesn't want to play? Oh well, as you used to say at certain times of the month, that's why God gave us mouths."*

*With that she reaches down, her fingertips grasping the swagger stick she's placed on the floor.*

*He opens his mouth to protest and she shoves the stick into it, wondering in a distracted way what his last lucid thought might be; whether there will be any similarity with the way her mind used to become scrambled by agony, by the instinct to survive, or even by welcoming the idea of death as a release.*

*She wants to thrust the stick ever further down into his throat, let her mind drag forward the horrendous images from her past once again. She wishes she could close her eyes and not open them till the choking and thrashing have stopped.*

*The wind howls again outside the window – of course, it hadn't ever stopped, but her mind has been focussed as much in the past as in the present. She wonders whether it is raging against her deed or roaring its approval.*

If only.

She seemed to have woken from a trance, to find herself standing, staring at the punch bag, which still swung a little, though she had no recollection of when the last blow had landed.

She sat, a sudden movement, all strength gone from her legs. It had seemed so real; she might almost have believed those were memories, not imaginings; that she hadn't fled to the stables that night when the monster had appeared in his bedroom window, cowering there before fleeing home. That instead she had taken her courage in both hands and dealt a blow for the abused. Maybe she had done it after all, in some sort of fugue state, like the one she had just experienced. Frightening how much detail was there, some of it information she had doubtless absorbed from a combination of the press and her discussions with the police…and some of it dredged from the murky depths of her childhood. There were times she wished she could remove certain pictures from the photo album of her past, but then she knew such horrible remembrances had been a huge driving force behind her setting up the social centre.

She had indeed struck a blow for those too weak and bullied to help themselves – that same night, but not directly as a result of it.

It was surreal and also somehow frightening to think that,

under cover of the bleak Cornish storm winds, by the fitful light of the moon that flickered through the darkness joining the 10th and 11th of November, someone else had turned up there. Someone possessing more courage than her. They couldn't have been filled with more hatred; no one could. Had they been watching him from that place too? She shuddered at the idea.

Sam looked in panic around her and at the bag, its final, gentle twitching seeming to replicate the last movements of a hangman's victim. She was used to lethargy and anxiety being pounded from her limbs, replaced by adrenalin. Where had it all gone, that feeling as the energy returned; her core strengthening; the punches more solid on the bag? Feeling terrified was something she needed to put behind her, and if the gym could no longer offer its usual therapy, then there was a new, lurking terror to deal with. Also, what if even the fact of Wright being dead would not bring her peace, only ghosts? There was no one left to exorcise, no crusade to act as a conduit for her anger and guilt. How would she silence the voices now if they refused to leave her alone?

Which brought her thoughts back to Logan's recent visits, both to her flat and, before that, his second call at the social centre. Her stomach had lurched, but from the primeval fear of being found guilty not of murder, but of inaction. Of silence. It had taken all her strength to see her through their discussions. His visit to the centre had tipped her over a different edge. Discussing Safebeds and downplaying the brutality of her uncle had reminded her of Angelina Miller and that poor girl's sickening story; a horrific tale and all too common.

Yes, Logan's visit had brought it all back – what Angelina had been through and why Sam had wanted to help her so much. That pain had resonated with her. Another girl who had waited too long, until she believed telling the police was not an option; who had feared that, in some way, she was responsible for what had happened to her.

The beast had woken. Sam had known that, Hydra-like, it

would always grow new heads, but if someone could just cut off one…it would be something. She had done what she could – one head had been severed – and yet, the awful irony of it, Sam found it so hard to deal with her part in that.

Because another creature was stirring, likewise disturbed by the DCI's visits: would she ever trust men again? And if not, how would her mistrust manifest itself? Even on the rugby field an incident like a few mornings before, when she had taken out the slightly cocky young player, might have added nuance and edge. Though that was nothing in the grander scheme of things, would that need to hurt be a concomitant symptom of a wider problem? Where once she had fought for justice within the system, would she now seek the paths of the vigilante?

Perhaps she was overreacting. Nevertheless, she had sensed in Logan someone who trod the roads less followed. The danger she feared was that those roads might lead him to the truth, and that could only mean trouble for her.

★★★★

Logan made his way through reception and headed for the doors that led to the various training areas and weights rooms.

"Hello?" The receptionist called to him, but he refused to break stride. "Excuse me!" Logan took almost childish pleasure in ignoring her, her voice reconfirming her identity, already revealed by her love of excessive black makeup around her eyes, as Janey. He remembered her smug smile from his previous visits. At last he stopped, but only because it suited him. "You can't just wander in and…"

His moment had arrived. It wasn't often he liked to pull rank, but from time to time, it felt good.

He produced his ID. "Detective Chief Inspector Logan; I believe you remember me well enough…Janey, was it?" He liked the impact of that. "Actually, I can just wander in – or are you asking me to get a warrant? Which I can if necessary."

He relished her silence before moving on through the doors.

Again, he was struck by the surreal sound of tortured cries emanating from these rather faceless, institutional corridors as members paid homage to their own, particular gods with bodies pushed to the limit. He had once visited the so-called House of Terror in Budapest, headquarters of both the Nazis and the Communists during the years when Hungary had been under their respective controls. This same peculiar juxtaposition of the civilised and the barbaric had struck him there too, and he had imagined how those rather anodyne walls must also have resonated with the screams of souls in torment. Two very different scenarios of course, until you closed your eyes.

When it became clear that Sam wasn't to be found, he headed back to reception.

"I thought Marshy was training here today." Once again, the look on Janey's face made him feel smug. *Yes, I know her nickname too. You have no secrets from me. Your inner sanctum is breached.*

"She was, but left about an hour ago." Janey's compliant response showed just how far her crest had fallen. Perhaps, thought Logan, she believed Sam might now be in some kind of trouble and was distancing herself.

He nodded and stepped outside. Before he had time to consider the next move, his phone rang, showing the station number.

"Logan…has he?…no, I'm on my way…no, don't worry about back-up; I suspect getting to his bedside through the officious medical staff will be tricky enough without the intimidating presence of more than one officer."

# 19

In the land of the blind, the one-eyed man is king – but who ruled in the land of the facially blind? At least those with prosopagnosia would be focussed on the crown! The news that Alastair Foster had stabilised and lurched one faltering step towards the light represented perhaps only the fluttering of an eyelid on a half-sighted eye, but it was something; another flicker to give Logan hope after the news about Lara's visit to the UK.

And how tough a cookie was Foster? He'd made it through being locked in a lightless cellar for days, miles from anywhere, with no food and little water, hearing Death's stertorous breathing beside him in the blackness every measureless moment. Despite himself, Logan had chuckled earlier at Pascoe's cruel humour, when he'd said that Foster's lifestyle had left him well prepared for a stint at Pennyweather Farm. On reflection, there might even have been some surreal truth in that.

Joking aside, Logan's desperate wish was that the walking corpse – not strictly true, as he wasn't yet out of bed – might be able to push open another door, even a crack, allowing a further tiny beam of light to fall across the murkiness of these recent deeds.

Foster's own presence in the whole sorry business was, on

reflection, not just a piece of the jigsaw, but an entire section of it. And what was all that business about the ponies – the RSPCA turning up to collect them the day before Wright's murder? What the hell did that have to do with anything – possibly nothing, but even a man like Logan, who believed in the finer details of the here and now, had always remained open to the possibility of energies leaving traces in the aftermath of powerful events, perhaps even influencing what followed. He was determined to ignore the signposts that stated 'Only A Weird Coincidence – this way'.

On reflection, the rather hackneyed image of the jigsaw was probably the wrong one; this was a chessboard where every piece was carved a different shape and moved according to its own rules, but still within the confines of the board.

★★★★

Having arrived at the hospital, Logan listened with forced patience to the usual warnings from the doctor – the patient was still in a critical condition, on life-support, being fed intravenously, not to be upset, etcetera. It wasn't until he stepped past the officers on the door, guarding the room in the ICU, that the full significance of those caveats hit him.

Of course, Logan had no true idea of how shabby a figure Foster had cut before all this had happened, but now he looked like a damned soul which had somehow been dragged through a fissure and escaped Hell. It wasn't down simply to a lack of food and water – through history, others had dealt with worse – there was also the haunted look in his eyes. Logan would have abandoned all hope of questioning this cadaver if it hadn't opened those same eyes at his approach. In them was etched the kind of torment that spoke of a man for whom full psychological recovery was, if not necessarily off the map, then a long road to travel. He had apparently not only heard Death's breathing, but felt the cold mist of those exhalations. Yet still he had refused to give in and welcome its embrace.

As he saw the fear in Foster's eyes, Logan wondered whether he himself now resembled Death, standing by the bed, silent and waiting. He sat in an attempt to present a reassuring, less threatening figure.

"It's okay, Mr Foster – I'm Detective Chief Inspector Logan. I'm here to help."

Was he? Sure, he was here to help himself. Yet his pity was real enough.

Foster said nothing, or if he did speak, the words manifested themselves only as rasping breaths and an occasional widening of the eyes. The lips barely moved.

"The doctors say you're making progress." Logan struggled not to burst out in nervous laughter at the sound his own words; a trite line from a third-rate film. He suppressed the smile with the practised ease of a man used to masking his mannerisms, before continuing: "I'm going to catch whoever did this to you."

The responses were the same as before, except the monitors suggested pulse, blood pressure and respiratory rate had increased. As he watched those machines and observed the readings, a dark humour surfaced, realising he might have been looking at some futuristic, more efficient version of his own processes; his AI alter ego! Leaning forward, he noted the impact of that movement on those monitors, so sat back again, speaking from a less oppressive distance: "If there is anything…any detail, no matter how small, that you can remember, please let me know."

The levels on the machines had steadied, but remained high. Was Foster's mind filled with nothing but images of blackness and torture? Part of Logan wanted to back off – a very small part. He had grown tired of endless night in the land of whatever type of blind.

"Can you think of any reason why someone might have wanted to do this to you?"

Nothing.

Wait! A breakthrough?

Had he imagined it, or had Foster given an ever-so-slight shake of the head. Now Logan couldn't help but lean in again. "Was that a no?" There it was again; another barely discernible movement... but was it confirmation, or denial?

Whatever – it was still a foot on the moon; an apple falling on the head.

Blood pressure, heart rate and respiration were definitely heading up the scale. How long before they triggered an alarm that would bring the staff running? Yet now, those readings seemed to be responding to physical exertion. Foster's neck strained in a slight arch; his eyes were widening. Had Logan already pushed him too far?

The lips moved; vapours of words, almost audible and not quite visible; a language learned in the company of the Grim Reaper.

If Logan had heard right, vindication was his.

He stayed leaning in, though in truth, it repelled him to be that close, and asked: "Did you say *woman?*"

Foster's croak of a response, before his head slumped back onto his pillow, was accompanied by the merest nod, faint and desperate.

If Logan himself had been hooked up to a pulse rate monitor at that moment, it would have been off the scale. Despite his determination to find Lara Wright, some part of him, perhaps altruistic, maybe simply naïve, had wanted to believe the female protagonists in this case were simply conductors of the lightning, not the wielders of its destructive fire. Yet surely now he had to acknowledge that part of his thought processes was flawed. Was it not, in reality, given his own experiences, a misplaced hope that lightning would not strike twice?

It seemed the old-fashioned tenets on which Logan had sought to base his life were being eroded case by case. In fact, they should have crumbled into the sea a long time ago. For him, the horror that a woman might be the perpetrator went deeper than the perfectly reasonable truth of them being just as capable of delivering a telling blow. He had, possibly without good reason, always needed women to be of better moral fibre than him. He hated to admit it…

*Why only now, Ben – surely your sister provided the earliest evidence right back in your childhood?*

…they were not some Earth Goddess on a pedestal to be worshipped by a bunch of hairy, spear wielding hunters; they inhabited the very same muddy plains.

Logan sat up straight, his mind racing now. Gill Scott was a black belt. He had seen Samantha Ingle crunch a muscular youth on the rugby pitch. Certainly, it wasn't beyond the bounds of possibility – Foster had probably never been a good physical specimen, judging by the comments of those who had seen him and yet…holy fuck! There was a link – the question was why? The man lived opposite RSM Wright. Had he seen something? Did he have to be silenced? If so, then why the drama; why not just kill him? All statements and reports suggested he had disappeared during the days around the time of the RSM's murder.

He puffed out his cheeks. Before he chased down this particular dark alley, he needed to be sure.

Foster might have drifted into sleep were it not for his open eyes, which stared vacantly into some other dimension. Excitement overcoming revulsion, Logan put his face close to the other man's. "How do you know it was a woman? Did you see her face; hear her voice?" Finally another creaking shake of the head. "Well how then?"

The high-pitched tone that emanated from the equipment by the bed was already generating a response of hurried footfall from down the corridor. Any minute now, Logan would have to back off. "Please tell me, Mr Foster, if you want me to catch this person."

Foster turned his head – the obvious effort required seemed incommensurate with the tiny movement – to look into Logan's eyes. The DCI didn't like what he saw there, but held his gaze. The parched lips compressed.

"Perfume."

★★★★

Logan had long ago given up on Venn Diagrams as a suitable analogy for this case – the flaw with that was it was based on circles; things, people that were rounded and whole. Now he realised that a spider's web was a much more appropriate image – hundreds of individual threads creating a sometimes invisible entanglement – and Foster's revelation at the hospital supported that. Was there a black widow waiting in the middle, destroying men for her own, as yet obscure, ends?

Looking at the manila folders on his desk, he was grateful for a change of perspective; a new pair of eyes, even if they were just his own, minus the scales. Now there was something to go on.

He sat. As he reached for the first file he stopped for a moment; remembered something Freddy Dessler had said to him during one of their exchanges. The psychologist had retained enough professional decorum and respect for his newfound interlocutor that he hadn't mentioned a name, but, to adapt an old phrase, a nod had been as good as a wink to a facially-blind man.

*"I remember a case where I had been asked to present a psychological profile of a suspect to the police. When it was returned to me, I thought nothing of it, but over a glass of wine one night I decided to give it further consideration, and the physical condition of the actual file caught my eye. It was pristine – had hardly been touched. That told me something about the officer who had requested it. Ultimately that ended up saving his life, the lesson being that one can turn over every stone, but sometimes one has to look at the stone itself."*

Logan sat for a moment contemplating those words. There was a lesson to be learned, but the irony was, the opposite applied to him right now – he needed to stop admiring the stones.

He reopened the first file with a sense of excitement. Also, he would revisit all three crime scenes – or rather four, he corrected himself; both farms in the Foster case were worth consideration.

It was still tempting to leave the files closed and start afresh, but he started leafing through, wondering whether the actuality of at least one female perpetrator might shed new light and cast some longer shadows. Of course, he would have to be careful to avoid assuming a woman was guilty of all three crimes, but he had to start somewhere.

As if to emphasise that all bets were off, the hammer blow came towards him from an unexpected direction as he flicked through the Kevin Miller file.

Looking through the crime scene photographs, he felt the hairs go up on the back of his neck and snatched up the phone to call his pathologist.

"Harj, are there any issues with your camera?"

Harj gave a puzzled laugh. "Issues with my camera? I assume you mean the one I use at crime scenes, or are you worried about the quality of my contributions to Instagram?"

"Okay, I acknowledge that question wasn't the clearest. Does the timer work okay?"

"Yeah, absolutely – spot on. Why?"

Logan lowered the phone, tutted to himself as he looked again at the photos and then carried on. "Forget that question, Harj – it was the wrong one. I should've asked whether the photos in the Kevin Miller file were taken over the course of half an hour, as the times seem to indicate."

"Yup, that'd be about right."

"Cheers Harj."


Within seconds he was on the phone to Pascoe.

"How did it go down in Torquay?"

"Gill Scott's alibi for the 10th checks out – she was at her martial arts club and then drinks afterwards for that evening until late."

"Mmm – I wonder if she, or Samantha Ingle for that matter, has one for the morning Kevin Miller was murdered."

"Kevin Miller?"

"Yes. I was going to tell you when you came in, but Foster indicated today his attacker was a woman. Maybe all three crimes have a female perp."

"A woman? Jesus!"

"I'm just trying to cover all bases, so get me that information from Gill Scott as quickly as you can. Speak soon. I'm off to pay Sheila Miller another visit."

"You don't think she did it?"

"No, the use of Wright's sword rather puts paid to that notion."

He fell silent. The remembrance of something passing and perhaps trivial caused all his cogs and wheels to grind to a halt. It might have been nothing. He would keep it to himself for the moment – not pass it to Pascoe for now. He would follow it up himself – just as soon as he'd spoken with Sheila Miller. As soon as... because it might also not have been nothing.

The distant, persistent, tinny sound of Pascoe's voice calling his name on the phone brought him back.

"Sorry, Pascoe. I'm going to see her because of the little matter of the clock at the crime scene being stopped at eleven minutes past eleven."

"You're kidding!"

"No. I mean, it's a long shot, but the timings on Harj's photos change and the clock in them doesn't."

As Logan approached his car in the station's multistorey parking, the sunlight beyond the edges deepened the shadows inside. Today they seemed to be alive. Were they laughing at or with him? He stopped and stared at one pillar, almost expecting the darkness to wander out and join him as he set off. These shadows were life companions for Logan – in many ways the ideal partners, though no less complex than the flesh and blood variety. Perhaps they offered sanctuary to all the disorder and frayed edges he could never allow himself; fickle guides, often lurking at the periphery of his vision; indistinct forms pointing; sometimes offering a glimpse, nothing more concrete than a sense that you had caught someone on the hop.

Someone like Sheila Miller as she answered the door.

That same instinct had tickled the hairs on his neck during his first visit on the day of the crime. Again, it had been just intuition; flutterings in the air; whispers. He'd put it down to Sheila Miller's own discomfort; the battered remains of her conscience niggling her for not regretting the murder of her brutish husband, especially when his mutilated body lay in the next room. This time, however, there was no shrubbery of context to mask her unease.

He noticed the strong smell of smoke, which hadn't been there on the morning of the murder; nor had she lit up while he'd been there that day. If he knew one thing about smokers – dying prematurely didn't make it onto the list as they lacked exclusive rights on that – it was that extreme stress and a drag on a fag went hand in hand. Her story went that she'd popped out for a pack when someone caused her to become a widow, and yet she appeared not to have indulged upon her return, even after making the gruesome discovery and with time to kill whilst waiting for the police to arrive.

Something still nagged Logan about the image of that muscular brute of a man lying facedown, having been skewered and then sodomised by a sword, with little apparent resistance. It was a something he would have to store away for later. Right now, his mind was wandering along an even more obscure path, down which the shadowy arm had pointed – a possible dead end, or the muddy way through a complex tangle of roots.

Certainly, there was nothing to suggest Sheila Miller had used cleaning or housework as any sort of, well, cleansing process to move on. If that had been the benchmark, one would have been forgiven for thinking that time had stood still. Rather, it was the lessening of the shadows beneath her eyes, which suggested the journey to a form of redemption had begun. Some would have thought it impossible to continue living in a flat where your husband had been the victim of a brutal murder, but Logan suspected the worst stain had been removed by that very act. Life could continue, courtesy of death.

Logan doubted there had been too many times in her life when Sheila Miller had half-smiled upon answering the front door, in particular when finding a figure from the authorities standing there. He looked around as he checked through the flat and was almost jealous of the slovenliness he knew could never be his. Perhaps she and Foster could get together if the latter made it through!

It was the only thing he in any way envied.

"How are you doing, Mrs Miller?"

"Alright, thanks. Still learning to breathe, know whadda mean?"

"Yes – I get that. Any contact with your daughter since…" He hesitated, caught on the hop by his own racing mind. Damn! It frustrated him that, thanks to the pace of events over the last few hours, he'd not had time to process Angelina Miller properly as a variable in all his calculations about the possible female killer. "… since the murder?"

Sheila Miller reached for a cigarette, much to Logan's dark, unspoken delight. "No – not expecting any either. Why would she come back? Doesn't matter that he's gone. It was me who didn't protect her, weren't it?"

Logan gave a slight inclination of the head; his attempt to agree without hurting her feelings.

"Anyway, look, that's not why I came. Could I just have another look in the…bedroom please?"

"Sure. Knock yerself out."

As he went through, Logan half-expected to find nothing had changed – that the room had been kept as a memorial to the death of the monster – but there were clean sheets and the place had been scrubbed, dusted and vacuumed, in noteworthy contrast to the rest of the flat.

He saw the clock, picked it up with gloved hands. It was still set at 11:11. He noted that it was battery-operated, but the battery compartment was empty.

In many ways, the clock was of lesser importance, given the sword had already linked two of the murders. The connection was no longer in question. Why, though? The oblique clue with the clock raised more questions than it answered in that respect – unless this was an elaborate game? Logan smiled. Was Fate intervening? Had the fingers pointed from the shadows again; prompted him to call on Sheila Miller just to set his chain of thoughts in motion?

He returned to the lounge. She hadn't moved.

"Mrs Miller, has the bedroom clock been stopped for a while?"

She looked up, puzzled. "I don't pay it no notice. It's not mine, it's…was his and he always changed the batteries."

"I just noticed it has stopped and there are no batteries in it now. But anyway…" He walked across to a chair and gestured. "May I?" He sat without waiting for a response.

"Can I get you a cup of tea or somethin'?"

"That'd be nice, thank you.

The mug, gripped by shaky fingers, crashed down onto the table. "What?"

Her complexion had been sallow to begin with, but now it turned from the colour of an unwashed sheet to a bleached one.

"I just asked why you protected the identity of the killer, Sheila?"

Sheila Miller reached for her cigarette pack, dropped it, picked it up and fumbled to extract one, while Logan continued: "Oh, I'm not saying you know her name. Perhaps I should have said her gender."

She sat with a thump. Logan allowed her discomfort to marinade in the silence. He went to take a sip of the tea, took a glance at the state of the mug and decided to leave it. He had only agreed to a drink as a means of putting his hostess off her guard before pouncing.

The silence continued. It was time to force things.

Logan leaned forward: "Sheila, abetting a murderer carries a jail sentence. You have just escaped from one prison; don't condemn yourself to another. I'm here alone for a reason. This is all off the record. The person we're closing in on – and make no mistake, we will arrest her with your help or without – is probably responsible for more than one murder."

That revelation caused Sheila Miller's gaze to lift from the floor. Still there was no response.

"Don't you see – with you speaking up for her, telling a jury what a monster your husband was, describing the dreadful things he was doing to you…" He saw her eyes widen. Some tricks, such as his double bluff, were just too simple. "Did you really think I bought the story of you nipping out for cigarettes and coming home to find him dead? If you stick with that, it makes you an accessory, or just possibly the prime suspect. Alternatively, if you speak up for her, then her sentence will be less severe."

Sheila Miller's hand shook as she took a deep, breathy drag on her cigarette. The sleeve of her shirt rode up on her arm and Logan thought he could see red marks on her wrists. His mind went back to the bruise she had attempted to hide with makeup on the day she reported the murder.

"Please don't make me insist on getting you medically examined," said Logan. He pointed. "I'm sure a check of those weals on your wrist might show them to be recent. He was an abuser, wasn't he? He deserved what was coming."

She dropped her arm again on instinct, though she knew the horse had bolted. Then she stubbed out the barely smoked cigarette before her body slumped.

"It was what she said, 'bout being a mother."

Wait! Confirmation she had actually been there when the

murder was committed. Logan, though his mind was working overtime to compute all the new information coming his way, struggled to assimilate that one. By his reckoning there might have been a vigilante, perhaps even the likewise abused daughter, who had come to avenge Kevin Miller's bullying. He had assumed Sheila Miller might have made herself scarce while it happened. He'd been fishing, but this was a potential whole different kettle of the things. She had been in the flat with the murderer!

Before he could ask anything else, Sheila pushed on. The dam, it seemed, had burst. "She seemed to understand – to know – what I've been through…and also how I failed, but at the same time, it was like she stabbed me anyway. And I deserved it. But she was givin' me another chance."

For Logan, the thrill of that disclosure reminded him why he loved being a detective. It struck him now – the extremes to which some men, and their endemic violence, had driven women.

In a tangential moment, he wondered whether he should now abandon all thoughts of ever finding that elusive woman with whom sharing the everyday might become a magical thing. Would all men now be tarred with the same brush? He shook free of the thought before utter depression could take hold.

"What did she say, Sheila?"

"Am I in trouble now?" Sheila Miller put her hands to her face and drew them down across her features in a gesture of utmost weariness.

"No. I'll make sure that you're not. I can say you called me today to retract your original story. In fact, call me, right now, so we have the call log as proof. You can plead trauma. You'll be fine – I'll make sure." He waited till she rang him from her mobile, answered and signalled that they wait in silence for a while to allow for the purported call. When they were done, he looked her in the eyes. "Now tell me what the killer said to you."

She closed her eyes. When they opened, Logan saw in them the afterimage of the dreadful place to which her mind had returned for a bleak moment.

"I can't remember the exact words – I didn't understand all of 'em – but I got what she meant. She told me…" Sheila Miller looked overwhelmed for a few seconds. "…told me that she'd been going to kill me, but understood now that I was also a victim."

Further revelations! Those were not words spoken to someone who was complicit.

"Where were you when she said this?"

Sheila held her wrists out. "I thought you'd worked it out. I was tied to the bed. She did that to me."

Logan's head was spinning a little. Of a sudden, his mind was in Wright's flat. "How did she do that to you."

"Honestly, I don't remember – she hit me when she came in…"

"In the solar plexus…" he saw the lack of understanding in Sheila Miller's eyes and pointed to his own torso, "…just here, in the chest."

"Yes."

Boy, had shafts of light started falling across the dark paths he had been following to this point. "I'm making a leap here, but I assume you were some sort of bait, left to distract…your husband and then…"

One look at her eyes told him he didn't need to pursue that line for now, or rather, he could fill in the blanks. Logan raised a hand of apology. "Sorry, you were telling me what she said."

"It was something about me suffering in silence, but…" Here she hung her head as if in shame. "She said men are brutes and their urges can be understood if not forgiven, but a mother's silence can't be forgiven. She told me never to forget that, and to make a fresh start."

Now a different silence hung in the stale room; one full of remorse and fear. She put her hands to her face again. There they stayed, while a sudden shaking seemed to wrack her body. At last, from behind her trembling fingers, came the sobs.

Logan found himself longing for the presence of a WPC who could sit with the distraught woman, but of course this discussion was outside the usual protocols. He'd got what he came for; now he needed to be away. Did that make him as bad as the others; yet another man leaving damage in his wake? He hoped not.

He rose from his seat; placed a hand on Sheila Miller's shoulder. When her face remained buried he knew it was time to leave, but not before he had texted Pascoe and asked him organise that WPC. Was she grieving for a lost daughter, or a lost life? As far as the latter was concerned, he hoped she would recover well enough to realise that things could move forward now, albeit carrying a burden. Regarding the former; well, he had to remain objective, but this was not the time or place to tell her that Angelina Miller had been on the list of suspects. Now he doubted her involvement – unless Sheila Miller was a supreme actress and they had agreed it all in advance to mislead the investigation, there was no way she would have subjected her mother to this ordeal. Also, surely, they weren't looking at yet another woman who'd mastered a martial art so she could overcome male brutishness. No more weird coincidences!

It was time to solve this farrago of a case, for everyone's sake. After ten lengthy minutes during which Sheila Miller only sunk further into her unshackled misery or grief, Logan spotted the squad car pulling up outside and was free to make his exit and begin hunting that resolution.

Having left the flat without further words exchanged, Logan was straight on the phone.

"Pascoe, call our friends in Torquay. Ask them to make a ranking officer and a WPC available to meet me outside Gill Scott's house in a few hours. Yes, another one! I don't know whether you had a chance yet to check her story for the day Miller was killed… no? Okay, well look, don't worry. I'll ask her myself."

# 20

He was relieved to find the street free from any journalists. On general principles, but also because whoever had spoken with the press before, it seemed it wasn't Pascoe. The little litmus test he had used with the DS when asking him to organise the WPC had shown up as loyalty rather than betrayal: Pascoe knew where Gill Scott lived and that Logan had been heading there now – he could have set the hacks running, but clearly had not.

Detective Sergeant Wimborne's handshake was firm, belying her stature. He found himself wondering whether she, too, was the proud owner of a black belt. She would be a useful ally if Gill Scott turned the wrong kind of physical; he would just leave it to them to fight it out between them. He looked around; saw no WPC. Clearly, in these times of cost-cutting, Wimborne covered all bases.

Taking in a face that was as stony as her suit was sharp, Logan couldn't avoid a twinge of regret; it seemed many of the young pretenders he was encountering in the force nowadays were achieving their goals at the expense of a sense of humour. Ironically that played something of a cruel joke on a prosopagnosia sufferer such as himself; how much harder it was to identify a particular colleague when confronted by rows of stern, emotionless faces atop clothing that also shied away from expressing personal differences. Then again, who was paying the price for that? Had the stifling inequalities of the old school drilled into these new ranks a perception that laughter and ambition were uneasy bedfellows? Such a pity. Still, you reaped what you had sown. He forced his train of thought to stop, because Wimborne's assertively professional features also ticked a good many of the boxes he labelled attractive, and no good could come from continuing that line of enquiry.

"Care to fill me in, sir?" She couldn't have chosen a worse opening line under the circumstances. And did he imagine it, or was it deliberate, because it seemed DS Wimborne looking at him in a slightly confrontational way, almost challenging him to commit the misdemeanour of grinning? He had decided already that sharing humorous thoughts with her would be a waste of time; when they had greeted each other, her smile hadn't reached her mouth!

"I'm here as much in hope as expectation," was his measured response.

DS Wimborne produced a notebook. "DS Pascoe told me you were coming over to ask Miss Scott directly about where she was on the fourteenth of November. As I also checked her alibi for the 10th of November at his request, which stacked up, by the way," she looked Logan straight in the eye; again, did he see accusation there? "are we saying that she's suspected of one, or even both, of these murders, sir?"

"I'm saying nothing, DS Wimborne. We have a blank canvas. Just keep your eyes peeled and tell me anything that rings untrue to your inner ear."

"Will do, sir."

Was she being smug, or were his inadequacies, which this case seemed to be mounting a concerted attack upon, making him defensive? This wasn't good. He felt like he was picking a fight in an empty room.

He rang the doorbell. Talk about out of the frying pan…

They knew Gill Scott was home. He had asked the Devon boys to monitor her movements, and today she hadn't left the flat. What did that tell him on this gloriously sunny afternoon?

The door opened. "DCI…Langan?"

Even if he hadn't recognised the voice or the haircut, the possibility that this was a dismissive greeting would have told him it was Gill Scott. It was either a clever response or that of an innocent woman.

"Logan." He gestured toward his colleague. "Miss Scott, this is DS Wimborne of the Devon and Cornwall Constabulary. I was wondering whether I could ask you a few more questions."

"In relation to Tom's death?"

"His and others." He raised an apologetic hand. "I know that sounds terrible, but…"

"It does. Come in anyway."

He entered first, sparing Wimborne the insult of treating her as anything other than a copper.

A glance around revealed that nothing had changed since the last visit — minimalist or transit camp? — except for one missing object; its absence intriguing, as was the lack of an offer of coffee this time. Gill Scott sat down; seemed to assume that they would too.

"So, how can I help?"

There was something different about her. On the previous visit she had been defensive, but controlled; this time, behind the bravado, there was nervousness, manifesting itself in a tapping of the foot that dangled in the air as she crossed her legs and a dryness of her lips that caused her to lick them — neither had been mannerisms of hers at their first meeting.

"Okay then — to cut to the chase, we have reason to believe that the recent murder of Kevin Miller of Boscawen, Truro, and a brutal, potentially fatal attack on a Mr Alastair Foster of Copton

Farm, Truro, which you may or may not know lies directly opposite your ex-husband's property, were committed by a woman."

"I don't know a Kevin Miller of Boscawen."

Was Gill Scott's lack of any surprise at this revelation a reflection of her confidence in a woman's strength, or an admission of
guilt, whether directly or by association?

"And I never said you did. Nonetheless, I'm here to see whether
you can shed any light; perhaps know a woman who might be
capable of those acts."

Gill Scott stayed silent.

"You'll remember that you were able to help us by identifying
RSM Wright's…" he produced a notebook and read, "nineteenth
century Sudanic African Tuareg, double-edged sword?" He didn't
wait for an affirmation. "This sword is of interest to us firstly
because it was the weapon used to murder Kevin Miller. Secondly
because I have reason to believe it was amongst the things from
your old house that you were keeping for your ex-husband to
collect, and thus in your possession."

In the inscrutability of Gill Scott's face, Logan saw confirmation of his earlier insight; that moment, during his call to Pascoe,
when he had remembered her passing comment about still having
some of RSM Wright's things in storage. This was why he had
kept that information to himself; he had wanted to avoid all chance
of forewarning her so he could see her eyes as she took it in. He
was used to watching closely; defining people by the slightest of
micro-movements in their features, or the even more damning
lack of any physiological response. It had been the slenderest of
chances. Now, he believed in himself again as a detective.

As much as the immobility of Gill's features, Logan had enjoyed
the slight but detectable catch in DS Wimborne's breath as she had
scribbled that fact in her own notebook.

He continued: "As you have made no reports of any theft of the
sword, this necessarily leads us to conclude that Miller's murderer
knew you, and therefore that she might have also been involved in

your ex-husband's murder. On top of this connection, we found links at that murder scene to the assault on Mr Foster."

"Would you like a coffee, DCI Logan?" Gill Scott was out of her seat without waiting for a response. Wimborne twitched, but Logan signalled with his hand for her to remain seated.

"Almost as much as I'd like a conviction, Miss Scott."

"I'm sure." Her words echoed from the kitchen.

She returned with three coffees on a tray. "I remembered how you took yours, DCI Logan."

Logan sipped at the coffee. "Indeed – better than you remembered my name."

She gave a little knowing nod of acknowledgement and sat again, though now somehow looking more composed. "So what leads you to the conclusion that these acts have been committed by a woman?"

He contemplated the cup before continuing. "Well, in the case of Kevin Miller, we have the rather damning testimony of a key witness who said the attacker spoke to her and was a woman. Call me Sherlock…" He sipped again at the coffee. "Then Foster, who is recovering, but not yet out of danger, told me that he smelt perfume on his attacker. There's nothing definitive about Wright's murder, other than that the victim appears to have left a bad taste in the mouth of every woman he's met."

"A more appropriate comment than you might know." The twist of Gill Scott's lips was more akin to a slash in the canvas than a smile. "So, other than me being a female and possibly having had that old sword of Tom's amongst his pile of junk, is there anything that's drawn you to me?"

"Oh, you're just my first port of call, but I'm sure you'll understand why, when I tell you I think the most obvious suspect is one Anna McGinty, formerly known as Lara Wright."

There are certain moments when the body is powerless to

prevent the primal instinct to move; to curl into a defensive ball or shift in a seat. For a man, it is often the sight of somebody taking a blow to the testicles, or observing a stiff-arm head-high tackle in a game of rugby; for a woman, perhaps the sight of a child in distress. How much worse for a mother, hearing that her daughter is a murder suspect. Gill Scott leaned forward. DS Wimborne fidgeted as well, and Logan sensed that this was already a more compelling, challenging test than the young police officer had anticipated.

He carried on: "So I would be very grateful if you could advise me as to her whereabouts."

"Why on earth do you think she's capable of something like this?"

"Well, she was in the country for the few days when these crimes were committed and has just made good her escape." He looked around the flat. "I'm guessing she might even have spent some time here." Once again, Gill Scott's eyes gave her away. "She's changed her name more than once and – call this a wild guess – I would imagine Wright was an abusive father, prompting her original decision to leave you all behind. Shed her skin, as it were. But then one day, she sees that same monster being celebrated in the Commonwealth's war commemorations. That's too much to bear. Justice needs to be done."

"How the hell does that tie her in with this…person from Boscawen, and the farmer?"

"The murders and the attack are clearly linked – but we'll take one step at a time." Logan put down his coffee cup with an intentional heaviness. "We're bringing her in, Miss Scott, for questioning at the very least. She's being watched as we speak."

"But Lara's just a slip of a girl. How would she take on these men?"

Logan pointed towards a bookshelf. "You've answered that question yourself by removing the photograph. A blue belt might not be your sixth dan black, but it still says that the two younger of those three smiling female martial arts proponents pack a punch."

He waited a moment. "Did she do it, Gill?"

Logan felt rather than saw DS Wimborne's head swivel at his use of the first name.

"No."

Gill Scott drained the last of her coffee. As she gave an appreciative look at the empty cup a peculiar expression formed. "I'll savour that as the last taste of decent coffee I'm likely to get for a while…I'm guessing."

Logan had been anticipating this, from the moment he had lobbed the grenade marked *Lara* into the middle of the room. "You mean as opposed to police station and prison coffee?"

She nodded. Again, there was a calmness to her. Perhaps it was relief. "How did you know I killed Miller?" The words were out. Logan tried to remain inscrutable and still his beating heart. "Oh, you don't have to pretend, DCI Logan; I know that's why you threw Lara into the equation – knowing I wouldn't let her take the blame. Well done you."

The squeak of the chair next to him pleased Logan. *Yes, DS Wimborne, sometimes it does take two to tango in this brutish world.*

"To answer your question, Miss Scott, although the words said to Sheila Miller could perhaps have been uttered by a daughter, they carry the ache – the knowledge – of a mother. The regret."

"I hope she learns from them."

"What did you say?" It was DS Wimborne.

Gill closed her eyes and her face was finally relaxed. "I told her that I had intended to kill her too, but I saw now she suffered enough – suffered in silence. I said that men's primal urges could not be forgiven, but they could be understood, if not comprehended. A mother's silence, on the other hand, could not, if it wasn't to protect her child. I told her never to forget that and make a fresh start without that piece of rotting meat I had skewered."

With everything out in the open, Logan leaned back in his chair. Almost unbelievably, he had a confession and felt able to release a little bit of tension in the line with which he had been trying to reel in his catch.

"How did you know about the Millers? Where did you find out about them?" Even as he asked the question, the penny dropped and he put his palm to his forehead. "Of course – Safebeds! Samantha Ingle."

"Do you mind if I have another coffee after all?"

"Um, sure. Knock yourself out." Logan was still a little stunned, both by the calmness of the request and by all the pieces, which were falling onto the table in front of him, some of them still not quite matching.

DS Wimborne rose from her seat and followed the hostess. Though Logan knew she wasn't the suicidal type, he wasn't about to argue protocols having allowed a convicted murderer to make themselves another drink in a room full of knives.

They continued the conversation in separate rooms, though Logan took the opportunity to text Pascoe and ask him to organise a squad car courtesy of the Torquay force.

"Are you saying my guess is correct, Miss Scott? I mean about Safebeds."

"Sam came to me, very agitated, a couple of days after my ex-husband's murder."

"Sam came here?" This was unforeseen.

"You had visited her; questioned her. It seems a combination of my ex-husband's celebrity leading up to the Armistice Celebration, the murder and your questioning tipped her over an edge. She said you were odd, obviously deeply suspicious of her."

Logan took a second to process that one. It was good to know his oddness had at least one positive side effect outside the dating world!

Gill carried on: "It surprised me – shocked me – when she turned up that night. She'd never had much of a regard for me. However, during her visit I found out why. She thought I had been turning a blind eye."

"To what?"

"To the...way my ex-husband was with her; the attention he paid her."

Logan felt his eyes widening. This was something else he hadn't written into the equation. Sam Ingle hadn't struck him as one of life's victims, whatever her anxieties or insecurities. Had he misread her?

Gill returned to her seat, DS Wimborne to hers and Logan continued.

"Are you saying he molested her?"

"I never saw that, as such – but perhaps, subconsciously, I chose to ignore signs. He was, with hindsight, a dreadful, disturbed man and it is to my shame that I ever married him, so perhaps I just closed my mind. I thought – hoped – he might have just flirted with her. She put me right on that score."

Gill squeezed her eyes shut.

Logan paused, weighing up how to ask the next question. "Did he behave in any sort of ...inappropriate way with Lara?"

It was only with a great effort that she opened her eyes again. "I thought not, but now I can't be sure, and that possibility raises images I can't banish. I do know he was a bully and there isn't a day that passes now when I don't beat myself up for not being stronger; just being grateful when his attention wasn't on me. I wasn't as tough as I thought. A martial art can only take you so far."

The three of them took a moment to reflect, perhaps relishing the silence and the absence of pestilential words.

Logan's head was spinning, and not from the caffeine. "So back to the question of Safebeds."

"Ah yes – well, it was a strange encounter; Sam's visit I mean. It became very heated, but also we hugged for perhaps the first time I can remember. She couldn't open up to start with, but she finally managed it by telling me the whole business of my ex-husband's death had disinterred memories of someone she had helped; an instance when she had taken a personal interest in someone disappearing via Safebeds. She told me about a brute; a monster who raped his daughter time and again, while the mother turned a blind eye, grateful not to be the recipient of his attentions. Then she told me it wasn't just daughters, it was nieces too." She looked Logan straight in the eye. "Sound familiar? I don't mean the rape."

"Did she suggest you should…"

"Kill him? No, no, no!" Gill raised a convincing hand of denial. "Despite how she looks, Samantha is a nervous and insecure woman, aware of her appeal to men, but unaware of the true impact she is having in the world. Her story of that girl's fate simply demolished the castle I had built for myself."

"She was also a lawyer, used to achieving results by inference. Can you be sure she didn't use you to wreak a little revenge on her behalf; that she didn't bring the trebuchet with her to knock down those castle walls?"

Both of them thought for a moment and Gill shrugged before continuing.

"Strangely enough, though I wasn't really sure I could go through with anything, I had assumed I would kill Sheila Miller too – I didn't just say that to frighten her. Perhaps I thought it might somehow cleanse me." She bit her lip. "How sick does that make me, I wonder? But anyway, what I saw unfolding in that charnel house they called a bedroom…well, I just saw red."

"But you made it happen. You tied her to the bed, didn't you, and set her up to be abused."

"She deserved it." Her pure brutality shocked Logan. "Angelina had told Sam in lurid detail the things that monster did and how compliant her mother had been, and then complicit by her silence when those same filthy, foul acts were inflicted on her own, his own daughter."

There was silence, but flowing from two very different sources, before Gill continued:

"As you rightly said, I had the antique sword amongst other things in my cellar. It seemed appropriate…a link."

Logan frowned. "To the first murder? Why would you want

to do that? From what you've told me, I'm assuming you had no involvement in Tom Wright's murder."

"It was me."

He stared at her. "I don't believe you – you're covering up for someone…and given the state she was in when she came to you, plus the fact that the whole Armistice commemoration thing had, to use your words, tipped her over an edge, my assumption now is that's Sam…" He paused, gathering his thoughts.

"You're wrong, I…"

Logan wasn't having this and spoke over the top of her, aware DS Wimborne was sitting bolt upright, not quite sure how to deal with this. "…especially given the nature of the crime, which I have always taken to have strong sexual symbolism. To me, she had the utmost motivation to kill your ex-husband."

"No!" There was an urgency in the loud confutation. "It was me."

Fibres snapped in the air. Logan and Gill held each other's gaze for the longest time. Nobody blinked first.

"Why?" asked Logan at last. "You knew nothing for certain about Sam's physical abuse till after Wright's death."

"That one's much simpler to explain. I hated the man and the way he was being bigged up in the press ate at me. Even then, I didn't set out to kill him. I just went to see him. He got aggressive, but he'd clearly forgotten I can look after myself. I wanted to have my say; wanted him to know how it felt to lie there helpless; events taken out of your control by fate. We might have left it there – me having my say with him tied to the bed – but no; he had to be a bully again, even under those circumstances, ridiculing me. Taunting me about other women; about how useless I was in bed." Gill looked straight at Logan. "All of that I could have handled – they were just words – but it was simply the arrogance of the man; the assumption that I wouldn't have the courage to follow through in any way."

The hand that Gill pressed for a few seconds against her forehead was shaking. She gathered herself and continued.

"The next thing I knew, I saw the swagger stick lying there and shoved it into his throat."

"What about Foster?" With doubts buzzing around his head like flies, Logan kept it simple, determined not to express his reservations and, in doing so, give Gill Scott the bricks with which to build another wall around herself.

"That I know nothing about."

"I believe you," said Logan.

"You do?" She looked taken aback.

"But what I don't understand is why you left the sword in Foster's field? At first I thought the killer was somehow taunting us? Standing facing you now, I know that isn't the case. But even you have to admit, it's a weird coincidence that you left it in the very place where the third victim lives."

"But coincidence is all it is. I think I just panicked; thought it might confuse everyone if I left it there, opposite my ex-husband's flat." She paused to consider something. "On reflection, maybe I wanted to link the deaths of those two beasts, even if it meant my being caught. What I have done is not easy for me to live with."

"The thing is… how much of a coincidence is it that the man who lived opposite your ex-husband was assaulted and kidnapped around the time of the murder, possibly just to keep him out of the way? How relevant is it that the attacker left a kind of signature at the place where Foster was found, less than half alive; a signature we believe we found both at Tom Wright's flat and perhaps also at Kevin Miller's?"

Gill said nothing, but then again, what could she have said?

Logan stood. "Gill Scott, you leave me no alternative, but to arrest you for the murders of RSM Tom Wright and Kevin Miller, as well as for an assault on Mrs Sheila Miller. You do not have to say anything, but it may harm your defence if you do not mention when questioned something which you later rely on in court. Anything you say may be given in evidence."

Logan saw the impact of those words on her features, as if all that had gone before – perhaps her whole life – had existed in a bubble, which had just been waiting to burst. Her chin started to twitch, while tears filled her eyes.

DS Wimborne was also now standing and produced her handcuffs.

"Those won't be necessary," said Gill, a hint of panic in her voice.

Logan saw an opportunity. "Sheila Miller might have thought the same about those cable ties."

An ironic smile spread on Gill's face, despite the circumstances. "Nice try, DCI Logan, but I used some manacles I found in her bedside cabinet."

Logan returned the smile, but it was tinged with sadness. "My mistake – I was confusing it with your ex-husband's murder. Strange you took cable ties with you that night when you just wanted to see Tom, but not to Boscawen when you intended to kill two people. Let's also not forget, the tenth was a night for which you have an alibi; a training session at your martial arts club in Torquay, followed by drinks."

She just looked at him – unreadable. "As you said, I do not have to say anything."


As Gill Scott was driven away in the squad car, Logan turned to DS Wimborne.

"I'm off back to Truro," he puffed out his cheeks, "just a little drive of eighty odd miles to see Samantha Ingle again. I'm almost certain Gill Scott was protecting someone, at least as far as the murder of RSM Wright was concerned."

"It was in her eyes, wasn't it?" ventured the DS.

Logan gave her a knowing nod. "Indeed – but not only. Bear in mind those eighty miles I just mentioned. Could she really have driven all that way after a training session and a few drinks?" He considered: "Ok, so say she did, fuelled by a cocktail of adrenaline, alcohol and anger – if that's the basis on which she turned up, if it was a heat-of-the-moment thing, for me, that doesn't square with there being no traces of any other DNA found at the RSM's flat. If she had arrived just wanting to have her say, as she put it, she wouldn't have taken measures to ensure no single trace of her presence could be found."

"And the cable ties, sir, as you pointed out. For the murder she did commit, she went unprepared."

The pair of them stared after the now distant car, lost in similar thoughts, as far as Logan could tell.

Wimborne broke the silence. "Are you saying you think this Samantha Ingle killed RSM Wright, sir?"

Logan puffed out his cheeks. "God knows."

"And the attack on Foster?"

"Even God doesn't know! I'm just hoping Gill Scott's arrest sets some hornets buzzing – and that I don't get stung."

"Any more cases like this, sir?"

Wimborne smiled. Logan wondered whether the resulting transformation in her features was the day's biggest surprise yet. The irony wasn't lost on him – in the world of the facially blind, such moments would never lose their power to rearrange everything you thought you knew.

# 21

A s he and Pascoe climbed the stairs towards Samantha Ingle's flat, Logan experienced a peculiar sense of déjà vu.

"I'm beginning to feel like some hybrid character from Greek mythology, doomed to open doors, behind which lurk various manifestations of a many-headed witch. What will she be today: monster, temptress, sorceress…murderer?"

The analogy had drawn an initial light laugh from Pascoe, but that last word cut it short. Clearly he was also a little confused. "But if Gill Scott has confessed, sir…"

"There's the rub, Pascoe." He saw the DS's blank expression – the Shakespearean reference meant nothing. "I mean I can't shake the feeling that Miss Scott's being less than straight with us."

"The sword links Gill Scott to Miller's murder , but not to her ex-husband's"

"Yes and no. The sword links Miller's murder to Gill Wright, but not to her ex-husband. As for the four ones, they were also present where Foster was imprisoned, and I believe Gill when she says she had nothing to do with that. No, she was visited by our friend here," he gestured towards Samantha's flat, "in a state of agitation. What if she felt guilty about the sins of her Tom Wright that were revealed in that visit, or better put, about being complicit by association and silence? What if Samantha revealed that with all the hero stuff in the press she'd gone over the edge and taken her vengeance, shown RSM Wright where he could stick his swagger? Maybe as well as finding her own beast to slay – Miller – Gill decides to atone by taking the rap?"

"But surely a confession's a confession, sir."

Logan stopped and turned on Pascoe, though he kept his voice down to a hiss. "Don't you want to see justice, Pascoe, rather than a clean book?"

The DS stayed silent, point duly taken. *Hypocrite!* said the bad angel, once again making a long overdue appearance from Logan's past, reminding him of all those blind eyes he had turned, but he brushed it away. That way led madness.

They continued up the final steps. "Then there's this whole, bloody eleven eleven business. I can't overlook it, but I don't understand it. What the hell has Foster got to do with this? Where does he fit in?"

Pascoe started repairing the bridge. "Yes, sir – maybe that's some sort of red herring. There's no apparent connection between him and the others, apart from geographical proximity to RSM Wright."

"Exactly! And if all the killer wanted was a safe place from which to observe the RSM's movements, surely that big, unlit field would have been enough, without resorting to extreme measures. Besides which, the attack on Wright strikes me as having been almost preordained; one which would have been committed on the 11th of November no matter what. And there in his flat we have the damned number connection again with the marks on that photo."

"And the clock at Sheila Miller's place?"

"Actually, I think that's pure coincidence. Anyway…"

They had reached Samantha's flat. As always when in the company of a junior officer, Logan resisted any obvious check of his tie length, or the need to knock with three separate sets of two taps.

The many-headed monster had lost none of its ability to surprise.

Upon opening the door, Samantha Ingle gestured towards her face. "I know how I look. I've not slept well for a couple of days."

Even someone not attuned to the finer workings of human physiognomy would have noticed the slight redness of Sam's eyes and the shadows beneath them, though the lack of any makeup was probably the biggest betrayer of all. Still, Logan was grateful for the sensory switch it had flicked

"I know there's never a good time for a visit by the police, Samantha." Logan stepped inside. He looked across at Pascoe for some guidance, but the latter seemed distracted, so interpreting the comment became a matter of chance. "I imagine things have been more than exhausting. Tell me about it."

"Would you like a coffee?"

Logan sensed the offer was perfunctory. "Thank you, no – I just put one out." He paused for effect. "At your aunt's place."

If Logan had been hoping for another of those moments when the body is betrayed by its reflexes, he was out of luck. Samantha Ingle was a trained lawyer. There was only some knowledge in her tone when she did reply. "Just put one out? Given you've come from Torquay, it must have been strong coffee – and you must have put your foot down."

"Well, I have serious news. That aunt, Gill Scott, has confessed to two murders."

As a riposte, it took some beating. Sam's eyes widened. There was no pretence. Still, her words contained a hint of defiance. "Then surely you should be telling her daughter."

"We would if we could find her." Logan looked around: a studied, overstated gesture. "Any help you can give us with that?"

"If the combined resources of the British police can't find her, I don't know how I can assist."

"I'm flattered you believe that." Logan's grin was sardonic and didn't reach his eyes, which now spotted something. He hoped his distraction hadn't registered with Sam and pushed on for the moment. "But actually we have found her. Our counterparts in Australia are just awaiting the nod."

He allowed the impact of the words to sink in before sitting in an attempt to lower any barriers. As always, Pascoe followed suit. Surprisingly, so did Sam, with a slight slump that, from her, spoke of exhaustion.

Logan knew he had the upper hand; that his next statement would push Sam well and truly onto the back foot, but made sure he maintained a measured tone as he continued: "Your aunt told me you had paid her an unexpected visit. Said you were agitated."

Sam gathered herself together with visible effort. "As I said, it's been a tough time. Certain memories have been dredged from the bottom of the lake where I'd hoped I'd abandoned them weighed down with stones. Please tell me more. What did she confess to? I'm guessing the murder of that bullying ex-husband of hers, but surely not that other lowlife from Boscawen."

Logan sat back. "Funnily enough yes – to both. But my opinion is the diametric opposite of yours. I get the murder of Kevin Miller – as far as I can ever understand skewering another human being with a sword away from active service."

"How so?"

"Well, she told me some of those dredged memories of yours had moved and upset her. Combined with what she saw as her oversights as both mother and aunt, it all proved to be a combustible mix."

"*Oversights?*"

"Oh come on, Sam – don't play me for a fool." He couldn't be sure, but it seemed to Logan the ripping away of pretence was almost a relief to Sam. "You told her…things that her husband had done to you; things she had hidden from, hands over her eyes, fingers in her ears for too long. She felt ashamed and thought that if she could deal out retribution it might make amends somehow. Save another soul. One you had already done your best to rescue – a certain Angelina Miller."

He could almost hear her jaw muscles squeaking as she clenched them. Now he leaned forward. "The thing is I'm not convinced – about her confessing to both murders. I feel she's protecting someone."

Sam said nothing, but her look of surprise seemed genuine; something Logan noted with interest before he continued.

"It's why I've been so keen to know the whereabouts of Lara Wright."

"You don't think Lara…"

"…is capable of changing her identity multiple times, including illegally; slipping back to this country; visiting her mother and her cousin, her former best friend; hearing things that drive her rage to the tipping point where she could commit murder? Well, let's just say I'd be interested in having a talk with her."

The hands of this woman, whom he had observed nailing someone twice her size on a rugby pitch, were shaking. Was this person capable of murder? Was she just scared that the game was up…for someone?"

Logan smiled. "You know what – does that offer of a coffee still stand? I know it's a bit of a cheeky request under the circumstances."

With the merest of nods, Sam headed into the kitchen. Logan could tell she needed to move.

As she disappeared, Pascoe opened his mouth to speak, but Logan gestured with a downturned palm for him to stay silent. He rose with stealth and headed for the object which had leapt out at him when he'd scanned the room. He was intrigued and, if for no other reason than to calm the OCD inside him, he picked up the roll of paper, which was about A3 size in length. It hadn't been there on his previous visits; of that he was sure. OCD was a double-edged sword; blessing and curse for a policeman.

The paper was slightly battered, but surprisingly did not possess the clothlike texture of a much handled document. Next to it on the table lay a ribbon, which he assumed had been tied around it. Some sort of present perhaps? Or a memento? Who had given it to her?

As Logan unrolled it, his pulse thundered in his ears and he felt his mouth go dry.

It was a child's drawing; a particular child – *Lara aged 6* was written in the bottom right-hand corner. Logan saw fields, trees, sky, clouds, filled in with the imprecise, brutal zigzags that often typify a small child's artistry; lightning streaks of colour.

But it was the image in the foreground, the only creature in the picture, which had caught his eye; a horse, or pony – it was hard to tell.

As Logan looked across at Pascoe, he knew his face reflected the lightbulb moment he was having. He gestured the DS across with an urgent, beckoning motion. "Look at this," he whispered.

Pascoe's frowned. "Mr Foster's ponies?" Logan shook his head; tapped the bottom right-hand corner. Now Pascoe's eyes widened "You're thinking Lara was here and gave her this for some reason?"

Logan started to roll the picture up again, but stopped at a very precise point, where a six-year-old's representation of a horse's legs showed as four parallel lines. Now it was Pascoe's turn to stand openmouthed.

"Eleven eleven!" It was an urgent whisper.

"I'm putting ponies and four evenly spaced lines of identical length together. I'm not sure about the eleven eleven thing any more…"

"How do you mean…" Pascoe tried to redeem the disrespectful interruption. "…sir?"

"I mean I am not understanding how it can possibly tie in as a date anymore; how applicable that can be." He glanced towards the kitchen. The clinking of crockery meant a few seconds more. He continued with a lowered voice. "I'm feeling increasingly that the link between the four lines and the date is a very tenuous one;

a misty lane that it's been easy to wander down. After all, as we've noted before, the eleventh of November brings back memories for so many veterans; some good, but many bad. The chances of some vengeful act are high. But the lines on the picture in Wright's flat, the scratches on the trapdoor and now…" he gestured with the picture, "…these lines on the picture, drawn by a little girl – whatever their connections with each other, if any, I just don't see any with the Armistice."

Hearing the sound of footsteps from the kitchen, they hurried back to their seats. Logan kept the rolled paper in his hand; a weapon of as-yet-unknown power, or a damp squib?

When Sam returned to the living room, she put down the tray of coffees and her hand reached for the cafetiere, stopped in mid-reach and was then withdrawn as she spotted the paper scroll. Once again, she seemed to recover her senses quickly.

"Like I said, recent events have been stirring a lot of memories from their resting places. I remembered a picture that Lara drew for me when we were just little girls."

"Sweet," said Logan, "and in its own way potentially pretty damning."

The coffee remained in the pot. With the other things that were brewing, the DCI reckoned he might as well continue.

"Well, at least two things in this …" he brandished the scroll, "connect Lara, to my way of thinking, with the attack on Mr Foster and the murder of her father." He started to unroll the picture again, held it once more at the point where the four parallel lines of the legs showed. "The pony and the four lines, which represent the date of Wright's murder and were also scratched into a door where we found Foster; the date he was imprisoned." Given this somewhat contradicted some of the views Logan had expressed to him a minute before, the DCI was acutely aware of Pascoe's reaction; the surprised turn of the head and a shift forward in his seat. In silence, he urged his junior officer to stay still and curb his less professional instincts. He pushed on: "We may not understand why Foster was attacked, but we believe Lara did it and these four lines support that. As I mentioned, she's being sought out as we speak."

"Foster wasn't imprisoned on that date. It's nothing to do…"

It seemed the words had come out before she could prevent them. The misinformation had worked. The pressure had told.

The three of them stared at each other in silence, until Logan, with the faintest of smiles, said: "Well then would you care to enlighten us? We understand why Lara, or her mother, or you would have killed RSM Wright – I say understand, though I don't condone – but tell me; why was Foster attacked? Where does he fit in? And who did kill RSM Wright?"

# 22

Sam looked less careworn, as if the unburdening was proving therapeutic, but exhausted nonetheless.

"He was a monster and for years I allowed myself to be weighed down by doubt. Had I somehow led him on? Was I flattered in my pathetic teenage way by his attentions?

"Having said that, they'd started before I was a teenager. I'd feel his eyes wandering over me, and pretty soon that activity was taken over by his hands. I know now that the problem – which should never have been left for me to solve – wasn't that I encouraged him, it was that I never discouraged him. Perhaps because my mother, or any other parents, weren't noticing, I assumed this was somehow normal – just some frightening rite of passage.

"The sad part was..." she shuddered, "...the sad part was, when he wasn't there – obviously he was away on active service for long stretches – I sort of missed being the centre of that attention." She gave the two detectives an almost penitent look. "How sick does that sound?"

In the light of their silence, neither judgemental nor conspiratorial, she continued: "That changed forever the first time he..." She stopped again and buried her face in her hands.

Logan glanced at Pascoe, whose jaw muscles were clenching. "Take your time, Sam."

Part of Logan wished to lose himself in empathy, as his junior colleague seemed to be doing; but another, drier part noted that as yet, there had been no confession of criminal activity. They would just have to let this tale unveil itself in the telling.

She looked up through the tears. "When he penetrated me for the first time. I felt just how wrong and sick the whole thing was. But I managed to convince myself, with some encouragement from him of course, that I would never be believed. Besides, he was an intimidating man and I was too scared to talk. He had this dagger, which he threatened to use to cut out my tongue if I ever told.

"Instead, my resentment towards others grew; for their failure to notice without me needing to say. My Mother. My Aunt. My Father, who was already off the scene and had, in any case, seldom been there.

"And Lara – my greatest acrimony was reserved for her." Sam rubbed her eyes. "You see, I tried telling her what was happening, but somehow always fell short of coming clean; perhaps out of embarrassment – of using the words; of describing it all in graphic detail. Perhaps, also, I couldn't quite bring myself to tell another girl exactly what her father was doing."

"Or you were scared of being called a liar?" ventured Logan.

"Maybe I was scared of destroying her life." Sam's features darkened. "But whatever; I told her enough, and she just turned her back on me.

"With no other means of escape, I started to withdraw to another part of my mind. You see, he would wait till Lara was out, or even send her out on some pretext. Then he would take me to her room and do…"

As Sam squeezed her eyes shut, Logan felt powerless. He was here possibly to arrest this woman, but saw in her the blameless embodiment of all the wrong that certain men could do. Silence was, for the moment, his only recourse.

Sam pointed to the roll of paper. "That picture hung on the wall above Lara's bed and I retreated into that safe place; that sanctuary. I allowed my mind to numb what my body couldn't."

And then — the strangest thing: Sam looked at Logan with something like pleading in her eyes, which filled with tears. "Do you…do you think there's a chance that a part of me actually enjoyed what was happening to me? Do you think I didn't tell Lara the full truth because I feared it might stop?"

She covered her face with her hands.

Logan didn't know what to say, nor what to do. Every possible verbal response sounded like a platitude when he rehearsed it in his mind. He wanted to put his arms around her, but simply by dint of being a man, felt he had no right.

"Do you know whether he visited these unwanted attentions on Lara as well?" The question came from Pascoe. Logan could certainly have hugged him; it was absolutely the right thing to say.

Sam appeared to regain her composure. "I don't believe so. She only intimated that she resented the amount of attention in general I seemed to get from him. Yet once I escaped to university, she became the target of his abuse."

"Did she tell you this recently?" asked Logan.

Sam managed a half-smile. "As an ex-lawyer, but more so as her kin, I'm not about to wander into that one."

"But you do realise that everything you're telling us makes you the prime suspect for RSM Wright's murder?"

Her eyes widened. "No! I didn't do it. I thought you said you suspected Lara even though my aunt Gill had confessed?"

"But neither of them would have drawn the four lines that mirror the horse legs from Lara's drawing on that photo. I don't know about Lara, but Gill didn't know all this history until after Wright's death, when you went to see her and told her everything that had happened."

"I admit, I had planned to confront him when all his bullshit became too much for me in the lead-up to the commemoration, but when I saw him standing at that window, with those night vision goggles on, he was such a…spectre, such a monster, I had to run and hide, even after all this time."

Logan nodded. "So that was you in the field."

Sam returned the nod. "As I said, I'd wanted to confront him. It was two evenings before the commemorations. The hero worship in the press had pushed me to the edge. Obviously, I wasn't alone in that." A painful smile followed before she continued. "Don't get me wrong – following the news of his death, I've imagined it gleefully; that it *was* me applying the coup de grâce. Wishing I'd been strong enough. Ever since the details were given in the press, I've pictured what it might have been like to go round there that night and be in the killer's shoes; be able to administer payback for what he put me through; continues to put me through when I lie alone and the lights are out. It's given my treatment of the punch bag extra meaning." She looked Logan straight in the eye. "But no, I'm not a killer."

"So you watched him from Mr Foster's premises. Guess I won't need an extensive search to match the DNA on the water bottle we found after all." Her gaze dropped again. "Was it you who attacked Foster?" Once more there was the merest of nods, and Logan leant in, hungry to bring further order to the disturbing chaos of this case. "Why did you scratch the four lines in the trapdoor when you imprisoned Foster? Was it the symbol of your sanctuary?" No response. "We've found the same signature at RSM Wright's premises."

Logan noted the blank look on her face; had seen it a thousand times on the faces of the guilty while they tried to play innocent, though hers troubled him – her mouth had opened in immediate protest, not in the territory of the actor – the liar – which is a split second later.

"I don't know what you're talking about."

That angered him, despite his sympathy for her. "I told you

before, Sam – don't take me for an idiot. It's hardly a long shot. Forensics have assured me the four vertical lines were scratched very recently, using a knife we found there. Are you trying to tell me it's pure coincidence that the same symbol was drawn on a picture at your uncle's flat?"

The way Sam spread her hands, shook her head and seemed lost for words disturbed him further. Logic dictated that the lines in Wright's flat formed a connection between Sam and Gill Scott only if they had spoken *before* Wright's murder, and he was increasingly convinced they hadn't. Logan glanced at Pascoe, who just returned his look with a tilt of the head. He turned back to Sam.

"Let's go back a step or two. Why did you attack Foster? Was it because of the conditions in which he kept the ponies?"

Sam seemed to jerk out of a trance, and nodded and Logan continued: "It was you who called the RSPCA the next day, wasn't it? You hated seeing them treated that way. It was as if the sanctuary of your troubled young mind, the one Lara had hanging on her wall, your place of refuge while your uncle committed abominable acts, had been defiled."

"I hid with those poor creatures till my uncle finally gave up his watch at the window. They were suffering from severe malnutrition, their ribs poking through, shivering and shaking, seeking some shelter from the wind in that ramshackle structure not worthy of the word 'stable.' One of them was lying down, weak and frail, while the other two stood by like starving angels of death. My anger, my disgust at the state of them fomented while I waited and I guess that, plus my frustration with myself for being a coward just came out. I'd seen a light on, so knew he was in. I couldn't help it – I was drawn to it like a moth. When he answered the door, I hit him flush on the solar plexus – all my love of innocent, abused animals and my hatred of abusers was in the blow."

Both Logan and Pascoe straightened in their seats, so taken aback by the sudden, blunt confession they were rendered silent for the moment.

"Foster was such a skanky, scruffy specimen, much as I'd expected he would be, that he collapsed; out cold."

"No need for a second blow to the jaw, unlike RSM Wright?" asked Logan.

Sam looked at him, her stare disconcerting in its frankness, but ignored the question.

Logan let it ride for now. However, that blow to the solar plexus of Foster, matching as it did the blow taken by RSM Wright, had become another curveball; another misshapen piece in the increasingly complex and confusing game laid out before him.

"I drove like a nun to Pennyweather Farm..."

"Why there?" Logan had to interrupt. In the debris and confusion resulting from the explosion of recent events, the fact that the farm had become a stage for this particular production had not been looked into. Distracted by other things, he had overlooked this. Hearing the name now reminded him of this error.

Sam gave the faintest of smiles. "For the disaffected, disenfranchised, or just doped-up youth of this area, the place has long been a legend. Of course, no one in their teens looking to hang out and enjoy a spliff really knows why the old ruin is there, but as a lawyer, I do now." For a moment, it was as if she put on a white wig and took a trip into her past. "It's unclaimed land; for some time, decades actually, there has been some confusion about who really owns it. There's not really any set procedure for checking into these things if you're planning to try to claim it; you can try checking the Land Registry, asking neighbours. Worst case," she gave another loaded smile, "you need to call in solicitors and all the costs that will entail. I think the residents of that area have enough land without wasting time arguing over a derelict building that comes with a nasty shadow of owner liability hanging over it and an awkward shaped piece of farmland, so they never go there. Perhaps they enjoy the barrier it places between them! Either way, given the..." her smile disappeared, "...trials of my youth, I relished the sanctuary of that old building and the chance to let my world evaporate, if only for a few minutes, in a smoky haze."

As Samantha gathered herself together, it was plain to see how the more recent memories had created a cold wind to counter the warmth of the older ones. "I stuck to the speed limits, but also prayed that the traffic lights would be kind to me. There weren't many, but if I'd had to stop and he'd come around, the noise would have been hard to explain, as would my reasons for driving his Range Rover.

"It was weird – by the time I killed the engine in the stable behind the derelict farmhouse, it felt as if I'd stumbled into some Shakespearean tragedy; all that pathetic fallacy stuff I remember from school, with the stormy southwesterlies matching the darkness in my mind and my actions."

Sam smiled, black humour surfacing now. She couldn't know the chill her description of the Cornish wind had set off in Logan's bones. He welcomed her moving on.

"My attention soon returned to my…let's call him a passenger, who was conscious now and thrashing in the back of the vehicle.

"I forced him out; he fell to the ground with a thump. I cut the ropes round his ankles with a knife I'd taken from his kitchen; dragged him to his feet. He was blindfolded. Even though I'd been in something like a trance when I hit him, that fog was gradually lifting and I didn't want him to know his attacker was a woman."

"Guess you overlooked the residual perfume."

"Ah, so that was your big break." Sam smiled again; strange how peace seemed to be descending – how visibly therapeutic this process was proving. "I grabbed him by the collar with one hand, placed the edge of the blade against his throat and whispered up close – too close with hindsight: "Try to run and I'll kill you."

"Then I marched him forward at knifepoint. I swept his legs from under him so he fell to the floor. Pulling back the battered old rug that I knew hid entrance to the cellar, I opened the trapdoor, cut the ropes on his wrists, and shoved him forward, down into the damp pit. There was a muffled yelp of pain. Something broken perhaps? In some ways I hoped so. Then I carved the four lines on the door."

"Why? Why do that?" Logan was leaning in, face tense as he tried to make the pieces fit. Sam appeared to think about it for a moment. Then, as if the effort of understanding her own actions was too much, she gave a helpless shrug.

"I know you want to find some sort of deep meaning behind that, but I'm afraid it's not something I can give you, at least not with any sense of premeditation. By that point whatever mixture of adrenaline and release was fuelling me had almost run dry. He must have pulled the gag off because I could hear his voice bleating from the darkness: *'Please! Where am I? Help me? Why are you doing this? Please!! Oh God, help me! Please, don't leave me here!'* Somehow hearing this tormentor of innocent animals reduced so quickly to snivelling and whining relit the last embers of my anger. I imagined those starving ponies, unable to voice their own pain. In their silent suffering did I see a pale reflection of my own at the hands of the vile beast that was my uncle? The four lines, as well as answering without letting him hear my voice – you see I was already starting to think like a lawyer again – were the necessary physical expression of that. Maybe they were the bone thin legs of the pony in Lara's drawing – a childhood sanctuary. Perhaps that was when I decided I would leave him there for four days because the marks looked like those made by prisoners in their dungeons or cells. I never truly intended to leave him in that hole. But once you turned up at the sports centre and I sensed you were going to be right onto things, he ended up being down there longer than I'd planned." She raised her hands in a gesture of despair. "I don't know; all I can say for sure is that they symbolised something primal and purgative. Then I just slammed the door shut on him, dropped the knife, replaced the rug and got out of there."

Looking at her now, Logan knew, no matter what had been driving her, it had taken all her willpower to walk away.

She continued: "I needed to act rationally again; do things. It's a long way back to Copton Farm from there. I stepped outside, taking deep breaths, enjoying the paradox of feeling calmer the more the wind blew. I remember smiling, funnily enough. So what if it was a long way. I was fit, wearing a tracksuit – people jog at strange hours. I'd had the foresight to park my car a few blocks from the RSM's flat so no one would see me return.

"It was done. Well, almost. I googled the RSPCA. That night, you harmed ponies at your peril. I looked back at Pennyweather Farm. That bastard would now have time to contemplate the meaning of thirst and malnutrition.

"So, I set off like some night runner of Bengal. I could smell the sea – you know how it is on wild Cornish nights. The wind was howling. I'm not sure whether it was raging against my deed or roaring its approval.

She let her head drop; shook it. "I don't think it was ever my intention to kill him. I'm sorry he ended up being in there longer than the four days, but once you turned up at the sports centre, I was wary of retracing my steps. I didn't know whether you would be watching me, Believe me, I am glad you found him."

"I believe you." Both Sam and Pascoe looked up at Logan. "Why else would you have left the picture of Pennyweather Farm for us to find?"

Now Sam's face lit with a sad sort of smile. "Is that what you thought? You're right that my conscience soon started to get the better of me, but that picture was for him. A reminder. I planned to let him out, but when he got home again I wanted him to spot that and to feel that he was always being monitored. That those ponies, or any other creature ever under his control, would have that watchful guardian that…that I never had." Her voice was a strangled mixture of anger and fatigue, but she still managed a small chuckle. "I had you pegged as an observant one from our first meeting, Inspector, but to have spotted that you must be…I don't know, an OCD savant of some kind."

Logan allowed himself one twirl of his signet ring. He wasn't the only observant one, it seemed!

Sam continued: "When I eventually plucked up the courage to go back, I saw you all there. I hid in the trees. I still don't know what it was that I felt when they switched the sirens on, which told me he was alive." Sam sighed and looked out of the window for a moment, seeming lost in thought. "But he needed to suffer. What was the point otherwise?" She looked back at Logan. "How are the ponies doing?"

Logan shrugged. "Okay, I guess. They were picked up."

"Please check for me, would you?"

"You're a one-off, Sam."

His tight smile wasn't mirrored by her. "You don't get it, do you? There is some innocence that can be saved."

Logan felt a slight reddening and with peculiar detachment noticed that he was spinning his signet ring again. Time to return to the matter in hand. "So, back to those four lines you scratched. You do realise that the same symbol was found at your uncle's flat …"

"Which I had nothing to do with."

He spoke over her interruption. "…which potentially links you with both crimes?"

"Or someone else."

Logan raised his hands in exasperation. "You've just confessed to one of them, goddammit! Plus, the fact that you admitted being in the field watching Wright."

"Not the night he was killed."

"Who are you talking about then, who's the *someone else* – Gill Scott? Are you covering for her? It doesn't fit. Why would she attack Foster…unless, of course, he witnessed her killing the RSM? Or is she a big animal lover too?"

Sam opened her mouth to speak but thought better of it.

"Or are you covering for Lara?" continued Logan. "Yes, that makes sense and it's why I was here in the first place. After all, she's the one who's behaved most suspiciously in this whole episode by coming all the way from the other side of the world and staying invisible. I happen to think Gill Scott is the one protecting some-body, as I've said before. If that's the case, who would that be if not her child?"

He saw in the coiled spring of her body that he was pushing her to the limit, but that went for both of them. He felt he'd been bending in circles for days like a bloody slinky in his attempt to make sense of what exactly had happened. It was maddening. This confusion, this disorder was everything he loathed about being a detective, yet at the same time resolving them was the very fuel for the engine that drove him to be one.

Logan rose from his chair with a sudden movement that seemed to startle both Sam and Pascoe. He sensed rather than saw their surprise; knew that two pairs of eyes were watching him. This was becoming as frustrating as hell. If the truth was unveiling itself, it seemed to be wearing a mask. As revenge for being abandoned, the lines of his beloved Venn diagram were circling him like some cartoon depiction of a blow to the head; the only things missing were the little birdie noises and stars.

He took a deep breath, shoving his hands in his pockets to prevent them betraying his agitation.

Okay, unsatisfactory though it was, he would settle for what he had – for now. For many a detective, this would have been a good day's work – confessions to both murders and the assault. Cases closed; top brass delighted.

If only. He never closed any case that wasn't neatly packed like the hand luggage for a budget flight!

He sensed he was still being lied to, but by whom?

He turned. "Very well, for the record, I'm truly sorry for the repeated ordeals you suffered at the hands of RSM Wright. It is my sincere hope that they will provide mitigation in the courts for what followed…but, Samantha Ingle, I am arresting you for the aggravated assault and kidnapping of Alastair Foster of Copton Farm, Chadstow…"

His words were drowned out by his own thoughts, as her face told him the sudden story of all he needed to know. It spoke of her innocence, of the murder at least. It gave him no pleasure to arrest her, but already it had provided a waymarker. This wasn't over.

She tried to stand – but didn't seem to have the strength. Logan signalled to Pascoe, who came forward with what appeared to be reluctance to fit the handcuffs to the perpetrator, which was how Logan needed to think of her for now, for the sake of remaining objective. There was an angry buzzing in the air; he had applied that kick to the hornets' nest. Enough of being messed around.

"Pascoe, contact our friends in Australia. Have them bring in Lara Wright, aka Anna McGinty, aka whatever identity she's assumed now."

"But sir, haven't we…"

"Just do it, DS Pascoe." He knew the elements which other people unified into his face brooked no contradiction. "We'll talk about it down at the station."

Sam appeared to have found some strength in her vocal chords at least. "What's Lara got to do with this if you have your confessions?"

He ignored her; shook his head. "What a bloody family! Just like you a few minutes ago, I feel like I've blundered into a Shakespearean tragedy. "I wish I was a writer. I could make a fortune out of this."

# 23

The two of them sat staring at the whiteboard.

"Like fucking Little Big Horn," said Logan as he took in all the arrows flying in different directions.

Pascoe spoke up. "I don't mean to be disrespectful, sir, but why all the negativity? One way or the other, as far as the powers-that-be are concerned, you've nailed the perpetrators."

"Have I?" Without even looking over, he knew what Pascoe's expression would be. "For Gill Scott at least, it's the difference between her being a double murderer or someone moved by emotion and a disturbed mind to kill a child rapist. Even allowing for mitigation, she's going to jail, but perhaps not for too long a stretch. I remain convinced that she is protecting someone." Now he looked across. "Your news about Lara would seem to support that."

"They still haven't located her, but she definitely boarded the flight."

Logan slapped the table and pointed. "You see! If hers isn't the behaviour of someone on the run, then what is?" He glared. "Find her, Pascoe. Tell them to bloody bring her in."

"Aren't we overlooking the fact that Gill Scott might actually have committed Wright's murder, sir? You seem determined to believe her confession is false, but worst case scenario we…"

Pascoe's observation trailed to a halt. They had been down this road before. There was a difference between justice and closing the file.

Logan took an absent-minded sip of coffee. "Well, I just can't shake the conviction – no pun intended – that Samantha Ingle is hiding something too, though I'm sure she's not a killer. I know I'm not the best judge of women…

"What do you base that on, sir?"

"What, my lack of judgement about women?"

They smiled, sharing a lighter moment before Logan continued: "She – Sam – might be physically fit, and I know she had all the motivation she needed, assuming what she told us today was true, but psychologically she's damaged and weak. Sure, she's capable of decking someone on the rugby pitch, or the measured physicality of a martial art, but only when it's an accepted part of the rules. Outside of that I just don't see aggression towards others as part of her makeup. Gill Scott is clearly stronger in mind, but I don't know. It was just the way she confessed – as if she stepped in to take the rap."

"I think Foster would disagree with you, sir – about Samantha, I mean."

Logan tilted his head in acknowledgment. "True enough, but whether she's capable of murder…she reacted to the treatment of another living being, not for reasons of personal vengeance. Plus, that attack was a reaction to her own failure to see through her plan to confront Wright. I think what she did to Foster would have drained her. Even reliving it was taking its toll. I can't see her returning to the same place the next night and going through with a premeditated attack on a man she admits terrified her. The attack on Foster was born of instantaneous distress."

As the pieces continued to refuse to fit together, Logan once again had the sudden need to be alone. He might have told Pascoe earlier that he was a useful sounding board, but right now the echoes were disturbing him and he found himself in need of the grand gift of silence. The dissatisfaction with this case's conclusion was prickling him.

Bloody women! They were like The Furies, cursing his every move in life. It may not have been a logical thought. It certainly wasn't a politically correct one; but it was how he felt.

He turned to Pascoe.

"Find Lara Wright."

He made the slightest of gestures with his head towards the door, saw that it rather threw Pascoe, who sat for a moment, as if confused by his sudden dismissal, before heading on his way.

Staring at the whiteboard again, he wanted to smash his fist through it. What was he missing? Was something lurking there in plain sight? Usually, this rectangular, two-dimensional world of melamine helped him to simplify the complexities of the universe he shared with others. He looked at the scribblings where, once upon a time, he had considered whether this was a vengeful crime by ex-squaddies. Had he missed something there? Had Pascoe? Logan wondered whether his own obsession with the dysfunctional triumvirate of Gill Scott, Samantha Ingle and Lara Wright had distracted him. After all, who was he to label any family *dysfunctional?*

However, deep down he remained convinced somebody in that family was hiding something to protect someone.

Back to the possibility of suspects from the army. It all seemed to hinge on whether Wright's newfound local celebrity status had acted like a poultice, drawing old wounds to a head and inspiring some bullied squaddie to finally act after all the intervening years. It just seemed too simplistic an explanation for a series of events which Logan remained convinced had complex connections,

He sat up straight. The attack on Foster had been shown as a random crime brought about by the ill-treatment of ponies. What connected the other two? Kevin Miller had no military connections and so it surely put paid to that angle.

Child abuse. Cut and dried.

But what about the four ones? He'd been trying to avoid getting sucked into that sphere because it was a connection that blurred more than it clarified…and yet even with that motif from Foster's prison door removed from the equation the bloody enigma of eleven eleven still nagged at him. The stopped clock in Miller's flat showing 11:11. Wright's murder on the 11th of the 11th, and then those four lines drawn on the regimental photo. It made less sense than ever, but he couldn't get out of his head that there was some message there. One he couldn't read. He believed those symbols would haunt him till he died; an unwanted, mocking addition to his catalogue of compulsions.

Grinding his jaw, Logan rose from his seat, picked up a cloth and went to erase Bovis' name. Something stayed his hand; perhaps just a copper's instinct. He disliked the idea of removing any thread from this tangled web and placing his hopes in the hands of fate. You couldn't untie a knot if you didn't have hold of all the strands.

Now his eyes flicked towards a recent addition to the board, where he had written *Falklands connection*, his way of referencing the photo in Wright's flat with the four lines drawn on it. Perhaps engendered by his own obsessiveness, Logan found a sudden, perverse pleasure in the balance of the three other squaddies and three wicked witches. Maybe there was a conspiracy. Had all of them colluded in the murder of the RSM, but then other matters had got out of hand?

But what other matters?

Something brought him up with a jolt. Outside blood ties – yet another in a series of apposite word choices during this case – did any of the women have any link with soldiers? What if Gill Scott, for example, had met, say, Bovis, and ended up having a fling with him, back in the day? Wright finds out, bides his time and takes it out on Bovis somehow. Years later Gill Scott finds out and exacts revenge on Wright. The pleasure of potential was ephemeral. Wright was a bully, according to family and colleagues. Presumably he would have psychologically tortured many a squaddie in his time. And would Gill Scott then go on to kill again, reliving her triumph over her demonic spouse with Kevin Miller?

No! Logan shook his head angrily. The flame of his instinct was still lighting a particular path. One of the threads, one of the witches, was missing. Finding Lara Wright was still hugely important. He just knew it.

Where the fuck was she!?

# 24

It was always bizarre to hear the dulcet tones of a newsreader summarising, in that succinct, emotionless manner, the details of a case in which you had been involved till it drained you and of which you had such intimate knowledge – the more so, when a nickname coined as part of police banter entered public consciousness.

*"In a bizarre twist to the case known in the media as The Armistice Killer, involving the murder of the war hero, former Regimental Sergeant Major Tom Wright, police have arrested his niece, the one-time barrister Samantha Ingle, in connection with an assault on Mr Alastair Foster of Copton Farm, a neighbour of Wright. This follows hot on the arrest of Wright's ex-wife, Miss Gill Scott, for the murders of the RSM and Kevin Miller of Boscawen, Truro, though as yet no connection has been made between Wright and Miller other than the proximity of their homes and the particularly violent nature of the two killings, both men having been found impaled on their beds. Devon and Cornwall Police have said that…"*

Pascoe tuned out the broadcast and raised his beer bottle in the direction of the screen.

"What this particular unit of the Devon and Cornwall Police says is cheers and good riddance. Here's to ridding the world of sadistic bullies and paedophiles."

He raised the bottle again in the direction of a picture on one of his bookshelves. "And here's to you, Uncle Lol; a true hero. I'm only sorry the death of these fuckers has cast a shadow over the real warriors. Still, at least the truth about Wright will come out during the trial. Guess we'll call that a Pyrrhic victory, to continue the DCI's beloved historic references."

He smiled. Uncle Lol had been right about the rumours of bullying and cruelty; about the corrupt salute which had taken the form of fingers on lips from the higher ranks; the covering up of one man's excesses to prevent besmirching the armed services. He had never doubted his uncle, but there was enough of the policeman in Pascoe to have wanted to see the evidence for himself. Or rather hear it firsthand. Lawrence Pascoe had been the most honourable of men; an old-fashioned soldier. He'd believed it would be enough for young Andy to present to the upper ranks the names of the three men and a description of the terrifying indignity of Russian roulette they'd suffered – but of course it wasn't. He'd been warned; the cabal would close ranks.

The piece of paper had been put in a drawer. Time had passed. New horrors replaced the old.

But again, the detective in him hadn't quite been able to let it pass. The drawer had been opened again.

He reached down and picked up the note. Pascoe's features darkened as he read it; firstly, because it brought back the vivid images of his uncle's passing – the tremulous voice asking other members of the family for a few moments with his nephew, and the even shakier hand, which had passed the note to him in secret – but also because…

*How he wished he could deny it, or close his mind to it*

…that very clandestine action had brought home to him an irrefutable truth; his uncle, through his silence, was as complicit in this matter as any other officer; something that had been borne out by his saying nothing until the day he died. Even in the note, written at a time when surely it mattered not what the upper ranks or powers-that-be thought, there was an element of obfuscation and blurring. It seemed loyalty to the army was Lawrence Pascoe's hamartia. Some may have believed he died of his wounds received in Helmand, but was there also an element of a broken heart? Or did he believe that all the soldiers who died as a result of flawed leadership were waiting like demons for those who gave the orders, so it was important to hide one's guilt.

Yet right at the end – of his life and the note, which were almost intertwined – it seemed Uncle Lawrence might have seen the light. Pascoe reread the last line now in an appropriate silence: *Nephew – Andy – see justice is done, in whatever way you can.*

And so it was that Pascoe had contacted Bovis a short time after his uncle's death – an objectionable man in many ways; the sort probably saved from a life of crime by the existence of the army. Yet that had made things all the more poignant; seeing the impact of Wright's bullying in Bovis' eyes. You couldn't fake that sort of recall. Pascoe had shared with him, for just a few minutes in a quiet English pub, images of horror which had reduced that tattooed mass of muscle to a brittle imitation of himself.

And there had been nothing Pascoe could do. Time passed and so, to some extent, did the anger. Yet he had pledged to himself he would protect the fragile beast that was Bovis, likewise his comrades-in-arms, from any mention in whatever form justice took. So what could he do?

Appropriate then, that war, or at least the commemoration of it, had presented the opportunity. If RSM Tom Wright had just kept his head down in the trenches, if he hadn't decided to soak up the adulation that should have been for others, and reap the temporary celebrity of the Armistice centenary to buy into the mythology of himself, he would probably still be alive. The pretence and showboating had angered another man, one anonymous colonel, enough to break ranks in the aftermath of Wright's death and ensure that, if nothing else, at least one person outside the armed services would know the truth. When the names he'd written on a beer mat had tallied with the ones on the list in Pascoe's possession, the young DS knew just sentence had been passed. There was a sense of relief. Of vindication.

But no peace.

Sitting outside the RSM's flat that night, he'd had no plan; certainly no intention of killing anyone. He didn't have it in him.

He was almost sure of that.


### One week before

It was all quiet on the Western Front – to coin what seemed an appropriate phrase – but not in the battle with his conscience; that most unforgiving of enemies. Nor in the elements, which seemed determined to spook him, with strong winds finding fissures to whistle through even in the almost hermetically sealed Volvo.

He had lost track of how long he'd been sitting in the car, but in due course a glance at his watch showed him that it was, indeed, Armistice Day. The lights were still on in the RSM's flat, but it was just possible now that the flame of battle had gone out in Pascoe's soul. Was he really going to cross swords with the local hero? What was he going to say? What had he ever been going to say? He accepted that the chances of him confronting Wright were almost zero.

And confront him with what? That he had stained the memory of Pascoe's uncle? Who would care, apart from Pascoe himself? That he had bullied three squaddies who were already terrified? War engendered strangeness; rewrote the rules – the laws of civility. Of civilisation.

Doubt and indecision were his fellow passengers now, occupying the back seats and filling the space with silent mockery.

Words from Wilfred Owen's *Dulce et decorum est* came to mind – *an ecstasy of fumbling* – as he rolled a clumsy cigarette. He was finding it tougher to sit here than at any time on any previous stake-out, perhaps because, on those occasions, there had always been a cut-and-dried definition of crime and punishment. What was the crime here; arrogance; injustice; bullying?

Pascoe threw open the door of the car; stepped out into the threatening windswept darkness of the Cornish countryside. He could almost smell the salt tang of the sea, even this far inland. It wasn't often that he smoked, so when he lit the rather misshapen cigarette, needing several attempts as the high winds compounded shaking hands, the headrush caused him to lean back against the car. He glanced at the lit upper windows, now seen through an appropriate fug of smoke and jumbled thoughts.

Every sense tipped onto its edge again at the sound of the footfall.

Not wanting to be seen loitering here at the back of the cottages, he leaned into the trees, throwing down the cigarette and praying that the smell of smoke wouldn't give him away – though his hasty orison, to borrow again from Owen, was unnecessary given the strength of the wind had almost carried the cigarette away, never mind the smoke. A security light on one of the garages was triggered and he crouched behind the car.

When the slight crunch of gravel told him that the new arrival had turned in towards the cottages, he risked a glance and knew straight away, this was not a resident; the way the tall, athletic figure was coiled in a cautious crouch, hesitant in step; the way it stopped, as if checking this was the right address.

A visitor at gone midnight – interesting.

The figure, clad in black, features and head hidden by a combination of woollen hat and hood, moved now in complete, stealthy silence up the iron staircase that led to the RSM's front door. Pascoe was grateful for the chance to focus on something other than his own doubts; be a policeman again, rather than a skulking ghost. Every fibre in him was alert, stretched by the certainty that a crime was about to be committed.

Could this be one of the triumvirate of squaddies, driven by similar outrage at the injustice of things? If so, then it wasn't Bovis; wasn't stocky enough. Pascoe had never met Penney or Bullard.

There was the lightest of taps on the door. Pascoe moved forward, taking extreme care not to let his weight draw protest from the gravel. As he reached the bottom of the steps, light fell on the porch above him and he moved out of sight behind the corner of the building. He heard growled words: "*What the fuck?*"

Pascoe felt, almost, rather than heard a sudden movement. There was the stifled choking splutter of breath being knocked from a body. Then silence. He took his ID from his inner pocket, which felt surreal given his intentions when he'd arrived some hours ago, and climbed, equally silently, to the top of the steps.

The door was still ajar and stepping up to it he saw a body on the floor of the hallway. It was sliding, pulled by the intruder, who was bent over it and who, on seeing Pascoe dropped the shoulders he was heaving. He made an initial lunge for the doorway, perhaps for Pascoe, but the DS had just about recovered quickly enough from seeing that 'he' was in fact a 'she' and lifted his hand, showing the badge.

"Uh-uh! Police!" he cautioned, trying to hide any panic.

The intruder still appeared to consider for a moment whether she could deck him before her shoulders slumped.

Pascoe was surprised to hear an undertone of humour in her voice. "Aw, guess you got me bang to rights." There was a hint of an Australian accent.

"Guess I did. The question is why and who are you?"

A stubborn silence. Pascoe reached for his phone and she raised her hand, all defiance gone.

"Please...don't! Just let me explain first."

Pascoe looked at the body. "Is he...?" She shook her head. Nevertheless, he ordered her to back away and then crouched by the body, placing his index and middle fingers over the carotid artery.

The woman answered before his fingertips could. "Oh, he's

alive…unfortunately." It seemed her courage was returning.

"Well then the least I need to do is call an ambulance." He lifted the phone again.

Once more there was that flip from deadpan humour to pleading. "Really, he's fine. I know how to hit."

Pascoe looked at Wright again and raised an eyebrow. "Evidently." He puffed out his cheeks. "Well let's at least move him somewhere comfortable."

He reached into his pocket and produced a pair of latex gloves. Well, it was a crime scene after all. To his amazement, she said: "Do you have another pair?" She showed him the backs of her hands, also gloved. "One of these just split."

Without questioning and, in truth, finding himself both intrigued and perhaps a tiny bit entranced by her, he handed her his second set.

With great effort they manoeuvred Wright's deadweight through the flat and into what looked like the main bedroom, where they laid him on the bed. All the time, Pascoe was tense, not just by dint of it being a crime scene with which he was technically interfering, but also because he knew one well-aimed blow from her would render him away with the fairies. Nevertheless, a thought made him smile, despite himself.

Curiosity got the better of her now. "Why are you grinning?"

"Oh, just the thought of waking from a blow to the head to find myself in bed with RSM Wright."

She burst out laughing, staggered back on weakened legs, but then put her hand to her mouth. "We need to be quiet," she said. "I don't know what the soundproofing is like in this particular renovation."

With that, she moved past him into the living room. He watched her carefully, heard the TV being switched on, followed by a babble of voices as she flipped through several channels before settling on some late night chat show, which appeared to have redefined chatting as talking over the top of everyone else. Pascoe had to admire her cunning.

"I lived in a place like this myself," she said as she returned to the bedroom. "Hearing my chavvy neighbours rowing, DIY-ing and screwing, in all senses, put me off these cottage conversions for life." Her features grew wistful. "Put me off screwing too…but thereby hangs a tale."

"You seem to be assuming you're not going to be arrested for this assault! The neighbours hearing something is surely not your main concern."

She gave him a forthright look. "No, that would be you I guess, detective. But then, we don't really know why you're here either, do we?"

As trump cards went, it was perfect, as was her timing.

Feeling somewhat powerless in the aftermath of her insightful comment about his own motivations, thrown by her cool acumen in this furnace of activity, Pascoe could only watch open-mouthed as she produced cable ties from her pockets and began to secure the unconscious man's wrists to the iron headboard.

"What the hell?" Now he stepped forward, still rather nervous about tackling her and confused by his own failure to call for backup.

"He'll be coming round soon." She didn't break off from her activity. "I said I'd tell you everything and I will…through him. Trust me. Please."

For whatever reason, he did. She finished the wrists and moved to fasten Wright's ankles to the foot of the bed; Pascoe continued not to prevent her. Then she spotted something and picked up a pair of night vision goggles, which she fixed in place on her prisoner.

"What are you doing that for?"

"I don't want to see his eyes. I want him dehumanised, so I can say my piece."

While Pascoe just shrugged, she started to slap the RSM on the cheeks, though there was a contradictory gentleness to the action. As predicted, he began to come round, coughing, seeming to choke.

"Quick," whispered the woman. "Please trust me. Just listen from the other room. You'd be just as able to prevent me leaving from there as well, if I try to make a bolt for it…which I won't."

Pascoe crossed to the window, shut it, found a little key on the sill and locked it. He smiled. "Just in case."

The woman reached into her pocket, produced a smartphone and gestured with it. "Just in case," she repeated and proceeded to activate the voice recorder app. Without thinking, Pascoe went to speak, but she put her fingers to her lips, laid the phone on the floor by the bed and then gestured for Pascoe to leave.

Then he did indeed step into a neighbouring room, presumably designed as a cramped second bedroom, but converted into some sort of regimental museum. He waited, doubting her silence, while the RSM's choking and coughing continued.

At length, that subsided. There was a series of sounds; violent jerks; the panic movements of someone regaining consciousness to find himself tied up. "What the fuck!? What the fuck!?"

If Pascoe's blood ran cold at the sound of the next word…

"Lara?"

At the revelation that Wright knew his attacker, it froze to bloody glaciers at the response:

"Father."

★★★★

He listened in horror.

The conversation was punctuated by occasional light footfall – he assumed Lara pacing in agitation on the carpeted floor – or the clanking of cable tie against bedframe as Wright threw whatever strength he had into trying to break his bonds. The episode was rendered all the more surreal by the vacuous tones emanating from the TV as the studio guests became increasingly peeved and waspish. Nevertheless, it provided perfect cover, as if Lara had made a pact with the devil.

Under any other circumstances, Pascoe would not have believed he could be in as much discomfort as the protagonists, but his very presence there, allied with his failure to step in and perform his duty as a policeman, left him squirming.

Yet, when all was said and done, the combustible nature of what he was hearing helped him silence his conscience.

"C'mon Lara, let me go."

"What – so you can slap me round a bit, like before? Part of me would like to see you try. But I know now – looking back, I'd have taken a thousand beatings from you if they'd prevented what you did to Sam."

"I don't know what you're talking about."

"Yeah, well, I never used to believe her either, to my lasting shame. I was probably jealous of her. In awe of her. Oh, not for that! Jealous of the attention. I didn't understand for years what exactly that attention entailed. I just stuck my fingers in my ears and failed to confront it. She seemed to have a hold over you."

"So your cousin loved me – so what?"

"Loved? Hah! A good euphemism, coming from you." There was more silence; more light footfall. Perhaps Wright recognised the danger he was in, because he didn't break that silence.

At last, Lara continued: "She told me all the…" the next syllable was drenched in clammy disgust, "…acts…you made her commit. God, it's no wonder mum taught us to defend ourselves. Only it was too late for Sam – she was already too terrified; too in thrall. Did mum, just by being a decent woman, make you feel so inadequate, emasculated, that you took it out on Sam?"

"Rubbish! You really believe that – of your own father? She's making it up." There was no word spoken by the RSM that wasn't tinged with panic, despite his dismissiveness.

"Yes, I do. It took a while till I was mature enough to recognise how she was broken in spirit; see beneath the beauty to find the beast you'd created."

"I've had enough of this. Let me go."

"How many times to do you reckon she thought that?"

"I'm your father, for God's sake."

"Yes, heaven help me. But God has nothing to do with you, or this night."

Pascoe was tempted beyond temptation to peep round the door and observe this dialogue, but he was scared he would give away his presence. He stood, jaw clenching and unclenching.

"Both of us ran from you. Sam told me once, when running was still just the dream of a young girl, that there was a picture on my wall and she would retreat into it; let her mind run away while her body let her down. It was a field with a pony. She said that pony, with all its gloriously innocent lack of artistic perspective, is seared indelibly into her mind, onto her retinae, as a symbol of good in the midst of evil."

"She used to say I was hung like a pony."

Pascoe could tell by the protracted silence that Lara had been stopped in her tracks; shaken to the core, like Pascoe himself, by what amounted to a sudden and shocking admission; as if Wright had decided enough was enough. If he was to be hanged for a lamb, or pony, he might as well be hanged for a sheep. The heartless laugh that followed was an even bigger disgrace.

Wright seemed to gain strength from the silence. "War does strange things to a man. You see humanity differently, once you've seen them try to wipe each other from existence. Few men come back undamaged."

"Bullshit!" Lara's hissed response echoed Pascoe's thoughts as he remembered his uncle. For sure, war took a sorry toll, both mental and physical, on many men and women; and it was they who were being celebrated and commemorated in ceremonies later that very day, partly also to make up for the shameful way many had been neglected in less enlightened times. But a man should never lose his core humanity.

"You wouldn't understand, little girl. But Sam understood. She was always older than her years. She came willingly enough – in all senses of the words." It seemed Wright was on a roll, determined to turn the tables. He'd had enough of being the victim this night and was lashing out. There was just a glimpse of the man Bovis would have both followed and feared.

There was a movement, followed by a threatening, hissing whisper from Lara: "Oh, if only I had the strength to smash your face to pieces with this now, I would. You effectively kidnapped her childhood, you bastard. She was more or less suffering Stockholm Syndrome. When I saw you on the internet, lording it in the press, I had to come back. The world needs to know what a viper it's been so keen to embrace."

"You can talk all the psychobabble bullshit you want, my girl…"

"Don't *my girl* me!"

"…all your Stockholm Syndrome crap. She was a slut, from young. Up the arse. In the mouth…"

"Like this, you mean!"

There was the sound of choking and thrashing. Pascoe stepped out. If what he found shocked him, that was nothing compared with the impact his sudden reappearance had on Lara, who appeared to wake from some nightmare. She looked at the swagger stick, which she was driving into her father's mouth, let go of it and stared at her hands, still clad in the latex gloves, which she now peeled from her hands in clumsy haste and cast aside, as if they represented contaminated skin. The stick was still lodged in the slavering mouth of the RSM, whose veins bulged in his head and neck. The nightmarish vision was added to by a pair of night vision goggles he was wearing.

Lara staggered back, looking openmouthed at Pascoe. "Oh my God! I nearly…"

Pascoe stepped forward and put one knee on the bed. "Yeah, well nearly isn't good enough." He grasped hold of the swagger stick and addressed Wright. "Oh, by the way, this is also for Bovis, Penney and Bullard – remember them?"

Despite the bravado, Pascoe was unnerved. If Wright has stayed silent, the DS might not have found the strength to go through with it. Instead, the word he tried to utter condemned him, distinctive despite the obstruction in his mouth.

"Cowards."

With that, Pascoe pressed down.

Then, out of the corner of his eye, he saw Lara step forward. Dismayed, he stopped, struck suddenly by the enormity of his actions and what he was condemning her to witness. Bottom line, this was her father. He turned his head towards her.

They exchanged a look. She walked past.

He heard the front door open; close again softly.

Throughout those charged seconds, the one constant had been the thrashing of the RSM. A few more seconds of pressure and that ceased.

When he was sure it was done, Pascoe climbed off the bed. His foot kicked something and he looked down to see Lara's phone still recording. An act of forgetfulness on her part, or one of extreme trust? He picked it up, flicked it off and stared at this small piece of hardware before pocketing it. It was now a repository for an inhuman act committed by two people, or perhaps one that was all too human. Part of him would have loved to see Wright flayed in a court of law and in the media for his confessions. Now, he would just be a veteran brutally murdered on Armistice Day. His legend would grow. If the recording could be redacted...

He looked again at the bed and had a sudden understanding of just why Lara had put the goggles on Wright. Pascoe could not have begun to think about the next step if those dead eyes had been watching him, accusing.

What had he done? It was for the common good, but it could never be good.

What had he done?

The time for answering that question would come. Now, though he wasn't trained in forensics, Pascoe did all he could to clean the scene, working quietly, trying to ensure there were no footprints or imprints on the carpets and floors, wiping the stick to remove any traces of Lara, though the gloves, which he also remembered to pick up, meant there would be no fingerprints. A bit of dirt from outside could as easily have been brought in by the victim and would be expected. Using the flashlight app on his phone, he scanned in minute detail for hairs. Lara had worn her hat the entire time, so his bigger fear was that traces of his own DNA might be found. There was no way he could preempt the discovery of the body and be first on the scene.

He would have to trust in fate and the sharpness of his eyesight.

Once he had done what he could, he switched off the TV, which had continued to provide an almost nightmarish soundtrack to events. Then off went the lights and he waited, trying not to move much and chastising himself any time he felt the urge to scratch his head, or dig at his nose, though he couldn't prevent a macabre grin spreading at the thought of being nailed by DNA from a stray bogey.

He stayed by the study window, which overlooked the front of the flat, glancing through the curtains, seeking any signs of movement outside. There was nothing. Darkness covered the world; the kingdom inside the flat was ruled by the silent figure lying in the other room.

At 3 a.m. he deemed it safe to leave. There would be no passers-by and it seemed the attempts to mask any sound or activity had been successful, as the neighbours had clearly not alerted anyone. If anyone had been curious about anything, they appeared to have given up the ghost.

An unfortunate phrase.

On exiting the flat, Pascoe had to pull the front door shut. To his guilty ears, it sounded like the gates to Hell had slammed. He had never killed a man before.

He trod with extreme caution down the iron steps, wanting to run, but needing to take his time. The security light came on and he felt for all the world like an escaping felon caught in a prison spotlight. He had to hope the occupants of the other flats were now in a deep sleep. At least the light enabled him to tread with care across the gravel, though he made sure to stay on the stones, not leaving footprints in the softer ground at the edges of the path.

Back in the lane that ran behind the cottages, he headed towards his car, relieved that he had left it in a secluded spot from which he could see the flat but not be seen. He glanced round, but saw no lights.

On Armistice Day, Pascoe had blood on his hands.

Perhaps it was this stark knowledge that caused his stifled cry when a figure stepped towards him from the shadows.

### One week later

The woodburner wasn't warming him anymore. He glanced at his uncle's portrait; knew that he wouldn't have approved of the ultimate sanction applied, nor have felt that an honourable justice had been done.

*He's in no position to be choosy,* uttered something from the shadows, *he did nothing in his life to seek justice.*

Pascoe shook his head to clear the thoughts. Wished he could shake the albatross of abrogated responsibility – his failure to mete out the justice requested by his uncle – from his shoulders so easily.

…and wash blood from his hands.

He reached into the pocket of his jeans and pulled out the phone, spinning it now in his fingers. What to do; what to do? Use this and Gill Scott was cleared of at least one murder. Lara's part in the recording couldn't be cut off the end, and so the search for her would intensify. But his late supporting role could, so if he handed it in anonymously he would be safe – except from his conscience, from which there would never be any escaping.

The sound of the doorbell made him jump, as it had for a number of days now; the seven, to be precise, since Wright's murder.

He slipped the phone into his pocket and opened the door. In she stepped, placing a kiss on his lips; a vision with Titian-red locks – which she then tore from her head, proceeding to scratch her scalp with relief and running her fingers through the short auburn hair. He remembered with a certain embarrassment how he'd almost jumped out of his skin when she had stepped towards him from the cover of the trees that night. Then again, it was under-standable that his nerves had been frayed.

The full implication of her having waited for him hadn't really struck home till she cried out in ecstasy a couple of hours later. The sex had, in many ways, been a release for both of them from the horror of their deeds and the guilt of their retreat...but in the silence that had followed, the grotesque fact of a woman sleeping with the man who'd just murdered her father had filled the dark-ness around them.

"How many of those things did you bring with you?" He pointed to the wig and laughed, enjoying the temporary relief that brought him. "Anyone would think you'd actually been planning a murder."

Pascoe knew straight away he shouldn't have said it. His features fell; the laughter dying like all things.

Her cool hand was on the back of his neck. "Stop worrying. He never did a single good thing for me in my life...except right at the end when he caused me to meet my partner-in-crime." She considered. "And to answer your question, I brought enough. At the very least, the police were going to be looking for his daughter and discover that she had slipped into the country." She kissed him again. "Luckily, the police included you. Not sure how things would have panned out otherwise. That Logan seems dysfunctional too – and that makes him dangerous." Lara held out a shopping bag. "Wine?"

He smiled and soon they were sitting in front of the muted TV, the soundless pictures casting onto their features the light and shade that their lives had become. It seemed his flashback had lasted but an instant, because the same news story was playing out.

Pascoe gestured with his glass towards the screen. "What do you think?"

She pursed her lips. "I think that mitigating circumstances will at least reduce their sentences. At the end of the day, my mother did commit a murder and Sam an assault."

Pascoe came to a decision. "On the subject of mitigating circumstances…" He removed the phone from his pocket.

"You still have that?" she said, sitting up, a sudden uncertainty in her eyes. "You told me you'd destroyed it and I assumed you must have when I wasn't arrested." There was an edge of panic in her voice. "Isn't that a bit dangerous…to keep it?"

He removed the memory card. "On here is all the mitigation the three of you need."

Her gaze was intense; hurt. "But…surely they have all they need already. Sam will tell of her ordeal; mum will tell the story of our lives." She pointed to the card. "But with this…I'm implicated." Her eyes widened. "And so are you, Andy, so are you."

She must have seen the shadow fall across his features because she reached out to him. "Oh, I wouldn't want to, Andy, believe me – but please understand: even if you edit out the part with you in…I couldn't go to jail for a murder I didn't commit. I don't have my mother's strength."

Pascoe found some humour in a dark moment: "I had to bite my tongue when your mother described you as a slip of a girl who wouldn't be able to take on any of those violent men." She placed her hand on his cheek and he tried his hardest not to flinch, saying instead: "This…" he sought the right phrase to describe their short, intense relationship so far, but nothing came to mind, "…

whatever this is we have, it really was born in blood, wasn't it? Our unholy alliance."

"There's only one solution, isn't there?"

She took the memory card from his unresisting hand, opened the door of the woodburner, and pitched it in.

Pascoe smiled: "I just wanted you to be the one..."

She threw her arms around him and gave a faux-coquettish look. "I thought I already was the one?" Cuddling up to him, she stared into the flames. "Nothing good would have come of it. Nothing good ever came of him."

"Except you," he replied, kissing her on the forehead.

She looked at him. "I'm damaged goods though, Andy. Don't ever lose sight of that."

"What do you think I am now?"

There was a pregnant silence, during which both of them stared at the TV screen. She broke it.

"Mum's strong – and she's riddled with guilt for everything she didn't see, or chose not to because of her own nightmare. I called on her after..." she paused. "Gave her a hell of a shock when she saw me." Lara gave a nervous laugh. "Seems I spent my time lately terrifying my parents and frightening people as I stepped out of hiding." She squeezed Pascoe's arm. "Sam went to see her as well. We live in a world of coincidences, do we not? I still find it incredible she and I were both moved enough by the past and the unfairness of the present to head down to Chadstow with the intention of confronting that monster. Enough of our old friendship must have held firm. We're like a..." she frowned, "...what was that many-headed-creature." Her eyes grew distant. "Anyway, one of us had the strength; the other didn't. Yet she was probably stronger in many ways, to be able to walk away.

"Going back to my mother, Sam told her everything. I backed that up during my visit. She'd always known there had been problems, but she was horrified by what she heard. I know her well enough to know she feels she's doing a righteous penance."

Lara shifted in his arms. "When she was teaching Sam and me taekwondo, she learnt tai chi as well. She said it gave her spiritual fortitude."

"There's a lot of her in you." Lara tilted her head at Pascoe's words. "You know, when she threw her head back and laughed, when DCI Logan and I were questioning her the first time? I had to be so careful not to say anything, but it reminded me of you and how you had been when we…" an uncomfortable memory caused him to pause for a moment, "…when we were at the RSM's flat and you burst out laughing at my comment. Sam laughed like that too. That sort of graveyard humour is a sign of strength."

"Yes, she'll survive – mum, I mean."

The brevity of the response rather threw Pascoe for a moment. "Will we? Obviously, we can't carry on like this."

She leaned away from him, the feisty Scott genes very evident. "Like what?"

"I mean with you on the run and me with blood on my hands."

"Well, you putting those four lines on that picture certainly helped our cause. Totally confused the plot and diverted any attention away from you – as did your leaking the nickname you guys had for the killer to the press."

"Maybe so." He chewed on his lip. "Unfortunately, it does mean it's left an awful lot of questions in the mind of DCI Logan, and he's not someone who stops. For example, there'll come a point where he discovers the girl living as Anna McGinty in Australia was never you and he'll reopen the ghosting enquiry." Pascoe pointed to his laptop. "As I have access to the systems and the paperless age can be a double-edged sword, I made a few deletions," he ran his fingertips through Lara's hair, "which will enable you to arise with a new identity like a phoenix from the flames… or disappear in a puff of smoke. Hopefully now he won't find you ghosted two identities, that there were two passport applications. Let's hope your other partner-in-crime, whoever she is," Pascoe raised his hands, "…and, like I said, I don't want to know – has shed her skin as effectively as you said she would and the Brisbane police waste plenty of time looking for her." Despite his concerns, Pascoe smiled. "Quite a mafia, the Safebeds network. Does Sam now know you contacted it years ago, when things at home were getting unbearable?"

"I doubt it – I've never told her and the details are all safe and sound, presumably in the cloud these days. Safebeds never divulge."

Lara mirrored his smile and took his other hand in hers. She kissed it and studied it. "Good to see you put those bloodied hands of yours to good use. She and I both got away from this country at a time when we needed to. She's a survivor. She's had a great few years in Oz and I think she enjoyed her couple of days back in the UK." There was a moment's reflection. "She won't let me down. Like me, she had to get away. Somewhere where she'd never have to be under a man's control again. With everything she went through, all the things that drove her to disappear in the first place, she chose not to make any friends in Australia that she couldn't just walk away from. Even if they find her the fallback is that she's obviously not Lara Wright, so she'll be fine.

"And in the meantime, I'll just hide out here. Your neighbours aren't exactly going to find it newsworthy that a young, single, handsome man has a woman in his flat. Plus, no one's looking for a girl with long Titian red hair and blue eyes."

"I might be."

Lara ran her hands through her cropped hair. "In that case, I'll grow it out."

"Thought you didn't want to be under a man's control again." There was just the hint of an edge in Pascoe's words that he couldn't mask.

She got up and looked flirtatious again. "There's control and control. Let's see if we can find some other work for those bloodied hands."

# 25

He was hoping that she would help to lift his dark mood, but given his history, he wondered why on earth he would entrust that task to a woman. Was he needy after all, as that other date had once described him, not that long ago?

At least this was a date with a difference – he'd already met her; seen how her smile could illuminate the darkest corners on the most complex and difficult of days. All he had to do now was recognise her. Given he had seen her in a sharp suit before, not the standard outfit of choice for a date, it depended on her not having masked that small scar at the corner of her mouth with makeup. There remained the problem of recognising her from a distance. There was no way he would talk about his condition yet, so he'd selected a meeting point he could drive towards in the hope that she would acknowledge him approaching. He wasn't ready for her to consider him weird yet.

He reflected that as days went it had been complex – a word he sensed did not apply to her, at least not with negative connotations. Intense, perhaps, but that was something different. He'd had his fill of complex, particularly the pursuit of it purely for its own sake. Intense was a calm, still lake; complex was that lake with ripples on it and no discernible source.

He, too, should have been calm. Arrests had been made and a file officially closed, but he'd been here before. Monsters were lurking way down beyond the light, beneath the deceptive tranquillity of his surface waters. Somehow, he needed to leave them there. For a man with his predilections, that was a huge ask.

But he didn't want to spend this evening talking shop. Even with his limited experience, he knew what a turnoff that would be.

He had hoped that the drive down to Torquay would ease his tension. Instead, the weather had closed in like grim imagery. He guessed the one positive to come from his discontent with the conclusion to the Armistice Killer case was that he'd been distracted from the usual destructive imaginings of how he was going to let himself down during the coming hours…or minutes if it went as badly as the Vanish woman.

Arriving way too early at the designated meeting place – what was the correct term for an embryonic tryst? – he parked up around the corner until he could arrive fashionably late. When he did so, he felt a huge pang of guilt on seeing what he assumed was her huddled figure in the doorway of the supermarket, sheltering from the strengthening drizzle.

She waved and his heart skipped the proverbial beat at the sight of this first manifestation of her dressing to impress. As she stepped out towards the car, Logan sighed, in part a reflex of despair at the sound of the clanking chains of desire, which would always keep men in thrall to women. It made a pleasant change to know this was a universal compulsion; something he shared with all mankind and needing no measure of guilt.

He thanked the fates that, for once, this woman was neither a fresh let-down from the void of the internet, nor the defendant or accused in one of his cases.

He made to get out of the car, but she was too quick for him and skipped around to the passenger side. In those few seconds, the combined wonder of firmness and denim displayed itself again;

as immutable as the Pyramids, more awe-inspiring, and definitely not built by aliens.

She leapt in.

"Hiya Ben. Ach, what a foul night! I'm sorry you had to drive so far." She looked at him in puzzlement. "What?"

He had taken in everything up to *Ben* and then his senses had scrambled.

"Hello, DS…" He slapped his palm against the steering wheel. "Oh, I'm so sorry – Miranda."

It could now have gone either way, but she chose to laugh. Then she looked at him. He was at a loss. Was he supposed to peck her on the cheek? All his other first dates had started with a handshake; well, that was out of the question. It was also a touch inaccurate – there was usually a handshake followed by a surreptitious scrutinising of the stranger's face for distinctive marks. Anyway, they'd already done the whole shakey-handy thing when they had first met.

She was still taking him in, but smiling that smile. "Yes, it is a bit surreal, isn't it. Especially as I thought you didn't like me when we first met."

He returned her smile with an uncertain one of his own. "Well, circumstances were a little different." Logan gave a sudden laugh. "But I'm determined not to talk shop tonight."

"It's a good idea," she agreed, "but probably not all that practical. Lucky we're in different towns."

And now she was pointing through the windscreen. "I know a great pub. This way."

She was remarkably easy to talk to about nothing; to be with – so much so that he was almost able to forget the CD case, which she didn't replace in the slot from which she'd taken it. Two tracks in, she removed it from the glovebox again.

"The Boxer Rebellion? I've not heard anything by them." She

nodded. "They're good."

They had to park some way from the pub. The rain was getting heavier.

Miranda frowned. "I'm such a girl; I didn't want to bring a raincoat on a date." She looked on the back seat. "Do you have an umbr…oh wait, there's a waterproof here. Is it yours?"

"No – oh good, actually that's Pascoe's. Feel free to use that, or indeed keep it. It's been littering up my car." Logan smiled. "Hope you don't mind walking into a pub wearing a police regulation waterproof jacket."

"Any port in a storm. Might get us served quicker!"

They dashed into the pub. There were enough people for it to feel sociable, but it felt like the sort of place that would be welcoming even if empty.

She must have seen him looking round and misinterpreted it. "Fear not, I have selected carefully. I have no wish to be questioned tomorrow either." She grinned and then, noticing him reaching for his wallet, stopped him. "No, the first round is definitely on me, you having driven all this way."

She ordered and as they waited, Logan couldn't help but take in how cute she looked standing there, hands thrust into the pockets of a coat way too big for her. She caught that glance too, smiled as if she had read his thoughts, but then frowned and rummaged in one of the pockets.

"Oh," she withdrew her hand, "it's just a marker pen."

There was a long pause. "Ben?"

Now she was staring at him, concern spreading across her features. "Is something wrong?"

Each time he tried to start a reply, he saw Pascoe's face – looking distracted across the throngs of well-wishers in Truro on what would have been the morning after, indeed the morning of, Wright's murder; his enigmatic expression, jaws clenching as both Gill Scott and Samantha Ingle threw their heads back in unexpected laughter at moments of extreme tension; his seeming lack of attention to detail in following up the enquiries with the regiment; the sense of abstraction in his hunt for Lara Wright.

"Ben...Ben, what's wrong?"

"I'm not sure anything is."

And maybe nothing was. Maybe Pascoe hadn't been wearing that waterproof jacket when they visited RSM Wright's flat the third time – except someone like Logan could not forget that he had been.

And perhaps the four black lines on the photograph in the RSM's study, the ones that made no sense, unless...Maybe they had been there all along and he'd just missed them the first couple of times round – except someone like Logan knew that they had not been. Whatever his many failings as a human being, his flaws were his strength where certain details were concerned.

And maybe, on reflection, when he had called Logan through into the study to look at that photograph, there hadn't been something in Pascoe's eyes and voice...

She had come with him, recognising a man who was onto something of huge importance; not even criticising his silence; waiting till he was ready to tell her the background. It was something for which he was hugely grateful. His pulse raced in tandem with the engine of his car as they made the long drive back to Truro.

There was a truth here somewhere, made up of a whole lot of lies. Of that, he had been convinced for some time. The one thing he had never really allowed for was that his own junior officer might have actual responsibility for the pieces not fitting together – or worse. As he explained to Miranda when he found it in himself to talk at last, it had never made any sense, once Samantha Ingle had confessed to her crime, that those four lines had been there in the RSM's flat. Nor would Gill Scott have known anything about the significance of the eleven eleven, the pony's legs, or anything related to it.

Logan knew something was wrong, but the facts were still swirling in the Cornish coastal winds. During the course of the eighty mile drive nothing settled, as if the slipstream of the car only made things worse. He felt the madness surfacing in the ordered compartments of his limbic brain.

Something else for which he hadn't legislated, along with the potential deception by his DS, was the cool of Miranda's hand on his as he gripped the steering wheel; anodyne to his pain. He sensed she wanted him to look at her.

"Sorry Ben, I know that's not very professional of me – but we're not on duty yet."

He smiled, hoping the sum of those fragments conveyed everything he wanted her to see on his face.


And impossible though it had to be, here they were, in what seemed like only minutes, outside DS Pascoe's flat. Logan knocked, though it felt like someone else's hand floating towards the door.

There was no reply. The car was there. Lights were on. He knocked again – waited.

Silence. He tried the handle.

It opened with shocking ease. Logan glanced at DS Wimborne and their exchanged look told of a chapter of darkness.

They went in.

"Pascoe?" No response. "Andy?"


They found him in the bedroom with a look of shock and dismay still etched on his face – half-dressed, totally lifeless, the essence of that missing elixir spread across the sheet in a red shape that might have been the outline of an unknown continent. DS Wimborne was plain Miranda again for a moment as she gripped Logan's arm.

Logan looked; took in the body on the bed. He spotted a piece of paper beneath the lamp on the bedside table. Picking it up, Logan read the shaky handwriting. The letter was addressed to *My dear nephew* and the DCI's eyes widened as he read the confession manqué from the now deceased Major Lawrence Pascoe, full of hints about some dark event concerning RSM Tom Wright, but stopping short of what he described as the *sordid details*. There was no such fudging on another piece of paper which was attached, written in DS Pascoe's hand and describing the shocking, cruel act that was the psychological torture of three soldiers, Bovis, Penney and Bullard by RSM Tom Wright in Iraq; how justice needed to be done where the army had failed. As damning evidence against young Pascoe, proof of motivation for the murder of Wright, it was the very definition of probably cause.

But this was DCI Ben Logan. Replacing the letter with care – Forensics would need to get here – his gaze lifted, scanning the room, looking at the walls before settling on some distant point, invisible beyond them. His eyes narrowed in understanding. A face floated in the ether, as it had through most of this case, features misty, indistinct, but for once, in Logan's world, the identity never in doubt.

"Lara."

## THE END